JENNIFER WILCK

The Perfect Secret

THE PERFECT MATCH BOOK 2

To Laurie, for being my plot genius, my sanity savior, and my coffee buddy.

To Lisa, for teaching me about adverbs (bad) and subtext (good). And for being a formatter extraordinaire.

To Miriam, for seeing what others miss and for loving my snark.

To Nancy, for helping me keep it simple and for really understanding my characters.

This book wouldn't be what it is without all of you!

Other Books by Jennifer Wilck

Scarred Hearts Series

A Restless Heart
Unlock My Heart
A Heart Restrained

Stand Alone Romance Novels

In The Moment
A Heart of Little Faith

**Harlequin Special Edition:
Holidays, Heart & Chutzpah**

Home for the Challah Days
Matzah Ball Blues
Deadlines, Donuts & Dreidels

**Harlequin The Fortunes of Texas:
Fortune's Secret Children Book 5**

Fortune's Holiday Surprise

CHAPTER ONE

It wasn't the sound of a body hitting the floor that registered right away. The thump was in the periphery, a noise that stood out a little more than the background conversations floating around her as Hannah chatted with friends after the concert. It was the silence in the aftermath that drew her attention to the mass of people who moved toward the opposite end of the lobby in the Jewish Community Center of Manhattan.

Through a tangle of limbs, she watched them assist a man who had fallen. Off to the side was a teenager, propelled out of the way by the ever-helpful gaggle, and who now looked as if she couldn't decide whether to dive back into the fray or melt into the ground.

Hannah's heart squeezed. She remembered too well what it was like to be a teenager. With a half-smile, the kind you give to a kindred soul, she walked toward her. "Everything okay?"

The girl kept her gaze focused on the grey-haired man being helped to his feet. "Yeah, the crowd pushed and someone backed into him and his knee buckled and... I tried to help, but they sort of took over."

She definitely had the "melt-into-the-ground" look.

"You know, if you kind of look through all of them, put your shoulders back and position your lips into a semblance of a smile, no one will notice how embarrassed you are," Hannah said.

The teen whipped around, straight brown hair swinging, and looked at her askance. "Excuse me?"

"Hi, I'm Hannah." She held out her hand, and after a couple of seconds the teen took it. "Growing up with three older brothers who took great pleasure in embarrassing me, I thought I'd pass along a little of the wisdom I've accumulated." She looked at the teen's red cheeks and shook her head. "I don't have any suggestions for how to stop a blush, though. Wish I did because it drives me crazy even today."

The teen drew her hands to her cheeks and closed her brown eyes for a moment. "Great, just great."

"Did you like the concert?"

The girl shrugged. "The guys were hot."

Hannah laughed. "I know, right? Especially the one with the deep voice."

Her face lit up. "Love him! Oh, I'm Tess, by the way. Sorry, my dad would kill me for my lack of manners."

"Your dad?"

Tess took a step toward the same grey-haired man who now limped over to them, leaning heavily on his cane. "Are you okay?"

Hannah did a double-take. When she'd seen him fall, she'd assumed by his cane and his grey hair he was elderly. Now, she vowed to get her sight checked. Tomorrow. Sure, his salt and pepper hair fooled her from a distance, but it was obvious he was one of those prematurely grey people, because his face was unlined, his eyes a bright piercing blue beneath black brows, his jaw square, and his posture straight and sure, despite his limp. His hand, which grasped his cane, was powerful and not marked with age spots. He was no elderly grandpa. He was gorgeous.

The man gave a shrug. "My pride is hurt more than anything else." He touched her shoulder. "Sorry if I embarrassed you." He turned his gaze to Hannah. "Do you two know each other?"

The hated blush heated Hannah's cheeks and neck. "Actually, we just met. I'm Hannah Cohen. Nice to meet you and Tess."

"Dan Rothberg."

She held out her hand. His handshake was firm and warm. This close to him, she could smell his spicy aftershave, and it reminded her of the clove-filled spice box they passed around during *Havdalah*, which signaled the end of Shabbat and the start of the new week. She'd always loved the scent.

Discomfort made lines form on his face, as if he was embarrassed that she'd seen what happened to him. Empathy washed over her, and she searched for something to distract him. "Did you enjoy the concert?" Hannah asked.

He started to respond, but was interrupted. "Dad, can we go?"

"Sorry," he said to Hannah. "I did. It was nice to meet you." Turning toward Tess, he nodded. "Yes, Tess, we can go."

She watched the two of them leave and wondered yet again how she mistook him for an old man. With a shake of her head, she returned to her book club friends.

"Do you know him?" Karen, her grandmother's best friend and one of the women in the book club, asked as she approached. "I've seen him and his daughter around, but he doesn't socialize. In fact, this is the first time I've seen him speak to anyone." She lowered her voice. "I think you two would be perfect together."

Hannah cringed inside. All she needed was for Karen Black, the "matchmaker," to turn her focus on her. She raised her voice and to the group, "Is everyone coming to our apartment next week for book club?"

Dan and Tess walked in silence down the Hoboken street toward home. He glanced at his daughter, but she was immersed in her phone. Her hair formed a curtain and prevented him from seeing her face.

"I wish you wouldn't walk and text. You'll hurt yourself, or someone else."

"I'm fine, Dad."

He held his tongue, though he wanted to say more, or at least comment on the tone in her voice. Her fifteen-year-old moods switched fast enough to make him dizzy, and he didn't feel like dealing with them. Maybe the best way for her to learn was to have something happen. Although with the unevenness of the sidewalk and the ambivalence of the other pedestrians, he was the one more likely to land on his ass. He gritted his teeth at the throbbing in his knee.

Getting knocked over in the crowd had made the pain worse, and he looked forward to returning home and putting his feet up. It was an unfortunate end to an otherwise fun evening. He'd enjoyed the concert more than he'd expected. The a cappella group had great voices and a terrific rhythm. He'd even tapped his feet and sung along on occasion. The beat-box rhythm, soulful harmony and Jewish music as varied as hip-hop and rock was a pleasant surprise.

As they waited for the light to change, the woman he'd met—Hannah, he thought her name was— flashed through his mind. She'd managed to make Tess smile. Maybe it was his mood Tess fought against, or maybe it was her age, but her smiles were few and far between.

Speaking of smiles, Hannah's was beautiful.

"Dad, Lexi wants to know if I can hang out with her tonight. Can I?"

He blinked as they approached the front of their apartment building. "Will her parents be home?"

She rolled her eyes as her thumbs moved at lightning speed on the phone keyboard. "Yeah, they are."

"Okay, but I want you home by nine."

"So early?" She widened her brown eyes and he melted, transported to when she was a toddler and thought he could do no wrong.

"Okay, ten. But no later."

"Thanks." She gave him a brief hug. Once inside, she ran past the doorman to the elevator.

Dan followed at a slower pace. Teenagers. They rode the elevator in silence to the third floor. Tess ran to the left toward Lexi's apartment, while Dan headed right toward their own. He grunted to himself as he unlocked the door, tossing his keys on the marble-topped hall table.

His leg hurt like a sonofabitch. He paused in the doorway of the bathroom. Staring at the medicine cabinet, he clenched his jaw, counted to ten, turned and went into the kitchen for a bag of ice. Before he could change his mind, he shuffled into the office. With a sigh, he sat at the table where his latest jigsaw puzzle, his go-to pain distraction, was spread out. Pulling over an extra chair, he lifted his leg onto it. With one hand, he held the bag of ice on his knee; with the other he played with the pieces. Out of five thousand pieces, he'd completed the outer frame, which left a ridiculous amount for the middle. He could look at the picture on the front of the box, but in his mind, that was cheating. Taking the easy way out always was. He'd done it before and look what had happened. He'd never put his daughter at risk again.

With a shake of his head to clear his mind, Dan focused on the puzzle. An under-the-sea scene, with multicolored fish and sea turtles and plants, the puzzle design was complicated and required concentration in order to match the exact shades of color. Although more old-fashioned than phone apps or video games, it was the perfect distraction to keep his focus off the pain. Out of the corner of his eye, a reddish-brown puzzle piece caught his eye and a vision of Hannah floated through his mind. The woman's hair was the exact color of the puzzle piece. He frowned. Woman? She was barely more than a girl and much too young for him to spare a thought for her. He winced as a shaft of pain sliced through his leg. *Focus on the puzzle.* Taking a deep breath, he removed all other thoughts from his mind.

The front door slid open, the click of the lock announcing Tess's return.

"Hey, you're home early," he said as she joined him in his home office. "Everything okay?"

She frowned. "Uh, no, it's ten o'clock, like you said. I'm going to bed. Good night."

He looked at the clock. Two hours had passed without him noticing it. "Whoa. Good night, Tess. I love you!"

"I love you too, Daddy."

As he went to his room, he marveled once more at the carousel ride that was his daughter.

The next day, Hannah walked during her lunch hour. Her heels clicked along the sidewalk in time to her breathing as she tried to blow off steam. The autumn breeze cooled her neck and temper, allowing her to take in the scenery. It was a beautiful autumn day in New York City. Skyscrapers stood in stark relief against the bright blue sky. The sun glinted off the windows, reminding her of a mirror ball. She would have enjoyed her walk more, but other things occupied her mind. Two things, in fact.

Why did clients have to be so difficult? She fisted her hands at her sides as she thought about their unreasonable demands. Pharmaceuticals made her yawn, but if she wanted a promotion and to develop her own client roster, she needed to succeed with what she was given. It was the only way to get a raise and be able to support her grandmother. She owed her.

Hannah had spent all morning trying to create an interesting angle to highlight her client's new CEO appointment. There wasn't one, and none of the large media outlets were biting. Even if she'd been able to fake interest in the subject, there was nothing earth-shattering about a new executive in a corner office. Her boss put Hannah in charge of crafting a successful news hook to be able to pitch the story. And Hannah was stumped.

As if that wasn't enough to fill her stomach with acid, there was Adam. He had the timing of a third-string, second-rate quarterback. How had she ever thought he was worth dating? And in all seriousness, she was never, *ever* answering her phone again without checking caller ID. Remembering his smarmy voice set her teeth on edge.

What started out as a fun set-up with the room-mate of her best friend's boyfriend had turned into anything but. Sure, he was funny and sexy with a great job at his father's law firm in New Jersey. But he was all flash and about as dependable as catching a taxi in the rain. He'd cancel plans last minute or forget they'd made them in the first place. Even now, a year later, she could taste her disappointment when he once again stood her up. And his attention span? A toddler possessed a longer one. She'd known from the start their relationship was casual. But as time went on, she discovered she wanted someone who understood her commitment to her family. She wanted more than a shallow hookup.

Hannah had broken it off with him a month ago and he'd seemed to take it in stride. Until today when he called out of the blue looking for a "good time," as he put it. In other words, he was in between girlfriends and horny. Lovely. Even now, thinking about what he'd said on the phone made her heart race, and not in a good way. Thanks to him, her concentration, along with the glimmer of an idea, evaporated.

Since her appetite disappeared as soon as she heard his, "Hey, babe," she walked during her lunch hour, trying to calm down and remember what she'd planned to suggest as a media hook. Her stomach had other ideas, though, and growled as she smelled the hot dog vendor on the corner. No matter how gross they were, something about those dirty water dogs appealed to her. She ordered one with mustard and a diet soda. When the vendor collected the money and passed over the food, she turned around and smacked into a hard body behind her.

"Oh, I'm so sor—"

It was the silver-haired guy from the night before. What was his name? Dan. "Hi," she said. His hand clasped her elbow to steady her as he balanced with his cane.

"Sorry, I didn't know you were behind me."

"Strange coincidence, isn't it? No damage done, no apology necessary."

He backed away with a hitch in his step, giving her room to move. But his hand was still on her elbow and not wanting to upset his balance, she followed, engaging in a silent dance routine. Meanwhile, others in line backed away. He frowned, took another step back and again she followed. His grip was firm, warm, and made the little hairs on her arm stand on end. A part of her didn't want him to let go. However, the practical side of her realized if he didn't do it soon, they would block the vendor or land on the ground. She looked pointedly at her arm and his gaze followed. His eyes crinkled, his mouth curved in a smile as he huffed a breath and let go of her arm.

"Oh, so that's how you do it," he said. "Next time I'll know better. Kind of weird, though, running into you here. Or maybe not weird, but..."

She laughed. He was awkward, charming, and chatty, which was a surprise after his aloofness yesterday.

"No worries, although maybe we should move out of the way." Hannah tossed a glance over her shoulder at the hot dog cart. "We're blocking the vendor from his customers. Or did you want to order a hot dog?"

"Yeah, I did. Wait a sec?"

"Sure." She moved to the side, surprised he didn't give her the brush-off, since yesterday he'd seemed eager to leave.

Moments later, he joined her. "I didn't mean weird before."

His body gave off warmth and an invisible string pulled her closer. "Yes, you did, but I understand. It is kind of weird."

His shoulders relaxed. "I also owe you an apology. You were great with Tess, somehow making her smile when I never seem to be able to, and I was surprised. I never properly thanked you."

"You're welcome. She's lovely. I enjoyed talking with her."

He tilted his head as if trying to translate what she said. His gaze compelled her to look, and she couldn't turn away. "Not many people say that about teenagers. Do you have any?"

"No, but I was one. And I have three older brothers, two of whom have children, and one of my nieces will turn thirteen this year, so..."

"So, you're well prepared. I thought so when she talked to you rather than playing with her phone or running away."

Hannah raised her eyebrows. "I doubt she would have run away without knowing if you were okay."

He shifted from one foot to the other, looking uncomfortable. Hannah had an urge to comfort him. "True." He cleared his throat. "Do you work near here?"

She looked around. Her thoughts had distracted her, and she'd walked much farther than she'd intended, almost ten blocks.

"Actually, no, I don't. I walked to distract myself and evidently, I did a good job."

They approached an empty bench and Hannah sat. "You can join me if you like." A part of her hoped he'd stay. This was turning into the best part of the day and she didn't want it to end too soon, not when she was getting to know him. With her luck, though, he would grab a quick bite to eat and return to work.

"Sure." When he lowered himself onto the bench, she warmed at his desire to stay a little longer. He took a bite of his hot dog with mustard and relish, resting his cane against his leg. She wondered if he'd been recently injured.

"What do you do?" he asked.

"I'm a PR exec at a large firm. I work with a big pharmaceutical company client. You?"

"Forensic accountant."

"Do you work nearby?"

He pointed to the cross street. "One block that way."

"Uh-oh, you may need to find a new hot dog vendor. I think we might have annoyed him with our two-step."

He laughed, more of a bark, and Hannah caught her breath. She got the feeling he didn't laugh often. Or maybe he did...she wasn't sure. But she liked being the one to make him do it.

Hannah took another bite of her hot dog and wiped her mouth. "So do you go to the JCC often?"

"Tess volunteers as a tutor. She's there more often than I am. I dragged her to the concert last night, though."

"What did you think of it?"

"I liked their rhythm. Can't say much for their 'hotness' though."

"Oh, you overheard us?"

He nodded and his cheek twitched. He was trying not to grin.

As they ate, she studied his profile. Close-cropped salt and pepper hair, square jaw, powerful shoulders. If she had to guess, she'd say late thirties despite the hair color. He turned and his gaze no longer brimmed with laughter.

"You have mustard...right...there." He took a napkin and wiped it off her cheek. His touch, even through the thin paper, branded her. Her face heated at the thought of how she must have looked, and his lips stretched into a smile. But to his credit, he didn't laugh, and he pulled away as if he sensed she needed more space.

"Thanks," she said. "Wow, I am just winning today, aren't I?"

"We all have our days."

She pulled out her phone to check the time. "I hate to eat and run, but I have to get back to work. It was great running into you...literally."

"I'm glad you did. See you around."

She threw away her trash, waved, and returned to her office. But after going about three blocks, she realized she hadn't gotten his phone number.

And he hadn't asked for hers.

CHAPTER TWO

Hannah's laugh was more breathtaking than her smile, Dan thought as he tapped a pencil against his desk. It had been a long time since he'd laughed, and longer since he'd made someone else laugh. Unless you counted Tess, but somehow, a teenager laughing at her dad didn't count in his mind. He'd been awkward, but somehow Hannah hadn't seemed to mind. Or at least she hadn't shown it. Best lunch he'd shared in a while. And she was beautiful. Auburn, shoulder-length hair that curled at the ends, blue eyes that could make him jealous of men who had been in her past. Her skin was pale, and her hands were small, delicate-looking.

He took a deep breath as Lisa, his co-worker, popped around the door of his office. "Hey, I'm having trouble with the analysis. I can probably have it to you later this afternoon. Is that okay?"

He raised his brows. "Yeah, that'll be fine."

He had a ton of work and needed her analysis before he could move forward with his project, but Lisa was a dedicated employee. If she said she needed more time, he wasn't about to deny her.

"Take a break and get a bite to eat," he added. "Maybe it'll help."

Lisa nodded. "Want to join me?"

He paused before answering. "No, I already ate. Thanks, though."

She saluted. "You know what they say about all work and no play. You should get out more, like maybe with whomever caused you to smile and stare off into space." With a wave, she left.

He jerked in his chair. Hannah had lightened his mood. Was it so obvious? He let himself dream a little as he thought about her. Maybe he should listen to Lisa and ask her out.

But as soon as the thought entered his mind, he dismissed it. He was a dad, focused on his daughter. The rest of his time was dedicated to his job. Eating lunch with Hannah was a spur-of-the-moment thing. He didn't do spur-of-the-moment. He planned, made lists, and weighed positives and negatives. He had no list prepared of reasons why asking Hannah out was a good idea. He had no plan formulated guiding him how to date.

The list not to date? That was easy. He was a single dad. His calendar was jammed with Tess's afterschool art classes, doctor appointments, and tutoring sessions.

And even when she didn't have a social life to rival the Queen's, his primary responsibility had to be to her, his secondary to his job. His knee had a bad habit of flaring up at the most inopportune times. The rest of the time, it hurt like a sonofabitch. Except...those reasons sounded stupid, even to him.

He frowned. Beth died seven years ago. There had been plenty of opportunities to date, but he avoided them all in an effort to be the best dad he could be, and to make up to Tess for...everything. In the beginning, he'd been recovering physically and mentally. Then there were the aftereffects. He massaged his knee with a wince. Things were under control now. He was under control. Could it work? Maybe. Did he want to? Kind of.

He juggled the pencil through his fingers as he cobbled together a new list, a list of what he knew about Hannah. She was younger than him. If he had to guess, by about ten years, which put her in her late twenties. Did age matter? He hadn't thought about her age when they'd eaten hot dogs. Maybe the age difference didn't matter.

He'd enjoyed her company. For a few minutes when they'd laughed during their hot-dog lunch, he'd felt carefree. Was relaxing so bad? Everyone needed to feel that way sometimes. And he hadn't in a long time. Maybe it was time. He reached for his phone and stopped, hand halfway in his pocket.

He didn't have her phone number. Maybe he should take it as a sign. If seeing her again was that great of an idea, he would've asked for it. He should accept his life as it was and forget about her. Returning to his desk, he reached for a folder.

He knew her last name. She was in PR. It couldn't hurt to do a little research. If he were unsuccessful, he'd put her out of his mind. He swiveled toward the computer and searched for Hannah Cohen. Multiple upon multiple options popped upon the screen. Maybe he should stop now, before he did something he'd regret. But an internal voice whispered not to give up.

The voice was a pain in the ass.

He scrolled through until he found her name listed as the media contact on a press release. Bingo. He apologized in silence for offending the voice in his head. He'd found her. He'd come this far, might as well see it through. Now all he had to do was hope she hadn't changed firms in the last six months.

Hannah stared at her computer as she put together the third round of media contacts for the client, based on the latest non-news news angle. This was ridiculous. Unless they had something earth shattering to report, few of her client's target media wanted to cover a personnel appointment, even when the person was the CEO of a corporation. And those who did didn't want to run huge articles on him—at most, they'd get a blurb on the business page. At least not without an interesting hook, which she was unable to produce at present.

Her phone rang and she grabbed it. "Hannah Cohen."

A throat cleared on the other end. "Hannah. This is Dan Rothberg. We had lunch together today."

Until she heard his voice, she hadn't realized she'd hoped he'd figure out a way to call. Her pulse raced and her neck heated. "Hi, Dan. Don't tell me, you're calling to gloat about the mustard." Because why else would he call?

A deep rumbling chuckle sounded on the other end. "Not this time."

This time. She smiled. "Well, that's a relief." Adam flashed in her mind. She grimaced as she thought about the reasons he'd call.

"I wondered if you'd like to go for a real lunch sometime. One without hot-dog vendors or wayward mustard."

Her stomach flipped, sank, and flipped again. He wasn't like Adam, was he? "Yeah, I would."

"Any chance you're free Monday?"

She opened the calendar app on her phone. "Wait, let me double check..." She had three deadlines and a nail appointment, but maybe she could work ahead. "Yes, I'm free."

"Excellent. What are your thoughts about Italian?"

Not innovative, but safe for a first meal with someone. "Love it."

"Okay, how about Piccolo Café on Madison between 37th and 38th. It shouldn't be too far from you."

She'd been there a couple of months ago when she and her best friend, Aviva, moved from the Jersey City office to the Manhattan one. The place had been full of hipsters with bad acoustics and squished together tables. Not great for conversations, but maybe he didn't know about the atmosphere. He was considerate, trying to make their lunch convenient for her. "No, it's not far. I know it well. They make a great fettuccini a la Bolognese."

"I'll meet you there at noon."

She mentally crossed off her manicure while rearranging her to-do list, hung up the phone and stared out the window. He'd spent time figuring out how to get in touch with her and put effort into finding a convenient place for her. She hugged herself as a warm glow suffused her.

Dan intrigued her. She wasn't sure what it was about him, but she didn't think he was good at the dating scene. Maybe it wasn't a "scene" for him, which was refreshing. Unlike most of the other guys she'd dated. Unlike Adam. Thinking about him put a damper on her mood. She shook her head to change the direction of her thoughts. She'd much rather think about Dan.

Hannah stopped by Aviva's office. "You ready to go?"

With a jump, Aviva turned around. "It's six o'clock already? I haven't gotten half of what I wanted to finish done. Ugh." She pushed away from her desk, picked up her purse, and followed Hannah out of the building.

The autumn breeze was chilly, especially with the sun low in the sky and blocked by buildings. Hannah shivered and rubbed her arms as they walked to the PATH station.

"Jacob and I are going to skate in Central Park this weekend, maybe see a movie as well. Want to join us?"

Hannah took a deep breath, stopped, and faced her friend as the PATH train whizzed toward Hoboken. "I appreciate how often you invite me to join the two of you, but I don't like to play the third wheel. Plus, I may have to work."

Aviva's face scrunched. Hannah knew she'd hurt her. She bit her lip.

"You're not a third wheel. You're my best friend. And I don't want to leave you out because I have a boyfriend and you don't at the moment."

Hannah gave her a hug. "You are the most accepting friend I've ever had. Inviting me along sometimes is fine. But don't be surprised if I don't come along all the time. It's painful sometimes. Doesn't Jacob mind?"

"Well..."

Hannah flashed a shrewd look at Aviva. "See?"

"Okay, I get your point. And his too, but don't tell him I said that. He's been right way too often of late, and it's driving me crazy."

Hannah nodded. "I promise. And, I have a date."

Aviva stopped in her tracks and pulled Hannah off to the side. "Really? Way to bury the lead. Who?"

"His name is Dan, but I'm not sure if it will last more than one time. Not to mention I should focus on getting a promotion. I don't want to sound superficial, but he's older than I am."

"How much older?"

She thought about it for a few seconds. "It's hard to tell because although his hair is gray, his face is young. But he has a teenage daughter, so maybe ten years? Is he too old, do you think?"

"Age matters a lot less now since we're older. It's not like we're still in school. How'd you meet him?"

Hannah told her about their meeting in the JCC and again at the hotdog stand.

"He sounds like he has potential."

She couldn't stop the smile from forming on her lips. "I never expected him to call. He's a little bit awkward about it so it's cute. We're meeting for lunch Monday, despite a part of me that thinks we shouldn't. I'm not sure how I feel about getting involved with someone who has a kid."

At the corner, Aviva gave Hannah a hug. "Nice to see you're optimistic. I'll see you Monday. And dress pretty!"

Hannah laughed at Aviva and walked the rest of the way to the apartment she shared with her grandmother. With a nod to the doorman, and a quick stop at the mailbox, she rode the elevator to the seventh floor and let herself in.

"*Bubbe?*"

"*Hannahla!* How was your day?" Her grandmother, Sylvia, waddled over and gave her a rib-cracking hug before she returned to the kitchen. "I have stuffed cabbage ready for dinner. Go change and we can sit down."

Hannah changed into sweats and a T-shirt before she returned to the kitchen to set the table. When she was finished, they lit the white Shabbat candles, sang the blessing, and sat down to eat. Hannah told her about her day.

"And how about you, *Bubbe?* What did you do today?"

"Oh, I played mah jongg with the girls in the morning and got my nails done this afternoon." She displayed her hand across the table. "Do you like the color? It's called Passion Fruit."

"Very pretty. Sounds like you had a nice day."

"I did. Do you have any plans tonight?"

"No, I'll relax, maybe work ahead a little. Unless you'd like to go see a movie?"

"No, there's nothing playing I want to see. Besides, you don't want to hang out with me. You need to find a handsome man your own age."

Hannah concentrated on her stuffed cabbage. What would her grandmother say if she knew about Dan?

CHAPTER THREE

onday, time dragged. Hannah half expected to hear the numbers of the clock scrape against the floor, creating ruts in the blue industrial carpet. The press release she was writing, discussing the goals of her client's new CEO, was stuck on line three. She'd sit down to write, and remember she needed a cup of coffee. So she'd go and get coffee, sit and be too warm. She'd adjust the thermostat and realize she should make sure her hair wasn't frizzy, since she didn't want Dan to see her look like the Wild Woman of Borneo. She'd return once again to the computer, and be too cold. Lunch could not come fast enough.

Finally, finally, finally, lunchtime rolled around. Hannah grabbed her purse and raced to the bathroom. After she fixed her makeup and hair, she walked to the Piccolo Café. As she approached the restaurant, she spotted him waiting on the sidewalk. Khakis with a razor-sharp crease fit him better than any she had seen before, and a flash of his sexy rear flitted through her head. A blue button-down Oxford, the exact color of his eyes, stretched across his broad shoulders and managed not to look rumpled after a half day of work. Silver-flecked hair glinted in the sun and a strong hand gripped his cane. The brown wood looked bronze in the sun, and for the first time, she noticed grooved cut-outs along the shaft, which added some artistry to it. He met her gaze and waved, a half-smile on his face, as he shifted his weight and pulled at his collar.

For some reason, his nerves calmed her. She exhaled, blew a strand of hair out of her face, and hurried to meet him. "Hi, sorry if I kept you waiting."

"I was early."

For her. Her stomach lurched and she pressed her hand against her middle to settle it.

He rested his hand on her upper arm. "Want to go inside?"

Warmth radiated from her arm to her fingertips. This close to him, she could smell his shampoo and a faint trace of his aftershave, and she wanted more time to figure out what those specific scents were. But they were in the middle of the sidewalk, and now was not the time to sniff.

Not to mention, she would look weird.

He ushered her indoors, and they followed the hostess to a table in the back of the rustic-looking dining room, his gait a little uneven as he limped.

"How's your day so far?" he asked when the hostess left.

"I'm glad lunch is finally here."

"Me too." His face reddened and he smiled, not holding her gaze for long, but long enough for her to admire his handsome grin. "The morning took much longer than I thought it would."

She wrinkled her nose. "I thought it was just me."

He shook his head. "I swear someone snuck into my office last night and slowed all the clocks. Every time I looked, a few minutes had passed, although it felt like longer, and every time the phone rang, I jumped."

"Why?"

He played with the edges of his menu for a moment, and she wondered what those fingers would feel like on her. When he refocused his gaze on her, her face heated and she took a deep breath. "Restaurant burned down," he said, "every road in the city closed, it's been a while since I've been on a date...I don't know."

She leaned forward with a smile. "Look at us. We made it."

"I'm glad." He touched her hand for a moment, his fingers strong, and a shiver ran up her arm. His words might be tentative, but his touch was warm, strong, and sure. His piercing blue eyes homed in on her and made it impossible to look away. His eyebrows were still dark, unlike his hair, which gave him a foreboding appearance, but when he smiled, his mouth stretched, drawing attention to his soft lips, adding a vulnerability to his features, and making her wonder what it would be like to kiss him. Would his kiss be soft and gentle or sure, in a take-no-prisoners kind of way? What would he taste like? Warmth pooled low in her belly as a desire to find out the answers to those questions blossomed.

They both jumped when the waitress appeared. "Are you ready to order?"

"Sorry, not even close," Dan said. "So, you said on the phone you'd been here before?" His gaze shifted to the menu and Hannah pulled her hand away.

"Yes, my best friend, Aviva, and I gorged on pasta while celebrating our move to the New York office a couple of months ago. Thanks for trying to find something near me. I hope it's not too far for you?"

"I like getting out of the office at lunchtime, and it doesn't happen often. When it does, I don't worry about how long I'm gone."

They chose their lunches and placed their orders. When the waitress left, Hannah leaned forward and rested her arms on the table. "I meant to ask you how you found me. Don't get me wrong, I'm glad you did, but I was curious since you never asked for my number."

He made a half-strangled sound somewhere between a laugh and a huff, and ran his hand over his short-cropped hair. "You told me your name and you said you were in PR. I found your name on a number of press releases. Then I took a chance you still worked at the same company."

"Wow, I'm impressed. Thank you for the effort."

He frowned. "Do people not usually make an effort for you?" His gaze was intense. She shifted in her seat. It wasn't a question she wanted to ponder, much less answer. Her discomfort must have shown on her face because he straightened his shoulders and shook his head. "I'm sorry, it was a personal question. Forget I asked. How long have you worked at Shelby Public Relations?"

Relief at being let off the hook mixed with surprise at his perception, and made her want to answer his original question. "Don't be sorry. As for working at Shelby? Since I graduated Washington University—first in their Jersey City satellite office, then, as I said, Aviva and I moved to their main office here. They offered me an entry-level job where senior executives mentored me and gave me the chance to work on a variety of projects. I've been happy there. Now I'm trying for a promotion so I can get my own client roster."

He winced. "I probably shouldn't ask, but how long ago did you graduate college?"

She chuckled. "I graduated five years ago. I'm twenty-seven."

He pulled at his shirt collar. "Not too bad, I guess. I'm thirty-nine."

She placed her hand on his arm. "Aviva said an age difference isn't bad now that we're out of school. Especially if the meeting is organic, like ours was." But he was older than she'd imagined. Would Aviva say the same if she knew his age? And did it matter?

He covered her hand with his and they sat in silence a moment until the waitress jostled his chair, and he flinched. "Oh, I'm sorry if I hurt you. Here, you ordered the penne a la vodka with chicken." She placed it in front of Dan and turned to Hannah. "And you ordered the fettucine a la Bolognese. Can I get either of you parmesan?"

They shook their heads and she left them in silence. The silence became awkward, and Hannah didn't know what to do to make it comfortable again. She didn't want to ask about his leg and make things worse. She rolled the fettucine around her fork and took a bite, the textures and flavors of the food distracting her for the moment—the al dente pasta, the tart tomato sauce, and the flavorful meat. When she looked across the table again at Dan, she grinned.

Leaning forward, she held out a finger. "You have sauce…right…there." She wiped it off his cheek, pausing for a moment to notice the rougher texture of his skin against her finger.

His shoulders shook, a deep rumble came from his toes as he laughed. "Guess we're even now." He wiped his face with his napkin.

"It appears we're both equally dangerous. We'll have to find neater food next time."

"Yes, we will." Once again, he squeezed her hand. *Good, there'll be a next time.*

He was off his game this afternoon. If he even had a "game" at all. It'd been so long since he'd been on a date. He didn't want to mess this up. As for his leg, she hadn't mentioned anything about it. With luck, she wouldn't. He'd see when it was time to stand up. In the meantime, a beautiful woman sat across from him. He smiled.

"What's funny?"

She stopped eating and watched him. He cleared his throat. "Mustard and tomato sauce."

"A horrible combination. I don't think I should let you cook for me."

He raised an eyebrow. "I'm a pretty decent cook. Tess will vouch for me."

"Really?"

"Well, if you're inclined to believe a teenager."

"It's hard being her age. I remember it well." She shuddered.

"Bad time?" If she had bad memories about her teenaged years, how would she feel about dating the father of one?

"Made worse by my three brothers."

"Older or younger?"

"Older."

"What are they like now?"

Her smile slipped and she bit her lip. "Older."

He took the hint and changed the subject, with more grace this time. "So, what kind of PR do you do?"

Sitting back, he listened as she talked about her clients: her pharmaceutical client's great charity work, but how it was impossible to get them the type of publicity they wanted; what she wanted to do five and ten years from now; how she wanted to be able to support her grandmother. He watched the sparkle light up her blue eyes, reminding him of sun glinting off a wave in the ocean. He listened to the lilt in her voice, and remembered how it'd washed over him at lunch the other day and made him not only eat with her, but pursue her. He asked questions and by the time the bill came, he felt as if he were back in the game.

As he paid, he turned to Hannah. "I'm glad we did this today. Any chance you'd want to do something again? Despite my age, being a parent to a teenager, my cane...I had an accident several years ago, injured my knee, and it never healed right. So, if you're looking for a star athlete, you should probably keep looking."

He held his breath, waiting to see what she said.

She nodded, and he finally released a breath.

"Do you have your phone on you?" she asked.

She'd said yes. He pulled it out of his pocket and handed it to her, his hand almost shaking in relief. She returned it to him. "Open your contacts."

He entered his password three times before it worked, opened the contacts app and handed the phone to her. She typed the same as his daughter, with her thumbs, whereas he used his pointer fingers. God, she was out of his league.

"I put my cell number in your phone. This way you don't have to search the internet for me."

Maybe it'd been a while since he'd dated. But when her eyes twinkled and her face glowed as it did now, he didn't care about anything but her. He grasped her wrist, sliding his fingers across the delicate bones in her wrist, feeling her pulse skitter beneath his skin. Her lips parted and an uncontrollable desire to kiss her filled him. Should he…would she…could he?

He stood there a moment, not moving or breathing. Such a short distance to cross, yet as wide as an ocean. Kissing her, tasting her, feeling her body against his—it was a fantasy he wanted to turn into reality. But not now. Because when he did kiss her, he wanted it to be perfect. And perfection needed a plan.

Hannah rode the elevator to her apartment that night after work, smiling every time she thought about her lunch with Dan. He was warm and funny. When he looked at her, really looked at her, her insides tingled, like effervescent soda bubbles. Imagine what would happen when he kissed her.

She slipped her key in the lock and opened the door. Voices greeted her and she stiffened, all thoughts of Dan's kiss evaporating. Gritting her teeth, she stepped into the hallway, dropped her keys on the desk, and hid her purse in the far corner of the coat closet.

Her grandmother looked toward her. "Hi, *Hannahla*, look who stopped by."

"Jeff." Hannah nodded to her brother and walked into the living room. His sandy hair was combed this time, his T-shirt and jeans cleaner than she remembered them being in a long time.

"Hey, Hannah."

"Jeff was telling me about his apartment." *Bubbe* beamed from her seat.

Hannah edged onto the corner of the sofa. "I thought you got kicked out of your apartment."

"Hannah!" Her grandmother put her hand on Hannah's knee, and Hannah reminded herself to be good.

Jeff stiffened a moment before he assumed a more relaxed pose. "No, it's okay, Grandma. Hannah, this is a new one. A friend and I sublet it from a guy he knows."

"A friend?"

He nodded. "Yeah, you don't know him, but he owns the restaurant I work at."

"So you have a job now."

"Mike's, a coffee shop in Hell's Kitchen. Waiter, busboy, you know."

She knew all right. Like all his other jobs, it would be short-lived, and result in him showing up asking for money. Or stealing it from someone's wallet, as he'd done so many times from her and from her friends.

"He's turning his life around, *Hannahla*. You should be happy for him."

Happy for him. Her brother, the screw-up. Her brother, the drug addict. He was always turning his life around in order to follow the drugs and the easy money. You could find him at the coked-up parties with shady friends and shadier dealings.

She narrowed her gaze. His eyes were clear and his hands didn't shake, but that meant nothing. He was a master manipulator and an expert at hiding his addiction. She couldn't see track marks on his arms, but he'd shot up other body parts before. Her grandmother might be fooled, and from her expression, she was annoyed Hannah didn't welcome him with open arms, but depending on him was futile. As a child, she could always depend on him to tease her, defend her, and cheer when she was sad. But sometime during his teenage years he'd changed, and now the one thing she could depend on was his need for money and the next fix. Thus, shoving her purse into the back of the coat closet.

"What do you want, Jeff?" Hannah said.

"Nothing."

"Sure." She tapped her foot.

"I mean it, Hannah. I just stopped by to visit."

"On your way where?"

"Work."

She crossed her arms and raised an eyebrow.

"I swear, Hannah. I've changed."

"Great."

"You don't believe me."

Hannah smoothed her hand over the green chenille fabric of the sofa. Its softness soothed her, but she couldn't be soft. She shrugged and heard her grandmother gasp.

"Hannah!"

"Relax, Grandma, it's okay," Jeff said. "She's got a right to be skeptical. But I swear, Hannah, I'm not the same person I was. I'm in a program."

"I'm thrilled you have a job and it's great you think this program will be different. But you'll be clean until the next hit or the next time something goes wrong. And every time you come here and swear things are different, you fool yourself and hurt *Bubbe*." *And me.* All the times he hadn't shown up when he'd promised came to the fore and she shook her head.

She rose and pinned her grandmother with a firm stare. "I'm going out. Make sure he's gone when I return." She switched her gaze to her brother. "And don't you dare ask for money." She'd started to replenish her savings account; she wouldn't let him drain it again. Jeff might not have any interest in paying back their grandmother for everything she'd done for them, but Hannah did.

Hannah strode to the closet, grabbed her purse and keys, and left the apartment. Tears she refused to shed clouded her vision and she paid little attention to where she went. Ten minutes later, she stopped at a bench. Her feet hurt. Slipping one foot out of its navy pump, she massaged it as pedestrians filed past.

People watching gave her an escape from her thoughts. A group of tourists pointed to the skyline, snapped pictures of the skyscrapers across the Hudson. Commuters poured out of the train station on their way home. Families walked through the park, kids raced ahead and parents followed at a slower pace. Young professionals headed toward the bars.

A street vendor walked by pushing a cart of roasted nuts. She wasn't hungry, but she wouldn't return home until she was positive her brother was gone. Across the street was a sushi place. As she was about to enter, her phone rang.

"Hannah, it's Dan."

Her throat clogged. "Hi. I didn't expect you to call so soon."

"Is everything okay? You don't sound like yourself."

He could tell her mood already? She took a deep breath. "Just some family stuff."

"Want to talk about it?"

Absolutely not. "Not really."

"I understand. I called because I wanted to let you to know how much fun I had at lunch today."

She turned and leaned against the sushi restaurant's façade. The heavy band around her chest loosened and she smiled. "I did too."

"Want to do it again sometime?"

"Lunch?"

"Well, I thought something more along the lines of the planetarium at night."

"Oh, like A Night At The Museum, except without the creepy dinosaurs come to life, hopefully," she said.

He laughed. "Actually, this place might have aliens. The next show is this weekend."

He was the father to a teenaged daughter. Regardless of how much she'd enjoyed herself with him, was this wise? She paused. "I'd love to go."

"Great. How about I pick you up at seven on Saturday, and afterwards we can have a late dinner. And if you change your mind, about talking I mean, I'm around."

CHAPTER FOUR

Dan hung up the call and gripped his phone so hard his knuckles turned white. What had he done? He didn't know if he was ready to date, or how it would affect Tess—he needed to make a pro and con list—and already he'd made plans to see her again.

The oven timer beeped and he spun around without thought. A shooting pain ran up and down his leg. "Tess," he called, fighting the urge to curse out loud. "Dinner's ready."

He held onto the counter, waited for the throbbing to stop, and counted in silence to keep his mind off of the pain. What he wouldn't give for a shot of something. Anything. The oven timer continued its incessant beep, adding a beat for his counting to keep up with until the pain subsided.

"Aren't you going to…oh…" Tess walked into the kitchen. Tossing a glance over her shoulder, she turned off the timer, grabbed an oven mitt, and took the baked chicken out. "Are you okay?"

"Just turned wrong. I'll be okay in a minute."

"Want me to get you some ibuprofen?" He shook his head and she continued. "It was worth a try. You look awful."

"I love you too." He cleared his throat and tried to make his voice sound normal. "How's the home-work?"

"It's getting there. I still have Spanish to study for."

"Want me to test you?"

"I have flash cards on my phone."

The table was set, and dinner was ready; he hobbled over to join Tess.

"The Abramsons want me to babysit again this Saturday night. I told them I'd check with you but I thought it was okay."

"Saturday? Uh, yeah, that's good, in fact." He served Tess chicken and asparagus.

"You sound weird."

He laughed. "You're tactful, you know that?"

She looked away and a blush crept across her cheek. "You sounded weird when you talked about Saturday. Do you not want me to go?"

"No, it's fine. I, uh, might not be home."

She dropped her fork. "You're always home Saturday nights."

"Well, this one I might not be."

"Where are you going?"

"To the planetarium."

"By yourself?" She made it sound like a museum trip alone was stranger than a trip to Mars. Which, he guessed, for a teenager, was the equivalent.

"No, with a friend."

She eyed him and it took all of his willpower not to look away. "Who?"

"Hannah. You met her at the JCC concert last week."

Tess's mouth dropped open; she closed it after a second or two. "So, you're going on a date? With her? You don't know her."

Dan resisted the urge to squirm. There was one teenager in the room. He wasn't it. "Well, we had lunch together today." For the second time.

"And now you're going out on a date?"

"Probably." What was his problem? Hannah was great. He'd enjoyed their lunch. He'd called to tell her that and asked her to the museum. She'd wanted to go with him. So why was he uncertain? How many young women wanted to saddle themselves with a grey-haired dad of a teenager who, from the sound of things, wasn't too keen on the idea?

"What does 'probably' mean?" She leaned forward and rested her chin in her hand.

It appeared his discomfort piqued her interest. Terrific. "I asked her to join me, but I may cancel." Because you haven't dated in twenty years, which is almost before Hannah was born, a little voice whispered. Well, not quite before she was born, but for sure before she hit puberty. He massaged his leg and frowned. And he expected her to want to go out with a guy with a bum leg?

"Why? Don't you like her?"

"Do you?"

Tess thought about the question for a few moments. Dan's stomach tightened the longer she took to answer the question. Why did her answer matter so much? It wasn't like he and Hannah were serious or anything. He wasn't sure he would see her again. But he waited for Tess's answer like he'd wait for a doctor's analysis of potentially troubling test results.

"I guess. I mean, I think it's weird you're going out with someone you don't know well, though. Do you guys even text?"

Well there's a ringing endorsement. He exhaled. He'd swear his breath came from the ends of his toes. "We talk." *She makes me laugh.* "But I might have rushed into things. I'm not sure this is the right time. What do you think?"

"I'm not the one who asked her out. You can't ask her out and then cancel. That's mean. Why'd you ask her if you don't like her?"

"I didn't say I don't like her. And I'm not mean." He took a deep breath. He could do this. The key was to remain in control and plan everything. Which he'd done for seven years since the disaster six months after Beth died. He'd cleaned up his act, put taking care of

Tess above everything else, and done nothing but remain in control. Maybe it was time for a little fun. He
deserved some, didn't he? Tess was out for the evening; it wasn't like he would be abandoning her or anything.

"Well if you're going to cancel on her, it's obvious
you don't."

"I'm not going to cancel!"

His raised voice startled him and Tess's smile told
him she'd baited him. With great success. Dammit. He
lowered his voice. "I'm not going to cancel...I don't
think."

By now, they'd finished dinner and Tess rose to
clear the table. "I don't get it. You can't make up your
mind whether or not you like her, whether or not
you're going to see her, but I'm the teenager who
doesn't know her own mind. Parents are so confusing."

Hannah plated the last of the snacks as her grandmother answered the door for the book club women.
This month was their turn to host. Hannah said hello
as the five women walked in. Of various ages, they all
had a common interest in reading and started this club
a year ago. Since Hannah and Sylvia were the hosts,
they'd chosen this month's book, a biography of Sonia
Sotomayor. As hosts, they were also supposed to lead

the discussion. After everyone had been greeted, Hannah pulled Sylvia aside.

"You'll lead the discussion, okay, *Bubbe*? I didn't finish the book."

"Of course, *Hannahla*, but I thought you wanted to read this one."

"I did, but I've been busy."

Her grandmother patted her cheek, which heated under her piercing gaze. "I've noticed you've been distracted. Anyone I'd be interested in?"

Hannah's face heated and she recalled her conversation about blushing with Tess. "*Bubbe*, please don't do this now."

Sylvia winked. "Don't worry, I'll cover for you." Turning, she headed into the living room.

With the wine flowing and plates filled with appetizers and desserts, the women made themselves comfortable around the room.

"So," Sylvia said, "thoughts about the book?"

Karen was the first to respond, of course. She was excellent at leading conversations, even when she wasn't supposed to. "I love reading about strong women and I found her journey interesting."

"I thought it was wonderful how she came from a tough background and has had such success in life," Sarah said. Sarah was a middle-aged recent member of the JCC. Hannah had gotten to know her in the last few months. Her comment reminded Hannah of Tess. When Sonia Sotomayor was growing up, a single-parent household wasn't as common, and made things more difficult. Now, it mattered less. Would it have any bearing on Tess's future? She shook her head. Tess's future wasn't her concern, although she wondered what Dan would think about the subject.

"The writing bothered me," Rachel said, her whiny voice setting Hannah's teeth on edge. Rachel complained about everything, even the books she, herself, chose.

"I don't know; the writing didn't bother me. Although the ending was a bit, eh," said Sylvia.

This was the part Hannah couldn't discuss, as she hadn't gotten there yet. As the women dissected the book, Hannah's thoughts wandered back to Dan. Back, hah. They hadn't strayed far from him all day.

"What do you think, Hannah?" With a start, Hannah turned toward Karen.

"I'm sorry, can you repeat the question?"

"Earth to Hannah," Jodi chanted. Jodi and Hannah teased each other often. "Where were you?"

"Oh, maybe she's thinking about the man she talked to at the concert the other night," Rachel said with a smirk.

Hannah's heart pounded in her chest. The last people she wanted to talk to about this were her book group. Not now, at least, when everything was new.

"Man? What man?" Karen asked. Oh geez, Karen was such a gossip.

Before she could respond, Rachel piped up. "She talked to Dan Rothberg and his daughter. You know the one I mean, he has a cane?"

Karen turned to her and Hannah sent a "help me" look to her grandmother. But Sylvia only shrugged.

"Oh right, I remember. He has the most gorgeous eyes. I've felt sorry for him after his wife died and all." Karen's gaze softened as she held Hannah's hand.

"Do you know what happened to him?" Hannah asked. "Or to his wife?" Maybe having a *yenta* here would help her get some information.

Karen shook her head. "Ladies, let's get back to the book."

Hannah gritted her teeth to keep her jaw from falling onto the floor. Karen, the gossip maven, silenced the rest of them, including her. Shame and curiosity battled in her brain. What in the world was going on?

Later, after they'd finished the book discussion, Karen pulled her aside. "I think it's wonderful you and Dan are friends. I have a soft spot for him, always have, and I wouldn't want to tell tales about him here. He's looked like he needed a friend. I think you and he are perfect together. It's his story to tell, and I hope he'll tell it to you sometime. Good luck."

He needed a friend? She thought they would be more than friends. At least she hoped so.

Saturday evening, Dan double-checked the address in his phone with the one on the building in front of him. 300 Newark Street, on the other side of Hoboken from where he lived. He walked into the lobby and gave his name to the doorman, who called up to the apartment. Thank God it wasn't some fourth-floor walkup.

"She'll be right down."

He waited in the navy and gold lobby, surrounded by large windows overlooking Hoboken's back streets. The elevator dinged. The double doors opened and Hannah stepped out. His breathing hitched and his heart beat like a snare drum. Trying not to stare, he admired the way her skinny jeans showed off her calves, the way her floral top hugged her breasts, and how her short black blazer accentuated her waist. When she approached, he realized her heels brought her almost to his nose. Her vanilla scent enveloped him.

"Hi," he said. Wow, great opening. "You look beautiful."

Her face took on a pink glow. He thought he might not have seen anything as appealing in a long time.

"Thank you," she said. "Your sweater does amazing things for your eyes."

All the air left him and he didn't know how to respond, what to do or how to breathe. It took every ounce of restraint not to leave his mouth hanging open. She reached a hand out to caress his arm. The pressure from her touch left a heated trail from his shoulder to his wrist. Was she admiring his arm or the wool?

"It's soft too."

That would be the wool. "Th-thank you."

Hannah patted his shoulder. "I guess as the father of a teenager, you don't get many compliments."

Just like that, he could breathe again. He chuckled, as much to relieve his tension as in reaction to her comment. "You'd be correct."

He placed his hand on the small of her back, ushered her out the door and into his car. He focused on maneuvering through the traffic on its way into the Lincoln Tunnel and hoped she didn't mind his lack of conversation.

"I imagine parenting a teen is tough," she said as they entered the tunnel. The artificial light gave off a sick yellow glow.

"It's not any tougher than any other age, just different. You get a glimpse of what they'll be like as adults, plus there's more adult interaction, when I'm lucky. Although usually her comments about my clothes consist of, 'Dad, you're not wearing that, are you?'"

Hannah laughed. "Gotta be great on the ego."

"Oh, I lost my ego a long time ago."

"Well, that's probably good for me."

He reached for her hand and squeezed. The contact was for a brief moment, but his hand retained the imprint of hers after he let go.

They parked his car and entered The Rose Center for Earth & Space.

"We need to start at the bottom." He pushed the LL button.

When the doors opened, they exited into the Cullman Hall of the Universe and Hannah turned in a slow circle. Between the initial sight of the glass cube and now the view of the Earth suspended from the ceiling bathed in blue lights, she was spellbound.

He couldn't take his eyes off of her, though. Her face glowed. Her mouth, a little open, made him want to kiss her. He wanted more. But it was too soon, too public, and he refocused his attention on giving her a proper experience at the planetarium.

"Never been here before?" Dan asked.

"No."

"Then let's take our time. Do you want to see the stars, planets, galaxies, or the universe?"

"Everything?"

Her enthusiasm warmed him. He placed his hand against the small of her back as he guided her toward each of the four zones. Dan started to think of the small of her back as "his" spot. His hand found its way there often. It kept them connected as he walked, somewhat awkwardly next to her. What would she do if he pulled her toward him and kissed her? Would she lean in or away?

After exploring for a half hour, and listening to her sighs of wonder, he ushered her into the elevator to the 1st floor and explored the Hall of Planet Earth.

"You know, if science had been this interesting in school, I might have developed a love of the subject," Hannah commented, as she investigated the various geological specimens.

Dan blinked, trying to scrub his mind of the image of her in a white lab coat, glasses, and nothing else. He cleared his throat. "I agree. I never much liked science in school, but I loved coming here." *I love it even more with you.* Dan pointed out some of his favorite rocks and minerals, as Hannah admired others. He preferred the ones with bright colors, while the history they revealed awed her. Her questions fascinated him and her observations illustrated things he hadn't considered in a long time. Her lips, as she spoke, entranced him.

Twenty minutes later, they made their way toward the Heilbrunn Cosmic Pathway. As they walked along the spiral path, Dan pointed out facts of interest. Her grip on his arm warmed him and he wanted to pull her against him and revel in her closeness. When they got to the third floor and the Hayden Big Bang Theater, Hannah gasped.

"Pretty amazing, isn't it?"

"I don't know where to look first."

They watched the Big Bang presentation. Or rather, Hannah watched the presentation; Dan watched Hannah. He loved listening to her questions, seeing the surprise and wonder on her face. Dan had come here on a regular basis since he was a kid. Each time, he learned something new, each time he couldn't wait to return. This time, he learned about Hannah.

And forgot, for a short amount of time, about the pain in his leg. In fact, in all the time they'd been there, he hadn't thought about the pain once. However, by the time they finished exploring the planetarium, Dan was hungry and his leg hurt. He'd miscalculated the amount of walking he'd have to do. Or maybe his leg muscles reacted to the tension of being on a date. Either way, he didn't want to miss out on enjoying his time with Hannah. He turned to her and eased his weight onto his other leg.

"I made reservations at Isabella's. We should be on time if we leave now."

He ignored the frown on her face and the way she seemed to glance with some frequency at his leg. He didn't need her worrying about him, although the pucker between her eyebrows made him want to smooth it out with a fingertip. Maybe it was good she was worried—it gave him something else to think about. As they headed toward the restaurant, Dan focused on walking. One he got there, he could sit and everything would be fine.

"Do you go to the rest of the museum as often?" Hannah asked.

Thank God she didn't ask about his leg. "Not really. I used to take Tess when she was young..." Dan paused and gritted his teeth as an uneven sidewalk jolted his leg. Dammit.

She sidestepped away and faced him head-on, grabbing his arms and keeping him steady, although he'd never admit to the purpose of her action, not even under oath.

"What are you doing, Hannah?"

She stared at him. He wanted to tear his gaze away, but he couldn't. Her eyes darkened until they were navy with concern. He wanted them to be dark with desire, though. "I know maybe I shouldn't bring this up, but you look like you're in pain. Is everything okay?"

He swallowed. So much for her desiring him. "It's fine." She arched an eyebrow and he relented. "My leg hurts. It always hurts. If I stopped doing things I enjoy just because it hurt, I'd never get out of bed." *I enjoy being with you.* He wanted to say it, but he wasn't sure he could risk it.

She squeezed his arm. "Carry on."

He blinked. When she returned to his side and hooked her arm through his free one, he blinked again. She'd accepted his explanation. Was it that easy? Maybe he should tell her how much he was attracted to her. Maybe it wouldn't sound crazy.

"What are we looking at?" she whispered out of the side of her mouth, pursing her lips together and giving him an insane urge to kiss them.

"What?"

"I assumed since we're standing here you must be looking at something, and I wanted to join in the fun. Or did you not realize we weren't moving?"

Her nostrils flared and she bit her lip. Dan realized she was trying not to laugh. Now he really wanted to kiss her, to capture her mouth with his, to make her his own. Before he could act on it, his stomach growled.

"Was that yours or mine?" She looked at him, an eyebrow raised.

His lips twitched. His breath hitched. He couldn't keep his amusement to himself any longer. It bubbled in his chest and he let it out as he shook his head.

"Okay, while I am older than you, I'm not old enough to be senile. Yet. So yes, I did know we weren't moving. But thanks for that. And yes, my stomach growled, because I'm hungry. Except I think I need to put eating on hold for a moment, because what I need, more than anything else right now, what I've needed all night long in fact, is to kiss you."

He reached his hand behind her neck and drew her close to him. This was what he'd waited for, her body close to his, the warmth of her nape against his palm. Tilting his head, he angled his mouth and brushed his lips against hers. A groan started in the back of his throat. Her lips were more delicious than he'd imagined. They were sweet and soft and for the moment, his. He deepened the kiss as her arms wrapped themselves around his waist. Good, because he didn't intend to stop anytime soon. Her body fit against his as if it was meant to—soft breasts against hard chest—he pulled her closer, wishing they could blend into one. When she sighed, he slipped his tongue inside her mouth. It was like honey, and he couldn't breathe from the sweetness.

Her fingers swirled against his back, leaving trails of fire. Shaking, he pulled away, though he wanted to keep her close. He rested his forehead against hers. Her pupils were huge, like his he suspected, her breathing quick. Her hands hadn't stopped moving and well, he wanted her to move them lower. But they were in the middle of the street and he wasn't an exhibitionist. He pulled farther away, took her hand, and led her toward the restaurant.

"Wait," she cried as he limped as fast as he could to Isabella's.

"What?"

"What about what I need?"

Before he could ask what she meant, she grabbed his head and pulled it down to her. She kissed him, hard, and pulled away.

"I wasn't finished," she said.

CHAPTER FIVE

Hannah squeezed her hands together so hard they hurt. She'd just kissed him in the middle of the street. Demanded to kiss him, actually. And that was after dismissing his pain. She hadn't meant to do that. She'd wanted to show him he didn't have to worry about it with her. But maybe he'd misunderstood. Her stomach tightened as she followed him to their table. There was no way she could eat. Not with him. His hand on her upper arm, as he pulled out her chair, stopped her from sitting.

"What's wrong?" His voice was low and made her stomach vibrate.

No point playing games. "I'm embarrassed."

"Why?" He let her sit before he eased himself into the chair across from her. She watched his face smooth out in relief as he stretched his leg under the table.

"That kiss..."

"...was many things, but embarrassing wasn't one of them."

She chewed on her bottom lip. It tasted of him—minty. He was right. Their kiss was hot, bone-melting bliss. His imprint still seared her mouth, her body still tingled from want, her heart still flip-flopped in her chest.

He reached across the table, clasped her hand in his and squeezed. "Don't be embarrassed."

Instead, she'd be turned on, all night if necessary.

He squeezed her hand again and with a nod, she leaned forward. "How's your leg?"

He dropped her hand, clenched his jaw, and stopped massaging his leg. "It's good to sit." His lips, to which she was developing an attachment, formed each word with care, as if he spoke a foreign language.

"Yes, it is. All our walking made me tired and hungry."

The restaurant was lovely. The dining room was decorated in pale gold with indirect lighting. Palm fronds softened the room. Large windows offered a view of the patio and the neighborhood outside. Red brick buildings glowed pink from the streetlights and the street still bustled at this time of night. Checking the reflection in the glass, she saw his shoulders loosen and his body appear less stone-like. She'd looked forward to this date too much to mess it up with an ill-timed question. Although she wanted him to know she was concerned for him, she didn't want him to mistake it for pity.

Hannah scanned the Mediterranean offerings on the menu the waiter gave them, grateful for something ordinary to think about.

"I've seen excellent reviews of their fish online, by the way," Dan said. When the waiter returned for their drink order, Dan looked up from his menu. "Do you want wine?"

"Mm, I'll have a glass of your Riesling, please."

"I'll have water."

If he didn't order wine, maybe she shouldn't either. "I don't have to get—"

Dan shook his head. "Not at all. I suggested it, remember?"

The waiter left with their drink order and Dan reached for her hand. "Relax, okay?"

She nodded, focused on the texture of his skin—harder than hers, yet soft at the same time. "I loved the planetarium. Now when I look at the night sky, I'll think of the planetarium's diorama of the constellations."

"I enjoyed watching your reactions. It's always fun seeing things through other people's eyes."

"What did you see in mine?"

He reclined in his chair, his lips pursed. "I saw delight and wonder. You're intelligent and appreciate beauty. You've got a great sense of humor, yet can be shy at times, and"—he bent forward—"you're an amazing kisser."

Hannah leaned back. "There's no way you could have learned all of that from watching me at the planetarium." Her mouth and her brain were out of sync as, in her head, she focused on the last thing he'd said. He liked her kisses. She resisted the urge to touch her lips. He was already laughing at her.

"Nope. Well, the delight and wonder are from the planetarium. The rest are my own powers of observation at different times. Although I'll confess I spent most of the evening thinking about your lips."

She bit hers, watching his gaze follow, before she decided to be brave. "Well, in that case, you'll have to add messy eater to the list."

"No more than I am. I'll give you a pass on it."

"Gee, thanks, you're so kind."

He shrugged. "What can I say?"

"Are you ready to order?" The waiter interrupted their conversation and placed Hannah's wine in front of her. She scanned the menu again and they placed their orders.

When the waiter left, Hannah shook her head.

"What is it?"

"Role reversal," she said. At his frown, she continued. "When I first met you, you seemed a little awkward or uncomfortable." When he started to speak, she stopped him by holding up her hand. "No, it was sweet, different from what I'm used to. Tonight, I'm the one who's awkward and you're the one cracking jokes."

He nodded. "It happens to the best of us, I think. At least I hope so."

She raised her shoulders and made her eyes go wide. "The couple who's awkward together..."

"Exactly. Would make a great dating profile—loves dates at the planetarium, awkward ones preferred."

She shook her head as she thought about the men she'd dated within the past six months. "Oh, think of the dating app possibilities!"

"I've never used them," he said. "My wife and I dated in college and married as soon as we graduated. Apps didn't exist then."

"Dating in college was much easier. Everyone I meet now seems to be aggressive, only interested in hooking up, and a little obnoxious. And they don't make much of an effort." She looked at him and wondered if he'd remember their previous conversation. When he nodded, she knew he did.

"Wow, I guess I'll take awkward any day."

"It's not to say they're all bad. It's just...they seem superficial. Like, as long as we're having a good time, everything is fine. But there isn't much depth. I love cracking jokes and fooling around as much as the next person. But not to the exclusion of everything else."

"You know, I think you've verbalized something I've tried to put my finger on."

"What?"

"I've got life down. Parenting, for the most part. As well as anyone ever can with a teenaged girl." He peered into his glass of water. "But I've done it to the exclusion of everything else. There's no...depth."

"How long have you been single?"

He dropped his hand to his lap. "My wife died almost eight years ago."

"Oh, I'm sorry."

He nodded. She watched him in silence, hoping he'd elaborate, not wanting to pry. After a minute, her patience was rewarded. His upper arm flexed, as if he were rubbing his leg. "It was a car accident."

"Is that how you hurt your leg?"

He startled. "What?"

"Your leg? You started rubbing it in a different way when you talked about your wife."

He grimaced. "You're pretty observant."

She watched him over the rim of the wineglass. He'd moved his hand away from his leg as soon as she brought his action to his attention. He looked lost. He moved his hand from his lap to the table to his neck, as if he didn't know where to land. This observant, kind man, who wanted depth, was terrified of what it meant. But he was still here at the table with her. She reminded herself she needed to move slowly, and she reached for his hand. His fingers were warm and he squeezed.

"My last boyfriend was the best friend of my best friend's boyfriend." She watched him figure out the relationship, mentally drawing a diagram until his face lit up.

"That could be problematic."

"It was at first, but now things seem to be okay. Except he calls whenever he gets horny." At the look of concern on Dan's face, she rushed to explain. "I've never accepted, of course, and he always seems fine when I beg off. I'm not interested. But I'm hopeful he takes the hint and stops calling."

"You're sure? Sorry, of course you're sure. You're an adult. How do your best friend and her boyfriend deal with it?"

The waiter came at that moment with their artichoke appetizer. Dan served her.

"Oh, this is sooo good," she said. The Parmesan cheese added a sharp bite of flavor and combined with the butter, the artichokes practically melted in her mouth.

Hannah swallowed and dabbed her lips with her napkin. "Getting back to your question…Aviva, my best friend, wants me to be happy. Her boyfriend, Jacob, understands Adam, my ex-boyfriend. So we're able to be friends." She paused. "Always being the third wheel is a little tiresome, though."

"You're lucky to have friends like them."

"What about you? Do you have friends like that?"

"I kind of pulled away from everyone when Beth died. Now I'm used to Tess and me being on our own and I'm not sure how to repair some of those relationships. But I hope to one day."

"I would think it would be difficult being thrust into the role of a single parent."

"It's a bit like riding a roller coaster without the safety harness. Tess is a great kid and everything I do is pretty much with her in mind."

Outside, they began a slow walk to his car. On the corner, while they waited for the light to change, he spoke. "I was going to cancel tonight. I'm glad I didn't."

His smile almost distracted her from what he'd said. "Wait. Why?"

"Because I wasn't sure if a date with you was a good idea."

"Why not?"

He exhaled. "Because it's been forever since I've been on a date, and there's this." He pointed to his cane.

"What made you keep our date?"

"Tess said cancelling would be mean, and if I like you, I should go out with you. She said some other things, but they weren't flattering to me, so I'll skip those for now."

Hannah smiled and stroked his hand. The hairs on it were soft; she traced his knuckles and tendons, moving up to his wrist and down to his fingernails. He moved his hand beneath hers to give her better access, and he watched, seemingly fascinated, by her movements.

"She seems pretty wise. You should listen to her more often."

He grasped her outstretched hand and they crossed the street. Once they reached the parking garage and while they waited for Dan's car, he pulled her close. "I'm glad I listened to Tess," he whispered against her hair. As he pulled away, he reached for her hand. "Don't tell her I said that, though."

"My lips are sealed."

Thirty-five minutes later, he maneuvered into an empty space in front of her apartment and put the car in park. She'd talked about a book she'd read as he navigated traffic. Now, she paused, bit her lip and he leaned forward, his lips brushing hers, like velvet on skin. She sighed and pulled him closer and he ran his hands through her hair as he cupped the back of her head and drew her to him. She reached for his nape, soft beneath her fingers. He explored her mouth with his tongue, as if he memorized her taste and texture, until the car grew warm and the gearshift dug into her ribs. When she whimpered, he pulled away.

"I'll call you." He stroked her cheek and tucked a stray lock of hair behind her ear.

Goosebumps ran down her neck and she swallowed. Pressing her hand against his, she climbed out of the car.

Dan sat in his living room with the lights out while he waited for Tess to come home. He shook his head. He managed his life by being super-organized, planning everything in advance. He controlled his leg pain in the same way. What made him think a date wouldn't require the same advanced planning?

Sure, he'd planned the activity and the dinner. But he should have figured his leg into the plan. He'd been so concerned about giving Hannah a good time, he hadn't allowed for ways to accommodate his leg. And she'd noticed. By some unknown random bit of luck, he'd handled it, but one of these days, if he weren't careful, she would ask more pointed questions.

A wry smile played about his lips. Despite everything, he'd enjoyed tonight. Hannah was funny and enthusiastic and compassionate. He could still hear her voice, throaty and soft, like perfectly aged whiskey. Whiskey he no longer drank.

And her lips. He could watch them for hours, the way they molded words, stretched into a smile, tucked between her teeth, or puckered for a kiss. He could still taste her—berry and white wine—and the memory of her kiss turned him on. Unless it was the taste of the wine...no, it was her kiss. He had nothing to worry about.

The sound of the key in the door pulled him out of his memory. He turned on the light next to him as Tess walked in the door. "Hey, Tess."

"How was your date?"

"Great. How was babysitting?"

"Zoe was cute, as usual. She had me do her hair, makeup, and nails and then she did mine." She held out her hands to Dan. He smiled at the orange and purple streaks that crossed her nails and covered her skin, remembering when Tess painted nails the same way.

"So what's Hannah like?" Tess sank into the chair next to him. Dan refrained from telling her to go to bed. For once she wanted to talk—he'd spend all night with her if necessary.

"She's nice. Funny and smart, too."

Tess winced. "Sounds great." Her tone implied anything but.

Dan nudged her. "Trust me, she is. I didn't think you'd want to hear other kinds of stuff."

"Eww, no. Where'd you guys go?"

"I took her to the planetarium, and afterwards, to Isabella's."

Tess sat up straight. "You took her there? I thought you were joking!"

"What? She liked it."

"Really? Or was she just pretending?"

He paused and considered Hannah's reaction. It hadn't seemed fake. He'd been careful not to overload her with too much geek data, which might fascinate him but bore others. No, he was sure she'd liked it.

"Her eyes didn't glaze over and she pulled me along to show me things she thought were interesting. So I'd have to say really."

"Weird. Are you going to see her again?"

This was worse than he'd expected, as he tried to keep from squirming in his seat under Tess's direct gaze. "I hope so."

"When do I get to meet her?"

"You've met her, Tess. At the JCC concert."

"I know, Dad, but when do I get to really meet her? If you like her enough to go out with her so often, I should at least get to know her better. Invite her over for dinner."

He glanced at his watch. "Shouldn't you be...in bed or something?" He regretted his eagerness to talk to her. Well, that was his feeling lots of times as the father of a teenager, but this time she was talking about Hannah. And for some reason, she made him feel like his mother was interrogating him, rather than his daughter. He needed to regain the upper hand. Somehow. "Dinner's a good idea, Tess. Just not right now."

"Why not? You're a good cook. Everyone has to eat. You can invite her here, impress her with your culinary skills, and she and I can get to know each other better. What's the problem?"

The idea had so many problems her compliment didn't hit him until after.

"Thanks," he said.

"For what?"

"For telling me I'm a good cook."

"You're welcome. But changing the subject won't work."

Damn. He ran a hand through his hair and remembered he needed a haircut. Turning in his seat, he grabbed his phone and added it to tomorrow's to-do list. "Tess, I think it's too soon in our relationship for this to happen."

"Too soon? What's too soon about it? You've been dating a couple of weeks, right?"

"Ten days." Was it only ten days?

"You have a daughter."

He nodded.

"So, it'll look weird if you keep me hidden away, like Mr. Rochester's wife."

"Oh, a literary reference," he said. "Nice touch."

She grinned. "I thought you'd appreciate it. As my reward, I think you should listen to me. I could always come with you somewhere if you don't want her at the apartment."

Letting out a sigh, he faced her. "Like a chaperone? Oh, sounds fun. Come here."

She stood and he pulled her into a hug. "I'll think about it. I'm glad you're okay with the idea of me dating."

Tess shrugged. "I don't know. I mean, Hannah seems nice, but do you have time to date? You always tell me how busy you are."

He pulled her into another hug. "No matter what I do, I'll always have time for you. I promise."

She leaped up and gave him a kiss on the cheek. "Goodnight, Dad. Love you."

"Love you too, sweetie."

Easing off the sofa, he limped into the kitchen and got a bag of ice from the freezer. God, he'd love some painkillers to take the edge off. But ice would have to do. Lying in bed with the ice on his knee, the taste of Hannah's berries on his lips, he wrestled with his thoughts. Was he too busy for a relationship? And how did Tess fit into all of this?

The next morning, Hannah still glowed from her date. Dan was complicated and guarded, but she saw something in him that made her want to stick around. She climbed out of bed and made her way into the kitchen. Her grandmother was already up, sitting at the table drinking coffee.

"The pot's fresh, *Hannahla*, help yourself."

Hannah poured herself a cup, added milk and sugar and joined her grandmother at the table.

"We need to talk about Jeff," her grandmother said.

Like that, Hannah's good mood dissolved. "Must we?"

"I don't like how you left things with him. He's trying. It would be nice for you to show him some encouragement."

Hannah took a deep breath. Her grandmother meant well, but she was an enabler. "*Bubbe*, he's done this before. He promises he'll change, but he never does."

"If you don't encourage him when he's trying, you're helping him fail."

"I've been burned by him too many times to have any faith this time is different from the multitude of other times."

Sylvia patted Hannah's arm. "You need to have some faith. He needs our support, not our condemnation."

"Okay, I'll try." They were empty words, but Hannah couldn't have this conversation any longer. She got dressed, grabbed her phone and purse, and headed out the door. Once outside, she let out a deep breath. Her grandmother saw the good in everyone, which was a great trait for a grandmother. Unless it blinded you to reality.

Her phone rang as she walked down the street and the caller put a smile on her face.

"Hi, Dan." She cleared her throat.

"Hey, Hannah. I wanted to tell you how much fun I had last night."

She paused and leaned against a building. "Me too."

He expelled a breath, reminding her of air rushing out of a balloon. "I'm glad. Tess thought maybe you didn't like the planetarium as much as I thought you did. I told her she was wrong, but..."

"No, in all honesty, I liked it. Everything else too." She started walking again.

"Hannah? Something in your voice is different."

She sighed at his perception. "Family stuff."

"Want to talk about it?"

Did she? Maybe he wouldn't want to stay involved with someone whose brother was a drug addict. Maybe he'd think she was unsympathetic. Maybe... "Maybe," she whispered.

"Where are you?"

She looked around. "I'm on my way toward Washington Street to do some errands."

"Meet me at Elysian Park in...twenty minutes."

"Are you sure?"

"Twenty minutes, Hannah."

"Okay."

She walked toward where Dan would meet her at the park. As she arrived, a taxi pulled up next to her and Dan climbed out. Concern showed on his face as he pulled her into a hug. The contact and the warmth made Hannah's eyes fill. She tried to wipe them without his noticing, but he tipped her chin up and wiped a stray tear with his thumb.

"Whatever it is, we'll fix it."

His desire to help touched her, but she was still scared her problem would turn him off. So she nodded and let him lead her toward a bench in the park. When they were seated, he took her hand in his.

"Talk to me."

The rasp of his skin against hers sent shivers up her arm. His hand was warm and solid and she wanted to trust him.

"My brother is a drug addict."

He stiffened next to her and she waited for him to say or do something, but he stayed where he was. His hand tightened around hers. After a moment, his thumb swirled over her wrist. She continued.

"He's been an addict for so long, it's hard to picture what he was like before." She turned a watery smile toward Dan. "He was such a fun-loving kid. I remember him always teasing me, but at the same time, he was my biggest defender." She quieted and looked across Hudson Street as the cars drove by. "And then somewhere he got lost."

Dan cleared his throat and placed a hand on her back. Was he pushing her away? A few seconds later, his hand moved, patting her back and she looked at her lap. "He promises to get clean, or he swears he is clean and he's not. And each time he comes to me and I give him money or a reference for a job, and he falls to pieces again and I clean up the mess. My other brothers won't have anything to do with him, it's always been just me. Well, me and Grandma, *Bubbe*. But I can't do it anymore, and *Bubbe* doesn't think I'm fair to him. She wants me to believe him. Except it hurts."

She rested her head on his shoulder. He sat as still as a statue, but moments later, he took a deep breath and molded himself to her body. Encouraged, she continued. "I need to support my grandmother. I'd like to believe my brother, but I've been hurt too many times to believe him because he says he's clean. Once an addict, always an addict. And if it makes me a bad person, well, then I'm a bad person."

"You're not a bad person. He's shown you he can't be trusted. You're acting on past experience."

"Then why do I feel awful? And why can't *Bubbe* understand my reasons?"

"Your grandmother, you're close to her?"

"I live with her."

"She sees the best in her grandkids. Maybe she doesn't want to see the bad. Someday, if your brother does get clean, he'll appreciate what you're doing for him. And maybe someday your grandmother will understand."

"I hope so."

"Hannah, I…"

She rested against his shoulder again and his voice faltered. He traced her spine with his fingers, sending chills up and down her back. Beneath her hand on his leg, his strong thigh muscle clenched beneath her touch. Leaning close, she inhaled his scent, a crisp combination of woods and musk with a hint of spice and her breath hitched.

She raised her head, looking into eyes so blue she'd swear they reflected the depths of the ocean, and all thought disappeared. The tips of her fingers traced his jawline and she leaned in, touching her lips to his with feather-light pressure. Their noses bumped and she felt the contrast between his smooth lips and the stubble surrounding them.

She pressed her lips against his and he sighed as he closed his eyes. Her tongue nudged his lips and he opened them, allowing the kiss to deepen. Their tongues tangled, danced, and explored, as her hands gripped his sides.

"Mommy, what are they doing?"

The high-pitched question snapped her out of the moment. She pulled away. His eyes were cloudy with desire and his breath came out as labored as hers. She buried her head in his neck.

"I think that's how this all started," he whispered, and she jumped away as he laughed. "Do you want to take a walk?"

She looked at him sideways. She wanted to ask him about what he'd started to tell her. But he'd comforted her. For the first time since she'd spoken to her grandma, she felt good and didn't want to mess it up. She took him at face value, deciding to save her questions for later.

They walked past the dog park and the playground.

"My wife and I used to bring Tess here when she was little. She loved the swings, always wanting to go much higher than either I or Beth would want to push her. I still remember the sound of her little voice yelling, 'Higher!'"

They watched the kids run around the playground. Hannah thought about Dan's memories. He'd always have memories of his wife—there'd never be a clean break. She would have to live in her shadow. Hannah looked at her phone. "Oh wow, I didn't realize how late it was. I need to finish my errands and get back."

They walked to the corner, crossed the street, and waited for a cab to come by.

When it pulled up, Dan turned to her. "Are you sure you're okay?"

She nodded. "Yeah, I am. Or I will be. Thanks for meeting me here and letting me talk."

He brushed the hair from her face. "Anytime. Anyplace."

She nodded and watched the cab pull away. Maybe he'd let her be there for him some day.

CHAPTER SIX

He sank into the seat inside the cab. Shit. Drawing deep breaths, he counted to himself, controlling his oxygen flow and lowering his pulse rate. But this time he wasn't breathing through physical pain.

His leg didn't hurt, or at least it didn't hurt any more than on any random day. His head hurt. His heart hurt.

He liked Hannah a lot. Whatever doubts he'd had from the night before disappeared when he heard her voice on the phone. He was honored she let him comfort her. When she stood at the entrance to Elysian Park, she'd looked small. That sweet, funny woman was alone and hurting. He wanted to fix things, to make her feel better. Power surged through him and he'd considered confiding in her. Because if he could feel powerful from trying to make her feel better, he wanted her to receive the same benefit. Maybe, this once, he wanted someone to be there for him.

She'd started talking about her brother's addiction, and it was as if someone punched him in the gut. She'd noticed him stiffen. He'd worked hard to relax next to her. He felt her hurt as a tangible thing. Once again, he wanted to take it all away.

It meant he couldn't confide in her, though he'd started to, no matter how much her expression begged him to when she asked about his leg. If he told her, he'd add to her hurt.

He gazed out the window at the cemetery where Beth was buried. It had been two years since he'd been to visit her grave. He leaned forward to tell the driver to stop, but hesitated before he could voice the request. At one time, he'd gone there often. He missed talking to her. Except when he'd visited, he did it so often, he felt like he couldn't stay away, sometimes going before work or in the middle of the night if Tess was away. It couldn't be healthy to visit that often, so he'd stopped. If he went now, would it make him want to start that up again? He couldn't risk it, and he let the driver continue on toward his apartment.

"Once an addict, always an addict," Hannah had said.

There was no way he could deny it.

"Hannah, how's the publicity coming for Fortex?"

She sighed. "They don't see the story here. Most outlets will put a notice in their 'New Hires' sections, or mention it in a brief news blurb, but I haven't been able to get anyone to bite on a profile. Despite their renown in the pharmaceutical industry, the company's not well-known enough to the general public. The story isn't sexy enough."

Jim looked at his watch and nodded. "Okay, how about you and I meet to brainstorm a brand recognition plan for them. Say around two?"

Thank goodness he understood. She nodded. "Yeah, that would be great. I've about exhausted all my current options."

He nodded, slapped the doorframe of her office, and left.

Stretching, she stood and walked to the kitchen to grab a second cup of coffee. Aviva stood next to the percolator. "Hey, Hannah, how was your weekend?"

"Good, for the most part. How was roller skating?"

Aviva frowned and leaned a hip against the counter. "What's *for the most part* mean?"

Hannah told her about her date with Dan and problem with her grandmother and Jeff.

Aviva drew her into a hug. "You'll have to introduce Dan to Jacob and me one of these days."

"I will. But..."

"But what?"

She looked around, making sure no one was coming into the kitchen. "I feel like he's holding something back. Like, he's completely there for me, but I can't get close to him."

Aviva patted her arm and turned toward the door. "Give it time, Hannah. Some people take longer to open up." As she reached the doorway, she turned and looked over her shoulder. "And others need to be told outright to talk." She winked.

Remembering Aviva's problem with getting Jacob to talk to her, Hannah nodded. Maybe it was time to stop tiptoeing around Dan and ask him questions outright. What was the worst he could do?

Dan stared at his phone after he hung up. Tess had called when she got home from school and wanted to know when he planned to invite Hannah over for dinner. There were so many problems with Tess's idea he didn't know where to start. Although he'd not dated before Hannah, he'd heard everyone talk about finding the "right time" to introduce your girlfriend or boyfriend to your kids. First and foremost, he had to protect Tess. When was the right time? When it felt natural? Well, it felt natural now. In this case, Tess was right.

Would Hannah feel like he was rushing things? It'd been barely two weeks. He wasn't trying to rush things, but he did want the two of them to get to know each other. Except if she got to know Tess, she'd learn things about him, things he couldn't discuss after their conversation in the park yesterday. He couldn't keep his past a secret forever, but deciding what to reveal and when could throw him into a potential minefield. Weighing the pros and cons would take much longer than he suspected Tess would give him.

He shook his head. When he'd made the spur-of-the-moment decision to call Hannah and ask her out the first time, he hadn't bargained on how complicated things would get. Or how fast.

His phone rang and he jumped when Hannah's ID flashed on the screen.

The universe was trying to tell him something.

"Hey, Hannah, how are you? I was thinking about you."

"Oh, that's good, I hope. I wanted to thank you again for yesterday. I needed to talk and it meant a lot to me you were willing to listen."

He heard the smile in her voice and his stomach tightened. "How are things with you and your grandmother now?"

"They're okay. Since I was able to get my frustration out with you, I was calm at home. For now at least."

"That's good."

"Mind if I ask you a question?"

He sat up straight. "I don't mind."

"You sound a little off. Is there anything *I* can do for *you*?"

He reached for a pen and gripped it hard. "Tess called."

"Oh, that's nice," she said. "Or is Tess the problem?"

"A little of both, in fact. She wants to get to know you." He froze, waiting for her answer.

"Oh."

That didn't sound good. Hannah was more verbose and didn't often answer with single words. "I don't want to rush things," he said. "I want to find the right time."

"Of course you do. And when you think it's right, I'd love to meet her."

Now would be the perfect time to invite her for dinner. He should. He missed her. But he couldn't. Because if she knew the truth, it would ruin everything.

As they hung up the phone, he cursed himself for his cowardice. She'd given him the perfect opening and he hadn't taken it. But he wasn't a spontaneous guy. He couldn't afford to be. If that made him a coward, so be it.

CHAPTER SEVEN

Hannah turned to her computer and ran a search: How to get a guy to open up to you. She reared back at the number of results—503,000,000 of them. Apparently, she wasn't the only one dating someone who didn't talk about his feelings. She needed a plan to help her get to know Dan better and to make him talk. At the top of the page was a simple list:

```
1.  Pay attention to body language
2.  Show appreciation
3.  Do something fun together
4.  Talk about things he cares about
5.  Don't make assumptions
6.  Be direct
```

Chewing on her lip, she evaluated the suggestions. Body language. He was the master at showing her he didn't want to discuss something. He turned into a glacier every time she asked if he was okay. Therefore, maybe it was time to ask a different question. Appreciation. Had she shown enough? Probably not. Okay, she could work with appreciation. Do something fun together. They had. The planetarium was lots of fun. But she hadn't gotten anywhere. Should she invite him to her apartment? Her grandmother was there, but she went out with her friends often enough. She flipped through her calendar. This weekend, in fact, her grandmother planned to visit Hannah's brother and their kids. She'd have the place to herself. She and Dan could hang out, watch a movie and maybe she'd try to cook for him. She wasn't the best in front of a stove, but she could put something together. Talk about things he cares about, don't make assumptions and be direct.

Okay, tonight, she'd make sure her grandmother's travel plans were set for the weekend and put her own plan into motion.

Tuesday during lunch, Dan paced in his office. Ignoring the painful flames his leg shot, pushing all thoughts of meds aside no matter how he craved them, he walked between his door and window and back, thinking of the ramifications, the possibilities, the complications involved in inviting Hannah to go out with him and Tess.

They'd just started seeing each other. If Tess got attached and things didn't work out, it would hurt his daughter, something he'd sworn after that fateful day seven years ago to never do again. But, she was fourteen, and she understood that not everything was guaranteed to work out. However, if Tess ended up disliking Hannah once she got to know her better, he'd have to break things off with her, and he didn't relish that idea either.

How much longer could he postpone Hannah finding out about his past drug addiction? He was overthinking. But he couldn't help it. Tess was right. He liked Hannah. A lot. He went to sleep with visions of her in his mind. He dreamt about her. He conducted imaginary conversations with her during the day. It was time for her to get to know his daughter. But could he risk it?

His jaw ached from clenching his teeth and as he opened his mouth to loosen his muscles, it dissolved into a yawn. He tried to stifle it when Lisa popped into his office. She winked. "Caught you."

Shaking his head, he stopped pacing and leaned against the heater under the window. "You did."

"Late night?"

He'd been awake past two worrying and planning and figuring. "Not really. Just didn't get as much sleep as I'd like."

"Did you have a chance to look further into those numbers I gave you?"

"Yeah, I did. There's no way Fortex is on the up and up. I mean, I know they develop important phar-maceuticals, but million-dollar donations to charity? And while I'm still waiting for confirmation from the charities, from the conversation I had with them, I don't think the numbers are accurate. I think we've got what we need to open an investigation." He rose and walked over to his desk. Putting aside his own prejudices against a pharma company, her work was solid. He rummaged through the papers on top until he found her report and handed it to her. "Good job."

She nodded. "Thanks. I'll get started filing the preliminary paperwork." As she headed out the door, she paused and turned to look at him. "Yes, you should ask her out."

He whipped around. "What?"

"No man gets that look on his face unless he's thinking about a woman. And you didn't sleep last night, so you must have been worrying. Go for it." With a wave, she left and he listened to her heels clack along the hall.

Was he that obvious? Oh hell. He grabbed his phone and punched in her number. Hannah answered and before he could chicken out—again, he blurted, "Brooklyn flea market. Saturday. I'll bring Tess so you can get to know her better." Whoa, that's not what he'd planned to suggest. Or how he'd planned to ask her.

"Well, hello to you too."

Damn. "Sorry…hello."

"Was that an invitation or a command?"

He ran his hand along the nape of his neck. "It was supposed to be an invitation."

"Hmm, you might want to work on your technique a bit."

He chuckled. "Among other things."

"I can't."

He sat up in his seat. Of all the possibilities he'd considered, her refusal wasn't one of them. Fool. "Oh, ah, all right. Maybe some other time..."

Her laugh confused him. "I can't, because I want you to come to my apartment."

Breath whooshed out of him. "You do?"

"Yes, I thought it would be fun to hang out together and get to know each other in a more relaxed situation. My grandmother will be away. Although you'll have to make do with my cooking, which isn't fabulous. So, how about we compromise? We can do the flea market first and the two of you can come to my apartment for dinner."

"That's a great idea, but in all seriousness, come to my place. Tess will be with us and..."

"You mean you haven't broken her of the habit of climbing on other people's furniture and writing on the walls yet?"

He loved the way this woman made his problems seem trivial. "I don't want to impose on you."

"You won't, Dan. Neither will Tess. I'm serious, let's do both. Besides, it might be better for Tess to get to know me somewhere other than her own home."

She had a point there. "All right, if you're sure. Tess and I will pick you up at eleven."

He hung up the phone and unclenched his fist. It was a good compromise.

The sun cooperated on Saturday morning and shined brightly, warmed the air and made Hannah feel as if it were summer again. With a last tip of her head toward the sky, she left the balcony, and waited for Dan and Tess outside the building. When their car pulled up, she opened the door and slid into the seat.

"Hi guys." Leaning toward Dan, she gave him a quick kiss on the cheek and waved to Tess.

Dan's face was red, which matched his red Henley. Hannah thought it was cute. He cleared his throat. "Tess, you remember Hannah."

"Uh, yeah Dad, it was only a couple of weeks ago."

She gave Hannah a small smile. Dressed in black leggings and a baggy grey sweater, her greeting was as colorless as her outfit.

"Hi, Tess. I'm glad you're joining us today."

"Thanks. Dad's not."

Really? Hannah frowned. Had she forced the meeting? She'd swear Dan suggested it first, but...

"Tess! Why would you say such a thing?" Dan faced his daughter, his jaw clenched.

"Because it's true."

"I needed to wait for the right time." He turned to Hannah. "Despite what she says, I'm glad you're here."

Hannah nodded. She hoped he meant it. "I hope you like to shop, Tess."

Tess nodded and reached for her phone.

Dan pulled onto the road. As he paused to let traffic go by, he reached over and squeezed her fingers, bringing them to his lips for a brief kiss.

"Okay people, we need to set some ground rules here," Tess said. "No mushy stuff, not when I'm sitting behind you. And two hands on the wheel, Dad."

Dan glanced into the rearview mirror. "Would you like to get out now?"

"Dad!" Tess slid as far down as her seatbelt would allow.

Hannah bit the inside of her cheek to keep from laughing. "Okay, Tess, don't worry, no mushy stuff with your dad." Maybe she could sneak a kiss later if Tess was occupied. Otherwise, it would be a long day.

Tess gave a reluctant smile. "Good to know somebody understands."

"Hey. Why do I feel like I'm outnumbered?" Dan asked.

"Because you totally are." Hannah winked at Tess.

Determined to win Tess over, Hannah joked with her and Dan. To her surprise, Hannah found Tess shared her love of Panic at the Disco; they talked about music and the band's best songs for much of the car ride to Brooklyn. By the time they pulled into the flea market, the tension had eased a little; she and Tess reached a reluctant accord and Hannah was mentally exhausted.

"Wow, this is huge," Tess said as they exited their car. What seemed like acres of white-topped tents filled with every vendor imaginable lined the market. Smoke billowed from grills where food vendors sold chicken and ribs, and what smelled like curry. Music played and people called to one another, their voices blending and providing a background harmony.

"Oh look, they have clothes!" Tess headed in the direction of a booth filled with colorful, flowing skirts and Dan gave a shout.

"Wait, Tess!"

She paused and looked at him.

"We're all doing this together, remember?"

Tess rolled her eyes. "Fine."

The three of them strolled the aisles, past fried dough, denim and leather clothes and sports collectibles vendors. Hannah inhaled the scents of fried foods and roasted peanuts, plus lots of sugar. They paused often to check on the quality of fabric, or to exclaim over some find they hadn't expected. After an hour or so, they'd covered about a quarter of the market. Hannah noticed Dan slowing down. As they approached an area set up for eating, she got an idea.

Turning to Dan, she spoke in a low voice. "How about you sit here for a bit while Tess and I go look at some clothes."

Dan's gaze narrowed and his voice became defiant. "I don't mind going with you." He folded his arms across his body and Hannah couldn't decide if she wanted to laugh at his predictability or admire his muscular chest and arms, which were emphasized by his stance. His red Henley was unbuttoned at the neck and gave a glimpse of dark chest hair. She consoled herself by rubbing her hands over his biceps, committing their feel to memory.

"I know, but it will give Tess and me a chance to bond over girl stuff. You don't have to sit here. You can explore on your own if you prefer."

He looked between Tess and the tables and chairs, and his hand gripped his cane hard enough to turn the knuckles white, as a brief flash of longing showed on his face. "You have your phones, right?"

Hannah and Tess held them up.

"Great, go do your thing, but text me and let me know what's going on."

"Just a sec, Tess," Hannah called. "Oh, and you might want to look the other way." She turned to Dan, stood on tiptoe and kissed his lips. They were minty with a hint of salt from sweat and she wrapped her arms around his neck. "We won't be gone long."

"Take your time. I want the two of you to get to know each other."

Hannah gave him one last, quick kiss before she turned to Tess. "You ready?"

"I guess. But you have to stop with the kissing."

The two of them wandered the clothes vendors, and stopped to check out the jeans.

"You're pretty smart," Tess said.

"Why do you think so?" Hannah held up a pair and looked in the mirror. With a frown, she put them back, unhappy with the color and cut.

"Because there's no way my dad could do this whole place, and you got him to sit without him realizing your plan."

Hannah turned to Tess. "I'm pretty sure he realized. I just suggested a way not to embarrass him."

Tess nodded and for the first time, Hannah noticed a hint of admiration on her face.

They moved on to a T-shirt vendor and the two of them giggled at "People Are Buggy," showing a cartoon of an ant with googly eyes on the front. Hannah picked out an "Eat Dessert First" one and paid the vendor. "You and your dad seem close." Hannah put her wallet away and grabbed the bag.

"He's cool. Sometimes. What about your family?"

She blocked the images of Jeff with red eyes and track marks on his arms. "Well, I live with my grandma and I have three older brothers, like I told you at the concert. Plus some nieces and nephews." Their smiling faces eased the pressure behind her forehead.

"Do you want kids of your own?"

Hannah smothered a cough. "I like kids, so yeah, someday."

"What about your parents?" Tess picked up and returned a silver pendant to the tray.

"My parents got divorced when I was in middle school and we lost contact with my dad." She swallowed, remembering the turmoil of those early years. "My mom died a few years ago." Blinking, she turned away so Tess wouldn't see.

"Oh. My mom died too."

"Your dad mentioned it. I'm sorry."

Hannah fingered some scarves. Tess picked out a yellow one and twisted it around her neck.

"Here, try it this way," Hannah said.

Tess admired herself in the mirror. "I was seven. It was a car accident. That's how my dad hurt his leg."

Hannah nodded. She didn't want to pump Tess for information, but she wouldn't stop her from sharing of her own free will. "I'm sorry. It must have been rough. The scarf looks pretty on you. Let me buy it for you?"

"You don't have to."

"I know."

Tess nodded and Hannah pulled out her wallet, paid the vendor, and they continued walking. Hannah's stomach growled; Tess giggled.

"We should probably head back to your dad and see if he's hungry."

They found him seated at a table, playing with his phone.

"Hey, what did you two buy?" he asked.

Tess showed him the scarf and Hannah showed the T-shirt.

"So I guess you enjoyed yourselves?"

"We did." Hannah looked at Tess for confirmation. At Tess's nod, Hannah's chest swelled. "But now we're hungry…or at least I am."

"I'm starved," Tess said.

"Good, me too," Dan said. "Let's eat."

Tess walked ahead to check out the food vendors. Dan pulled Hannah aside. "Thanks for the break."

"Break? What break?" She winked at him. She wrapped her arm around his waist. Nothing else needed to be said.

CHAPTER EIGHT

"**W**as I right or was I right, Dad?"

"I don't know what you mean." He tried to maintain a straight face, but thought she noticed the strangled sound of his voice as he tried not to laugh.

After finding food—hero sandwiches, sodas, and chips—they ate their lunch at the same set of tables and chairs where he'd rested. Hannah and Tess told Dan about their time together; the rapport they were building warmed him inside. Now, as they checked out the last of the vendors, he linked arms with Tess as Hannah rushed ahead to check out a vintage dealer.

"Yes, you were right," he said. "I'm glad you got a chance to meet."

She shoved him playfully with her hip so he turned to her, one eyebrow raised. "Really?"

Biting her lip between her teeth, she reminded him of when she was five, and the way she looked at him when she wanted something, brown eyes like chocolate coins seeming to fill her entire face. Beth had always been able to resist, but not him. Never him. He staggered as the memory swamped him.

"Did I hurt you, Daddy? I didn't mean to."

Giving her a quick squeeze, he shook his head. "You? Hurt me? That could never happen, kiddo. Promise."

She unlinked her arm from his and walked to Hannah. By the time he caught up with them, they were deep in conversation. They pulled apart and Tess giggled.

"What did I miss?"

"Oh...nothing," Tess said.

Girls were so secretive.

Hannah grabbed his hand. She was soft and warm and...to hell with Tess's admonition, he wanted to kiss his girlfriend. He tipped his head and pressed his lips against hers. She tasted fruity. Hoping she could read his desire in his expression, he pulled away to look into her face.

"Eww," Tess said. With a toss of her hair, she moved on to the next vendor.

Hannah's eyes twinkled. "Tess and I bonded, don't worry."

"I'm not," he said. "I figure as long as you don't say *eww* every time I kiss you, or roll your eyes, we're good. Are you finished looking around here?"

"Leg hurt?"

She'd never been this direct before. *Breathe*, he told himself. It's a natural question. He was rusty because other than Tess, no one talked about his leg. "Yeah, some, but don't stop because of me."

"I'm not. If there was something I really wanted to search for, I'd suggest you sit and wait for me. But I'm good. As long as Tess is ready to go, we can leave anytime."

He pulled her into a hug and inhaled the scent of her auburn hair. He believed the scent of her could melt away all his pain. "As long as I'm with you, I don't care where we are. Tess, are you ready yet?"

Tess sauntered over and frowned at his arm around Hannah's shoulders. "I guess so."

"Great, let's go to my apartment," Hannah said.

She stayed pressed against his side as they walked to the car. He wasn't sure if she did it because she wanted to be close to him, or if she was giving him something to lean on. If he were honest with himself, he'd admit he leaned on her a little. But he wouldn't analyze it. Her touch was heaven. Her fingers curled through his belt loop and stroked his side, her hair tickled his neck. There was no way he would say anything to push her away, even if Tess thought it was gross.

He was curious to see her apartment. Knowing she lived with her grandmother, he wanted to get a glimpse of Hannah, the granddaughter, even if the grandmother wasn't home. Would it be an old-lady apartment that Hannah inhabited, or did Hannah leave her mark on it?

Neither talked much about their families. They both had pasts they kept close to the vest.

"Come on in." Hannah unlocked the door. "Make yourselves at home. The bathroom is down the hall if anyone wants to freshen up."

Dan nodded to Tess as she went in search of it. A green fuzzy-looking sofa, obviously from her grand-mother's era, was modernized with up-to-date geomet-ric pillows in green, blue, and copper. Two comforta-ble-looking beige chairs sat on either side of an end ta-ble with a lamp that made him do a double-take—it was a woman's leg in a black high-heeled pump with a black lace and bead lampshade. Obviously, *hopefully*, Hannah's influence. A beige and black carpet was soft under his feet and lots of books and photos lined shelves and were scattered around the room. The pho-tos interested him the most.

"Those are my parents on their honeymoon in Mexico." Hannah rubbed his back. "Those are my brothers at my college graduation and those are my nieces and nephews last summer."

She didn't specify which brother was the drug ad-dict and he didn't ask. Not now, when Tess was com-ing down the hall.

"So what should we watch first? Your choice, Tess." Hannah offered drinks and popcorn.

She handed the remote to Tess, who scrolled through the streaming services. "Oh, this one looks good." She highlighted "Breakfast Club."

Dan turned to Hannah. "Are you okay with it?"

Hannah nodded; they started the movie. Tess sprawled on the floor, phone in hand, leaving Dan and Hannah the couch. Dan sank into it and stifled a groan.

"Need anything?" Hannah asked, her voice low, as she sat next to him. "Tylenol? Ibuprofen?"

Need anything? So many, many things. He swallowed. What he wouldn't give to accept painkillers, even over-the-counter ones. "Ice, if you have some."

She stared at him for a moment, rose and went into the kitchen.

Damn, he should have said, "you." But he wasn't sure what she meant and he couldn't take it back. She came back with an ice pack, and he waited for her to hand it to him.

"Where's the best place to put it?" Her eyes twinkled and the constriction in his chest eased.

He guided her hand to right above his knee. His hand covered hers, rough over smooth, warm on top of cold.

"Is this better?" she asked, her voice a whisper.

With a nod, he leaned against the cushions, drawing her to him so she rested against his shoulder, her hand on his thigh, above the ice pack. His muscle twitched. He couldn't tell if she touched him out of sympathy or a desire to heal him. Maybe she touched him because she liked him. And with Tess sitting six feet in front of them, he couldn't ask.

When she stroked his leg, it was the first time in seven years he found it enjoyable. Probably due to the fact she didn't wear a white coat or carry a stethoscope.

He liked touching her. For the past five minutes, his arm had been around her, his hand stroking her shoulder. He played with her hair, whose silkiness and array of color—various shades of reds, browns, and gold—delighted him. But she didn't have an injury she tried to avoid discussing. And he would look like a fool if he assumed she touched him because she wanted to, and it turned out she pitied him.

He clenched his jaw. Dammit, he was too old to be this unsure of women.

"You two finished with your smexy times?" Tess half-turned to them, her hand over her eyes. Dan wasn't sure who was more mortified, he or Hannah. Hannah was a deep shade of red, which he found adorable. A suspicious heat flooded his face.

"Focus on the movie." He reached for Hannah. "We're getting a drink of water."

He hoped the movie continued for longer than its hour and a half run time as he led her down the hall, ignoring the kitchen. She opened a door and pulled him into a bedroom. Perching on the end of the bed, one hand clenched in a fist, she watched him.

He cleared his throat. "Would it be a stupid question for me to ask you why you were touching my bad leg?"

"People always say there's no such thing as a stupid question. However, they obviously hang out with a different set of people than I do."

He chuckled and sat next to her. "So is that a yes?"

"How about it's a maybe, until you tell me what you're thinking."

"I think I don't know if you're touching me because you're attracted to me or because you want to fix me."

"I didn't know you were broken."

"And I didn't know you avoided questions so well."

She ducked her head. "Sorry." She shifted away from him and sat sideways, cross-legged on the bed. "I'm touching you because I like you. I'll admit I was careful so as not to hurt—"

He stopped further conversation by pulling her against him and kissing her. She liked him. It was all he needed to hear. Her mouth was soft and alluring. Relief and desire mingled as the kiss lengthened. He wanted to taste every part of her, but Tess was in the other room. As if she'd read his mind, she sighed and he dragged his mouth away.

Her mouth was irresistible. It looked delicious and he ran his fingers over her lips, along her jaw, and through her hair, drawing her close. Forehead to forehead, he slowed his breathing.

"I hope that answers your question," she said with a whisper.

"I think I should ask more of them, if that's the answer I get."

"I've never been the one reluctant to answer questions."

He reared back. "What do you want to know?"

She bit her lip. "Lots of things, but Tess is in the other room, and I don't want to make her feel left out."

He pulled her close and kissed her forehead. "I love how you care about my daughter's feelings. Let's go back and join her. We can talk later."

When the movie ended, Tess picked up her phone and texted with great speed. Dan shifted uncomfortably in the chair, and for once it wasn't due to his leg.

Tess came to him. "Dad, Lexi's having a crisis and wants me to come over. I know I'm supposed to spend the time with you and Hannah, but do you think she'd mind?"

Hannah glanced over her shoulder at them as she walked toward the kitchen. "I know I shouldn't eavesdrop, but I wouldn't mind, if it's what you want. You're more than welcome to stay for dinner, or leave to be with your friends. Either way is fine with me."

Tess looked between Dan and Hannah. "Are you sure?"

He swallowed. A few minutes ago he'd wished Tess wasn't here and now, his wish was answered. Was it okay to accept it? What kind of father wanted his daughter to leave? Did he do his duty and force Tess to stay, with the chance of making her resent his relationship with Hannah, or did he follow his heart and allow her to go? Once again, the big brown eyes won out. "I'm okay with it as long as Hannah is. And as long as Lexi's parents are home." It was one evening. It would be okay.

Tess started to roll her eyes, but a look from Dan stopped it. "Thank you, both!" she said.

Hannah came over. "I enjoyed spending the day with you."

Tess hugged her, and Dan saw the shock and pleasure in Hannah's expression as she returned the hug.

"Bye, Dad. I'll be home by ten." She waved.

Before she left the apartment, Dan yelled, "Don't forget to text when you get there!"

"So, dinner for two." Hannah turned toward Dan as he approached.

He pulled her into his arms, his lips met hers and he gave in to all the desires he'd withheld in front of his daughter. His hands slid through her hair, massaging her scalp and when she opened her mouth, he slipped his tongue inside. She tasted sweet and he sighed against her mouth. "I hope Tess leaving doesn't cause you a problem."

She pressed her breasts into his chest, her hands sliding around and cupping his ass. "Not at all."

God, he wanted her. Leaning against the counter, he spread his legs, pulling her between them. She moaned, or maybe he did. He couldn't tell beyond the rushing in his ears.

The rushing transformed into a buzzing, and he pulled away, heavy-lidded and aching.

Hannah took a step back. "The oven is pre-heated."

"What can I do to help?"

"Um..." She spun in slow motion.

"Well, let's start with what are you making?" he asked.

"London broil, roasted vegetables, and bread."

"Okay, do you need help chopping?"

"No, I'm good."

She set the broiler, slid the meat inside, and moved on to the vegetables. She'd said she wasn't much of a cook, but she seemed pretty comfortable in the kitchen. When she finished, she pulled a stool from under the sink, stood on it, and disconnected the smoke alarm.

"What did you do that for?" he asked.

She turned on the faucet and washed her hands. "Well, in case I misjudge the broiling..."

He laughed and handed her a dishtowel. "Should I be worried?"

"Probably a bad idea for me to say anything other than no. Now, what would you like to drink? I have wine, beer, soda?"

His mouth grew dry at the thought of taking a long pull on a frosty brew and he swallowed reflexively. Never again. "I'll have water."

"So, you don't drink, right? I mean, it's the feeling I get from you."

His stomach clenched. *Please don't let this line of questioning force my hand, not now.* "I don't mind if you do." He reached for the napkins and silverware and followed her lead, hoping she'd drop the subject, although they were getting closer and closer to a time when he'd have to answer.

She smiled as she set the table. "Is there a reason for you not drinking?"

Dammit. His gut tightened. "Family history."

"Got it." She nodded.

No, she didn't have a clue, but he wouldn't debate the point with her.

Returning to the oven, she turned the meat and uncovered the vegetables. The aromas made his mouth water. Despite her concerns, no smoke billowed.

"Since you ordered the peach dessert the other night, I bought a peach and plum cobbler for tonight. I assumed you weren't a chocolate person."

Another assumption she shouldn't make—he liked chocolate too much to allow himself to have it—but an assumption he couldn't correct without starting an avalanche of other questions. "It sounds delicious. But you should have said something. I would have been happy to provide dessert."

"Don't worry about it. You can take leftovers home for Tess." She pulled everything out of the oven. "It must be hard to balance things."

It was. "Do you want me to slice the meat?"

As he began, he admired the cut of the meat and the meal in general. She was a good cook, if looks were to be believed. "Excellent job. It's delicious."

"Thanks. It's my grandma's recipe. She's a wonderful cook."

"It's obvious you take after her. You didn't even have to disconnect the smoke alarm!"

Hannah let out a deep breath as she brought everything to the table. "Previous history indicated otherwise. My grandmother, although supportive, is not convinced I won't starve you tonight. I think she told me ten times how to cook everything."

He savored the flavor of the London broil and looked around the dining room. It was a nook off the kitchen, nothing fancy, but homey. A sideboard held Shabbat candles and some China serving pieces. On white walls hung a Chagall print and an old-fashioned wedding portrait. He pointed to it with his fork.

"Your grandparents?"

Hannah nodded. "Yes, I love that one. They were married forty-five years. What about you? How long were you married?"

The meat formed rocks in his stomach. He didn't want to have this conversation. "Ten years."

"Tess said you hurt your leg in the car accident when you lost your wife."

His fork clattered to the table. "You talked to Tess about this?"

"It came up in conversation."

He pushed his chair back and ignored the shooting pain running up and down his leg from the sudden movement. "You pumped my daughter for information while the two of you were alone?"

Hannah's eyes widened. Her hands clamped her silverware hard enough for Dan to see her knuckles whiten. "Whoa, wait a second. I didn't pump her for information."

He rose, nostrils flared. His heart beat hard, and spots formed behind his eyes. "What, she told you the information out of the blue?"

Hannah stood and leaned toward him, but he backed away. He didn't want to be near her right now. What else did she know?

"It wasn't out of the blue. Tess asked me about my family. I told her my parents divorced, and my mom died a few years ago. Tess said hers did too, which I knew. She mentioned, on her own, you hurt your leg in the accident, which you hinted at earlier. There was no *pumping* for information."

Her air quotes would have been cute if he weren't angry and he paced from the dining table to the sofa and back again, trying to fill his lungs with air, while ignoring the pain in his leg. He didn't know how to get out of this argument without talking about things he didn't want to discuss with her. Things he couldn't discuss with her, given what he knew about her brother.

He stopped next to his seat. Her cheeks were red, her neck splotchy. She was angry too. Somehow, knowing her emotions helped cool his anger and allowed rational thought in. Analyzing what she'd said, he realized maybe it wasn't as much of a problem as he thought. She knew when it happened. Big deal. He rubbed the back of his head. "Yeah, I may have over-reacted just now."

As the words exited his mouth, it was apparent that was the wrong thing to say. If her eyes could shoot lasers, he would duck.

"You think? Don't get me started on the Fort Knox storing your personal information." She pushed past him into the living room. "We've dated for almost three weeks and I know next to nothing about you. You clam up every time I start to get close. You freak out at the thought of Tess telling me anything." She stood in his personal space and dared him to avoid her gaze. "You're my boyfriend. What is the point of my getting to know your daughter if you won't let me know you?"

She was furious and she was beautiful. Her chest heaved, drawing attention to her cleavage, framed by the dark blue V-neck sweater that hugged her curves. Her creamy skin—other than her neck, which was mottled from emotion—glowed. Not that he wanted to make her angry, but, man, she was amazing when she was.

She was also right.

It was that thought which made him swallow. He needed to move forward with care. Because he sensed this was a turning point. He had a choice to make and he'd better choose wisely. He was her boyfriend, which made her his girlfriend. His girlfriend deserved an-swers. "You're right."

Those two words acted like a pin touching an over-inflated balloon. Her anger disappeared. A part of him was sorry to see it go.

"What would you like to know?" He lowered him-self into the chair. His anxiety rose as he gripped the edge of the table, waiting for her response. He'd meant the question, but it was a big one, filled with many pos-sible scenarios.

"Tell me about your wife." He must have shown his sorrow, because she followed up quickly. "I don't mean the painful parts, but there must be something you can tell me—what you loved about her, what kind of mom she was, her favorite color. I need something to make her human, otherwise she's this fantastical be-ing I can never hope to come close to."

Of course. If the roles were reversed, he'd want the same thing. "I don't need you to be like her. I like you as you are."

Memories flooded through him. Hannah and the apartment disappeared, replaced by scenes from his old life. "We met in college—UMass." In his mind, he en-visioned the campus, the rolling hills surrounding it, the college town nearby. "She was a film major and I was an accounting major. We met at a party one night and were together from then on. She was sweet with a typical artist personality. She doted on Tess. She was a terrible cook. I mean, burned-water bad."

"So that's why you're a good one?"

A weight lifted from his chest as he remembered the first time Beth cooked for him—smoky apartment, charred food, nervous smiles, tears. "I didn't like the idea of starvation—it's a painful way to go."

"Yeah, I've heard that."

He reached for her hand. It was soft and smooth and grounded him in the present. "What else do you want to know?"

"Would you tell me about the accident? I can't keep feeling like I have to tiptoe around every possible mention of it."

He didn't realize his hand was clenched until she started to massage it. God, if he'd hurt her...but he hadn't. He blinked and loosened his grip. "It was a drunk driver. We drove through an intersection and he t-boned us. On Beth's side. I was driving." He closed his eyes, images of the crash flashing through his mind, sounds of squealing tires, crumpling metal and shattering glass piercing his eardrums.

"I'm sorry."

"Me too."

"And your leg?"

"Shattered in six places, held together by screws, plates and a lot of luck." Smells of the hospital replaced the garlicky scent of the London broil and he wrinkled his nose. "I didn't mean to make you feel the way you did. I get focused on moving forward and I don't like to dwell on the past. But I know you need information—"

"It's not information as much as I need to know you. Yes, the information helps, but it's also the intangible stuff I need."

He pulled her close. She leaned against him and rested against his chest. She was warm in his arms and he nuzzled her hair. "Boyfriend, huh?" he asked.

She angled back to look at him. "Does the word bother you?"

"No," he said. "I like it. And I like the sound of girlfriend too."

He sat with her snuggled against him awkwardly at the table, the rest of their food untouched, feeling more comfortable than he had in a long time. For now, he was safe. But in the back of his mind, worry niggled. His safety net was wearing thin.

CHAPTER NINE

Hannah hummed to herself as she arrived at work on Monday. Not only had she spent a wonderful weekend with Dan, and gone shopping with her grandmother, she'd thought of the perfect idea for her client. She waved to the receptionist as she entered and made a beeline for Aviva's office.

"Lunch today?" she asked, sticking her head around the doorway.

Aviva looked up. "Wow, you look cheery."

Hannah nodded. "I had a great weekend."

As Hannah walked down the hall to her office, Aviva yelled after her. "Thanks for keeping me in suspense!"

She stopped at Jim's office. "Good morning. Did you want to meet later?"

Five minutes before her scheduled meeting with Jim, she grabbed her files and walked to his office.

Jim waved her to a seat. "So, I looked over your rebranding ideas from last week and I think our best bet might be to partner with another brand. It will give them the benefit of another brand's expertise and—"

"Jim, I'm sorry to interrupt, but I thought of a new idea yesterday."

Jim leaned forward and steepled his fingers.

"When I was trying to find something to make the CEO stand out from everyone else, there was one thing that struck me…his philanthropy. Now, most CEOs make some sort of donation to charity, but if you look at his figures, his percentage is huge." She handed Jim the financials and watched his eyebrows rise. "Someone like him will possess a social conscience and would want their business to reflect it as well. What if we suggested *cause marketing* to him—his company could partner with a charity, donate a percentage of their profits to the charity and sponsor a fundraiser? It makes them look good and it associates the corporation with whatever cause they're passionate about. It makes them look less like a cold, uncaring corporation and more like a world citizen."

"I love the idea and I think they will too. Can you draft a proposal?"

Hannah's heartbeat sped up. "Sure, what do you want me to include?"

He walked over and leaned against the desk. "Hannah, I want you to handle all of it. I'll provide you any support you need; I'll be your sounding board, whatever. But I want this to be your baby. You created it; you should get to run it. Okay with you?"

She gripped the arms of her chair. "Absolutely."

"Great. Let's talk to the client this afternoon." He looked at his watch. "Say, four o'clock?"

Hannah checked her schedule. "I should be able to put something together by then."

She left his office, positive she was floating, and started toward Aviva's to share her good news. But halfway there she stopped. She wanted to tell Aviva, and she would at lunch. But at this moment, the first person she wanted to tell was Dan. Sometime within the past three weeks, he'd become important. Releasing a breath, she raced to her office, shut the door, and dialed Dan. He answered on the third ring.

"Guess what," she said, heart pounding, breath coming in gasps.

"You're having an asthma attack?"

"Funny guy. My boss made me lead on a project I created." She told him the entire story, filling him in on the problems and her solution involving pairing with a charity to take advantage of the company's already huge charitable donations.

"That's terrific, Hannah."

"Listen, I've got to go and put everything together for my meeting. I wanted to tell someone and you were the first person I wanted to speak to."

"Call me tonight and let me know how it went."

Hannah dragged herself home that night past eight o'clock. After several hours of drafting a proposal, she showed it to Jim, who loved it, and hinted she was working her way toward promotion. The client loved it as well, and was running it up their food chain.

She'd spent the rest of the time drafting next steps and researching answers to their questions. There would be a full in-person meeting next week where she'd present the complete plan. Between the adrenaline high from her success and the hard work it entailed, she was beyond exhausted. Now, all she wanted was food, a long soak in the tub, and bed.

She unlocked the door, stepped over the threshold, and froze.

Jeff.

His voice, his cadence, rang through the apartment. Her stomach dropped. Acid burned the back of her throat. She couldn't do this. She couldn't deal with him—the empty promises, the suspicions about his motives, the furtive hiding of her purse so he wouldn't take her money. Her grandmother? She couldn't deal with her either—her pathetic hope that all would be okay, her disappointment when Hannah refused to participate.

Her heart pounded and her hands grew clammy as she tiptoed backward, exited the apartment, and returned to the lobby. Breathless, she staggered to a chair in the corner behind a palm frond. All she wanted was to curl into a ball in the security of her home, but this place wasn't it. Dan was. The urge to call him, to hear his voice, overwhelmed her. She dialed his number with shaking fingers and waited for him to answer.

"Hey, Hannah." The sound of his deep caring voice, her end-of-day fatigue, her excitement from work, and her disappointment about Jeff came to a head and her eyes misted.

Her throat clogged and she croaked, "Dan?"

"Hannah, what's wrong?"

She started to cry.

"Sweetheart, talk to me. Please."

She took a deep shaky breath. "Jeff is here. I'm exhausted and I wanted to eat and take a bath and talk to you. I don't want to deal with him." She started to cry once more.

"Come over, right now. Hop a cab and take it to my apartment."

"I don't want to bother you and Tess."

"You won't. I want you to come."

She paused. Wouldn't it be better to stay here and wait for Jeff to leave? "Okay."

"I'll wait right here for you, sweetheart."

This was stupid. It was beyond stupid, and if she carried a thesaurus in her purse, she'd look up how beyond stupid it was. But a thesaurus would weigh her down and prevent her from running away. And right now, as she shifted from one leg to the other in front of Dan's apartment building, she wanted to run fast and far, from his apartment, from this town, from everyone.

She didn't want to show how afraid she was, or how needy. She didn't want to be the one with the drug-addicted brother, or with the sweet but enabling grandmother, or maybe with the good-at-listening/bad-at-confessing boyfriend. She wanted to be someone else, only she didn't know who or how to find her.

The cab pulled away and she was about to take her own advice and run when Dan came outside. From the way he'd spoken on the phone, she expected him to swallow her up in a hug. While the idea had appealed to her in her lobby, right at this moment, the thought scared her to death. He must have read her hesitation in her body language, or maybe there was a sign blinking over her head: Prickly, Proceed at Own Risk. Either way, he stopped a few feet away and watched her, one hand on his cane, the other in his pocket.

"Hannah." His voice was deep, yet soft, and made her stomach flip flop.

She gripped the strap of her purse tight enough for her nails to dig into her palm, making her wince. His gaze tracked the movement, and the cause, and returned to her face.

"You don't want to be here, do you?"

She shrugged. What "here" did he mean? Because although she'd lumped him into the list of things she wasn't sure she wanted, she knew she didn't want to be without him. Maybe.

"Sometimes if you let someone into your space, it changes the *here* and makes it more bearable."

She raised an eyebrow. Did he really say that?

He chuckled. "I learned it from a wise girlfriend."

"Do you have a lot of those?"

"Just one, in fact. Not only is she wise, but she's so beautiful she stops traffic." The corners of his mouth twitched and his gaze slid to the side.

She turned and watched people maneuver around them, muttering under their breath.

"I don't think they admire me right now." She moved out of the way, toward him.

"I am."

"Why?"

"Because you're beautiful and strong and you know when to ask for help, even if you don't think you want it."

Okay, she would definitely scratch him off the list of things she didn't want. "I don't feel any of that right now," she whispered. The tears she'd suppressed at the sound of his voice on the phone threatened once again, and she looked away. If she was forced to stare into those amazing lake-blue eyes one more second, hers would overflow, and she refused to turn into a puddle on the sidewalk.

His shadow on the pavement moved closer and the tips of his shoes touched hers. She would not turn into a puddle.

He stroked her arm, from shoulder to wrist. She wouldn't look at him and she wouldn't turn into a puddle.

"I used to do this to Tess when she was a little girl." He leaned his cane against the building and brought her hand toward her center, walked his fingers up her stomach until they touched her chin, which he tipped until their gazes met. She wouldn't turn...oh hell.

Tears ran down her face. He folded her against his body, wrapped her into a hug like a cocoon, and held her. What was she afraid of? For the first time since she walked over the threshold of her apartment and heard Jeff's voice, she was home. He was warm and safe and smelled like spice, evoking images of being tucked in under a blanket on a cold, winter's night, *havdalah* candles flickering in the darkness. Everything slipped away—the car horns, multilingual conversations, and rumbling trucks—everything except him.

She swallowed and shifted against him. He pulled away half an inch to look at her.

"I made your sweater soggy," she said.

"I know."

"I'm sorry."

"I'm not."

She bit her lip and he traced it with his fingertip.

"Come inside?" He grabbed his cane.

With a nod, she let him take her hand and lead her into the building. The lobby was nondescript—beiges and greys—and seemed the exact opposite of the man who held her hand. He was warm and alive and soft, yet strong.

"Come upstairs?"

His implicit understanding she might need to do this in stages touched her and she squeezed his hand as they walked to the elevator. When it arrived, he ushered her inside, hit 3, and leaned her against him, balancing his cane in the crook of his elbow. Her back touched his hard chest muscles as they rode three floors. His arms wrapped around her middle like a seatbelt, and she stroked the sinews and tendons in his arm through his sweater.

When they arrived on his floor, he stopped her before his door. "Tess is gone. I suggested she do her homework at her friend's. I thought you'd be more comfortable that way."

Hannah ran her hands over her hair and wiped her eyes. "No, I don't want to banish Tess because I'm here. It's her house; she's free to move about as she wants."

Dan stroked her cheek. "It's okay. She was happy to go." He opened the door.

"I don't want to interfere between the two of you."

Dan walked over to her and took her hand. "Tess will be fine."

Hannah looked at him wide-eyed. Behind her, the elevator door opened. In front of her, Dan's expression begged her to stay. With a sigh, she followed him to the kitchen.

"Would you like something to drink?"

She should be thirsty after all those tears, but she wasn't. Wrapping her arms around her middle, she sighed and shook her head. Dan walked to her and took her in his arms. He was solid and she let out a shaky sigh. He kissed her mouth with extreme gentleness before he pulled her away from him. "Go make yourself at home."

The apartment was homey. Clearly, the kitchen was used by someone who liked to cook. Stainless appliances, black-marbled counter, and wine-colored walls, with enough space to prep and chop and whatever else one did in the kitchen. The pots she could see were good ones; there were ingredients stored on the counter—ones that were used, not placed there for decoration—and there were bowls of fruits and veggies. She shook her head. What did she expect—processed food boxes everywhere? The man said he cooked.

She walked down the picture-lined hallway into the living room. Right now, she wasn't ready for a peek into Dan's family life. She had enough difficulty handling her own. The living room's floor-to-ceiling windows prevented it from looking like a cave. Deep blue walls, large leather sofas and chairs, and soft beige carpet.

Lots of bookshelves filled to capacity with books painted a picture of Dan and Tess's life. On the bottom shelves were children's books. As the shelves rose higher, there were young adult books, romances, and mysteries. It was obvious some of the books were Dan's, such as several on photography and architecture. Others, like the romances, might have been left over from his wife. A few self-help books caught her eye and she was about to take a look at them when Dan cleared his throat.

"We're big readers."

"I can see. It's nice."

"Come sit down." He led the way to the oversized sofa and eased onto it. He patted the seat next to him and she snuggled into him.

"Do you have any aspirin or anything I could have? My head hurts."

"I'm sorry, I don't." His gaze slid to the side before he returned his focus to her. "Do you want ice?"

"No, it's okay. It'll go away soon."

No painkillers? Really?

He stroked her back and she yawned. The emotions of the day caught up with her. His rhythmic caressing made her eyelids heavy. Beneath her ear, she could hear the reassuring beat of his heart. Her hand on his chest traced the outline of his muscles. The quiet strength of this man amazed her. His willingness to support her stunned her, though by now, it shouldn't.

"Do you want to talk or just sit here?" His voice was pitched low. She could feel its rumble beneath her ear.

"I don't know what there is to talk about. Nothing has changed. Jeff's still an addict, my grandmother still wants to enable him. I'm the bad guy."

He kissed the top of her head. "You're not the bad guy. Someday, they will both see that as well. Why was Jeff at your apartment?"

"I have no idea. I opened the door, heard his voice, and left."

"So he might still be clean."

She pulled away. "Are you defending him?"

"No." He stared at her. Sincerity, along with something else she couldn't name, reflected in his gaze. She relaxed again and Dan continued. "I'm saying there could be any number of reasons why he was in your apartment. Since you didn't go in, you don't know what the reason was. Right?"

She swallowed. "Right."

"I'm pointing it out because there are many sides to a story."

"In all honesty, at this point, the only thing that will make me feel better is for him to disappear. And he won't, not when my grandmother encourages him."

His breathing hitched and he coughed. "What can we do to make things easier for you the next time he shows up?"

"I have no idea. Although talking to you and knowing you support me does help."

The hand stroking her back paused, before resuming. "I'm glad. And I'm glad you know I support you, because I do."

She met his gaze, sharp with concern. This close, she could see the varying shades of blue around his pupil, the short dark lashes framing his lids and the faint lines at the corners of his eyes. She'd never noticed those lines before and they only added to his appeal. Licking her lips, she watched his pupils dilate and his lids lower a fraction.

She licked her lips again to see what would happen—his nostrils flared and his breath warmed her face. Reaching out with a finger, she traced his lips, which parted at her touch. Lowering her finger, she ran it across his jaw line, feeling the rasp of his stubble brush her fingertip.

He leaned against the back of the sofa, and she trailed her finger down his neck and over his Adam's apple. It bobbed as he swallowed. She let her finger move lower, to the collar of his shirt beneath his sweater. Starched cotton, warm skin, and hard collarbone contrasted with each other. She traced the outline of his shirt, making a V against his chest where the top button opened.

He grasped her hand, holding it in place for a moment before he raised it to his mouth and kissed her fingers. His breath was warm; each touch of his lips against her fingertips sent shards of heat from the ends of her fingers up her arm straight to her chest.

Straightening, she took both hands and ran them through his close-cropped hair. Why did she never think salt-and-pepper was sexy before? Trailing her hands down the planes of his face, she leaned forward and touched her lips to his.

Like a match to a tinderbox, he reacted, bending forward, grabbing her to him and pressing his mouth against hers. They toppled against the sofa, her underneath him, while his mouth devoured hers. His hands roamed from her hair to her waist and back, leaving hot trails in their wake. Heat pooled in her belly. Her breath came in gasps as she plunged her tongue deeper, gripped his body harder and pressed herself against him. Hard melded with soft, boundaries blurred. She lost the ability to tell where she ended and he began.

His hands continued their journey to cup her breasts. The touch was blissful torture, making her shudder as he unclasped her bra and caressed her. All logical thought disappeared. The world around her telescoped to his hands on her body.

She raised her arms above her head and he pulled off her shirt. Hypersensitive to his touch, her body tingled as the fabric dragged against her skin. He flung it away, taking first one breast and then the other in his mouth, sucking gently and making her toes curl with desire. Need made her anxious. With shaking hands, she pulled at his sweater.

"We need to take this off," she whispered. She flung it off of him and unbuttoned his shirt.

His hands stilled, a look of uncertainty flashing across his face.

She climbed onto his lap, took his face between her hands, and forced him to look at her. Lowering her mouth to his, she kissed him on the lips.

"I want you," he whispered.

"I want you too."

"But I won't take advantage of you," he said.

She pulled away and her skin grew chilled. "You won't take advantage of me."

"The first time we have sex, I want it to be because we both want it, not because there are external reasons pushing us together."

Desire mingled with appreciation and frustration. Her heart rate slowed. Her hands curled into fists. How long would she have to wait until the "time was right?"

He wanted her. God, he wanted her more than he'd wanted any woman in a long time. Kissing her, undressing her, touching her, meant more to him than just fooling around. He hadn't engaged in any real relationship since Beth died. Whether it was due to a lack of desire or a lack of opportunity, the first time he'd considered a relationship as a possibility was with Hannah. Was wanting her normal? He felt the same pull to be with her as he had for the painkillers. Except this was Hannah and she wasn't a drug. People felt a pull to anyone they were attracted to, right? More so when they were starting to think their feelings might be serious...he couldn't go there. Because how could he think about whether or not he loved someone he wasn't honest with?

He shifted—his leg would stiffen if he kept it one position too long—and he frowned. It didn't bother him with her. Was it because of what they did, or because of her?

He needed to be open and honest with her—about his own addiction and what it had caused. But he couldn't do it now, not when she was devastated about Jeff.

"I hear you thinking." She maneuvered herself out from under him, and turned on her side, elbow propping her head. She looked like a goddess—an angry goddess—and Dan licked his parched lips.

He saw the masked frustration in her eyes and in the set of her mouth. Even if he did want to share his thoughts, how could he tell her he was a recovering drug addict when she'd talked about wanting nothing to do with her brother? He was too old to be taken over by pure lust without there being some underlying deeper meaning, regardless of how far he'd let things go. How could he share his feelings if he couldn't let himself identify them? He cared about her. He thought about her when they were separated, looked forward to sharing things with her when they were together, and shared her joy and pain when she expressed them.

So why couldn't he tell her? Why couldn't he risk it?

She'd hate him when she found out the secrets he kept.

He opened his mouth and closed it.

"Okay…" She drew lazy circles on his chest. "How about I start? Thank you."

That got his attention. He'd expected her to yell at him. "For kissing you?"

She punched him in the arm. "No, eww, no. For listening, for forcing me to come inside when I wanted to run away, and for making me feel better."

He let out a breath in a rush of air. "I'm glad you trusted me enough to let me do that. As for this…" Her eyes softened.

"We shouldn't have sex if we're not ready for it. And although I thought you were ready," she gave him a wicked smile, "you seem conflicted."

She was pretty perceptive. "I am, but not for the reasons you might think. Or maybe for exactly what you thought. I'm not—"

"Talk. Don't worry about what I might think, or not. Just speak."

He swallowed. "I've been attracted to you from the start, but I didn't invite you here with the intention of having sex. I asked Tess to leave because I wanted you to feel free to talk to me." He paused, played with her hand, which somehow found its way into his grip. His smile was rueful. "There's a whole different level of planning required with a teenager."

"Yeah, I was a little wary of her presence."

"I don't do this," he touched her lips, "for the hell of it. For me it has to mean something."

"So, what does it mean?"

"I'm serious about our relationship. I want to see where it goes from here."

"Then why do you look worried?"

I'm afraid to tell you the truth. And he'd never get any further than this unless he found a way to tell her everything.

CHAPTER TEN

Hannah gripped the door handle of her apartment. Thanks to the conversation with Dan, she knew what to do about her brother. But it didn't make it any easier. She took a deep breath, reminded herself Dan understood her point of view, and pushed open the door. At first, the apartment was quiet, but as she took a few steps inside, murmurs from the kitchen made her stop.

Dan had prepared her for this possibility. Straightening her shoulders, she walked into the kitchen.

"Hi *Bubbe*, Jeff." She hugged her grandmother and nodded to her brother.

"Sweetheart, where were you?"

"I'm sorry, I should have called. I was with Dan."

"Who's Dan?" Jeff sipped a cup of coffee.

As far as she was concerned, her brother abdicated any and all rights to know about her life the second he took his first injection of heroin. If her grandmother weren't here, she wouldn't deign to acknowledge his presence. But Hannah wanted her grandmother reasonable when she talked to her later, and this was the second time she'd seen Jeff when he wasn't high, so she answered.

"My boyfriend." She walked over to the sink and helped herself to a glass of water. "You're still here," she said, over its rim.

"Well, Grandma was worried. I thought I'd keep her company."

Hannah's chest burned at the irony of her brother providing support to her grandmother, but she bit the inside of her cheek and kept silent. "Why did you come in the first place?"

He waved an arm over his shoulder toward the living room. "I needed bedding and Grandma said she had some extra."

Hannah swung around toward her grandmother, who nodded in affirmation.

"Bedding, huh? Well, I'm home and I'm going to bed. Sorry I worried you, *Bubbe*." She bent, gave her a hug, turned, and walked toward her bedroom. Locking the door, she got undressed and lay in bed until the front door closed. When she was sure Jeff was gone, she returned to the kitchen.

"Jeff left." Her grandmother's disapproving tone made her cringe, but she kept to her resolve.

"I want to talk to you, *Bubbe*."

"I don't think I'm going to like this conversation."

"We need to have it."

Her grandmother sighed and paced the living room. Returning to her chair in the kitchen, she sat, folded her hands on her lap and looked at Hannah. "Okay, go ahead."

"I know you love Jeff, and I know you love me. I also know you want to do what you think is best for us. But your vision and mine are different." She knelt by her grandmother and took her hands. "I can't be here if he is. I'd never tell you not to have him here, but I would like to know ahead of time so I can make plans to be somewhere else."

"Is that why you stayed at Dan's so late?"

"Yes. I came home from work and heard you two talking. So I left."

"He's trying, *Hannahla.*"

Hannah shrugged. "I still can't be in the same apartment."

"So you're abandoning your brother?"

Hannah's ears burned as the first stab of guilt sliced through her. She didn't want to abandon him, but she couldn't continue to watch her grandmother enable him. "He abandoned me when he started using. I'm protecting myself."

Her grandmother shook her head. "This isn't right. Am I supposed to call you whenever he comes over? It would feel like I'm warning you. About your own brother."

"I know, but it's the best I can do."

"You won't change your mind?"

"No."

"I don't approve. I think you're making a big mistake, and I hope you can somehow find it in your heart to forgive him. Because he's trying."

"I love you, *Bubbe*."

Hannah's grandmother shook her head. "I love you, too, sweetheart, but you were raised better than this, *Hannahla*. Everyone makes mistakes."

The next day at work, Hannah's office phone rang.

"Hannah Cohen."

"You're sexy when you're professional, you know that?"

Hannah's face heated. "I didn't expect you to call at work."

"I missed your voice.

"Aww, you're sweet."

"Really, that's all I have to do to get that reaction?"

"Well..." She smiled as he chuckled on the other end of the phone.

"I'm in your neighborhood this afternoon. Want a visitor?"

"Really? What are you doing over here?"

"A meeting. I know we talk all the time, but I want to see you."

"I'd love you to stop by. I can introduce you to my friend, Aviva."

Was it okay for her boyfriend to come to her office? She'd seen others do it. As long as they didn't spend too much time, it would be fine.

Besides, she missed him too.

Later that afternoon, Jim stopped at Hannah's office at the same time her intercom buzzed: "Dan Rothberg is here to see you."

Jim frowned. "Expecting someone?"

Great timing. "My friend is in the neighborhood and asked if I'd mind if he stopped by. It'll only be for a moment."

"It's fine, I'll catch you later."

She walked to reception. "Hey, Elise, here I am. Dan's here?"

"Yes, and he's sexy, if I might add."

Elise, in her early sixties, found something sexy about every man who crossed her path, so Hannah laughed and gave her a wave before she headed into the reception area.

Dan wore a light blue Oxford shirt open at the neck and grey slacks with the end of his navy tie sticking out of his pocket. He was conservative and dashing and all hers. Her stomach flip-flopped.

"Hey," she said.

"Hey, beautiful." He pulled out a bouquet of flowers hidden behind his back. They were violets in purple, yellow, and white.

She wrapped her hands around his hand holding the flowers and buried her nose in them, inhaling deeply. "They're beautiful!"

He smiled. "I saw them and thought of you." He gave her a chaste peck on the cheek, withdrew his hand and pulled away.

"Would you like to come inside?"

On the way to her office, she introduced him to Aviva. The two shook hands.

"It's nice to meet you, Aviva. Hannah speaks of you often."

"She speaks about you as well."

Before the conversation could go any further in a direction she suspected she didn't want to hear, Hannah tugged on Dan's arm. "My office is this way." As they said goodbye to Aviva, she gave Hannah a look and Hannah's face heated. They'd have to talk later.

Hannah told him about her conversation with her grandmother.

"Are you alright with how things turned out?"

"Yeah. She's not thrilled with the way I choose to handle it, but she accepted it, which is huge for her."

"Good, I'm glad you were able to work it out."

"I also...had an idea."

"What kind of idea?"

She played with things on her desk, moving the stapler back and forth, straightening the paper piles, until Dan placed his hand on top of hers. She read kindness and compassion in his expression and swallowed. "I think I need to find out more about my brother."

"How do you mean?"

"Well, he says he has a job. I thought I might go and check it out. That makes me a horrible person, doesn't it?"

"No. It makes you a human being. And a pretty open-minded one."

"Why?"

"Because you're not blindly believing him, but you're willing to consider he might be telling the truth. And the only way for you to know is to investigate. It's not a bad thing, Hannah."

"Even if it's my own brother?" Her voice was a whisper and she stared into her lap.

"Especially if it's your brother."

She let out a breath. Her smile wobbled as she met his gaze.

"I hate to leave this soon, but I have a meeting to go to," he said.

She hugged him. His chest was hard, his heart beat against her ear. It was solid, steady, and strong. More than anything, she wanted to leave with him, but she still had work to do.

"Thank you again for the visit and the flowers."

"Anytime."

Dan reviewed the paperwork Lisa gave him. It was the fourth time he'd looked at the numbers. They hadn't made sense from the beginning, and after weeks of tracing and backtracking, he'd concluded Fortex was funneling company money somewhere, using philanthropy to hide it. Now it was time to figure out where "somewhere" was.

"Lisa, it's Dan. Can you meet me in the conference room in a half hour?"

For the next half hour, Dan made a list of the expenses and deposits, as well as the backup documentation he had. By the time he walked into the conference room, he was ready.

"Thanks for meeting with me." He eased into the chair, put his files on the table, and handed a stack to Lisa. "Based on your findings and my digging, I'm pretty sure Fortex funneled money somewhere, but I'm not sure where. So, you take the expense side, divide it among your team, and let's track the money. I'll do the same with my team on the deposit side."

Lisa whistled. "I thought it looked hinky, and I'm glad you agree." She shuffled through the files. "Going to be a lot of work, but okay. I hate it when companies that seem good from the outside are bad. Dammit, this will cause damage for a lot of people, not just their employees. People depend on them for lifesaving drugs."

Dan stifled a shudder. "I know, which is why we need to keep things quiet as long as possible. If word gets out they're siphoning money, it can affect their grants, their hiring ability, and their reputation for years to come. And I don't want it to happen if we can avoid it."

Lisa nodded.

He returned to his desk massaging his leg. His mouth dried at the thought of taking something—anything—to relieve the pain, and dizziness washed over him. He waited for it to pass, inhaling through his nose and exhaling through his mouth. When he could focus again, he redirected his thoughts to the investigation and its ramifications. He hated investigating pharmaceutical companies—it hit a little too close to home— but it wasn't like he could say anything. And he hadn't overstated things with Lisa. Whenever a company was accused of bad financials, the effect spiraled out, tarnishing everyone who worked for the company, even if some of the employees were innocent. Add research or fundraising into the mix, and the beneficiaries of the work were affected as well.

He needed to identify the guilty party in Fortex's structure and do as much damage control as possible.

CHAPTER ELEVEN

Hannah panicked as she sat in her office a day later. There were rumors circulating that Fortex's CEO embezzled funds. No one knew the source, but the financial papers picked up on it. Her phone had been ringing for hours.

No matter how many times she and her colleagues spoke to the CFO, he swore up, down, and sideways there was nothing going on with their finances. It might be true, but the papers were going to have a field day with this. Only a week ago, she'd begged the media for coverage, now she'd give anything for them to ignore this. She tried to create other stories for the media to pursue, none of which resulted in any bites. Everyone was yelling at her. If she didn't figure out the source of these stories, she would lose her client, or worse, her job.

Jim stuck his head in her office. "How are you doing with developing case histories for some of Fortex's medical success stories? Your marketing plan will take too long to develop. We need something positive now."

Hannah swung her chair around and pointed to a stack of folders on her desk. "Fortex is a huge pharmaceutical company. I've got calls out to everyone on their case study list and I'm waiting to hear from them. In the meantime, I've drafted the bare bones, so all I have to do is plug in the specific information."

"Good. When you're done with it, put together a media list for which publications we plan to target. We've got to get them some positive publicity or we'll lose them." He turned to go, but paused and fixed her with his penetrating stare.

She shivered. That stare made him a star with the clients. It freaked out his staff, though. Hannah had never been the recipient of it. She didn't like it.

"We need to figure out where the rumors originated."

She gulped. "I know."

Looking at his retreating back, she shook her head. How in the world was she supposed to figure out who started the rumors?

The next day, Jim was waiting for her when she arrived at work. "Hannah, can I see you in my office?"

His tone brooked no argument. "I'll be right there." Her stomach plummeted and her head began to ache. She straightened her posture, smoothed her hair, and walked to her boss's office. His back was to her when she reached it, so she knocked.

He swiveled, motioning her inside. "Sit down. The other day your friend visited you. Dan Rothberg?"

Hannah caught her breath. "Yes, he's my boyfriend. Why?"

He leaned on his desk and steepled his fingers, resting his mouth on their tips. "The same Dan Rothberg who works for Lorpman LLP?"

"Yes, that's the name of his firm. Why?"

"We have a huge problem."

Her stomach dropped. "What do you mean?"

"Lorpman is the firm investigating Fortex, and Dan Rothberg is the lead investigator."

"Wait, what?" She leaned forward.

"Your boyfriend is investigating their financials. If Fortex finds out you're dating him, they'll think you've given him information and access."

"I don't understand. Dan is the one investigating Fortex?" She sank onto the nearest chair and gripped the armrest. This couldn't be possible.

Jim pulled up a photo from the internet. It was a professional headshot from Dan's office's website. Same salt and pepper hair, same to-die-for blue eyes, same smile-crinkles around the eyes, same lips she couldn't get enough of.

"They have no idea how he found and accessed this information."

"Neither do I. He's good at his job. I didn't know he was investigating them."

"Still, we've got to figure out what to do here. We can't put our business with them at risk."

All the oxygen siphoned out of the room. "You know me, Jim. I've done nothing wrong."

"I know it's all in the perception, Hannah. Even if you didn't say anything on purpose, it's easy to slip. To say something you think is harmless but isn't. There's no telling what you gave away by accident. And if the client finds out, it's not just your job that's on the line."

Her head pounded harder as her pulse rushed in her ears. She couldn't afford to lose her job. If this got out, her reputation and her ability to be hired any-where, would be impacted.

"They should be more concerned with the illegal-ity of what they've done than who I date."

"They're a company, Hannah, and they're fighting for their livelihood. That's what they're focusing on now, and what we have to do as well. I have to do dam-age control."

There was nothing left to say. She rose and re-turned to her office, where she shut the door and dropped into her chair. She would have to take herself off the account. It was either remove herself, or further harm her company and ruin any remaining chance she had of a promotion. It shouldn't be a big deal, but it was, because she was counting on success with Fortex to get her a promotion. Grabbing her phone, she punched a number onto the keypad.

Dan's deep, familiar voice answered. "Hey, Hannah."

"What did you do?"

Dan pushed back in his chair, sending it rolling across the chair mat. "What are you talking about?"

"You're the one behind the Fortex investigation?"

He frowned. How did she know whom he was investigating? "Yes."

"They're my client."

Oh shit. "They can't be." He mentally reviewed all the things she'd said about her job, fitting them together like the pieces of a puzzle. They clicked into place and he shook his head. How had he never noticed the similarities before?

"Well, they were. I have to take myself off the account."

"You mean your boss found out I'm investigating them and realized I'm your boyfriend?"

She nodded. "He thinks I shared information with you. If I don't remove myself, I may lose my job. I'll definitely lose my reputation."

"That's ridiculous. I'll contact him and straighten it out."

"No, you can't. You'll make things worse."

"You're right. If you'd told me the problem, you can't say you've never spoken to me about it. Shit.

Hannah, I'm sorry." Dan waited for her to acknowledge his apology, but she remained silent. "Hannah?"

"I have to go."

Her voice sounded thick, and it hit him after she hung up she'd been crying. He'd made her cry. Lunch sat like a weight in his stomach. For some reason, making her cry bothered him more than losing her the account. Not that it didn't bother him as well. It did. But there was a professional distance he could put into place, a knowledge that once all of the evidence was presented, her losing the account before things crashed around her might not be all that bad.

But making her cry?

He'd seen her cry when she talked about her brother. The thought of her crying over something he'd done slayed him. His chest tightened. There had to be something he could do. Anything.

He was halfway out his office door when her request penetrated his brain. She didn't want him talking to her boss. But there were others to whom he could.

Dan was sitting at her dining room table munching on one of her grandmother's muffins and chatting about her grandmother's mah jongg group when Hannah arrived home early from work.

She came to a dead stop in the hallway. What the hell? Why was he in her apartment?

Her grandmother was feeding him, the Jewish grandmother equivalent of promising him her hand in marriage. He was listening to and participating in a conversation about the new versus the old mah jongg card and seemed to be enjoying himself. Anger, shock, and embarrassment threatened to overwhelm her.

The aroma of her grandmother's raisin muffins made her stomach growl.

"*Hannahla*, don't stand there, come in. Dan and I were talking."

She marched to the table and perched on the edge of the chair.

"Are you hungry?"

She was angry, not hungry. But good luck telling her grandmother. Jewish grandmas solved all problems with food. *Bubbe* held out the plate of muffins. After waiting a moment, Hannah took one and nibbled on the edge. She'd never be able to swallow more than a morsel or two. Already, the tiny bit she'd bitten off turned to sawdust in her mouth.

Placing a glass of milk in front of her, her grandmother headed toward the door. "I'll let you two talk."

Hannah tracked her grandmother as she left the room, and she raised her hand to cover her cheek where her grandmother had kissed it before she left. The silence in the room was heavy. Needing something to do, Hannah stood and skirted the perimeter.

"Awfully chummy with my grandmother."

She focused her gaze somewhere between his chin and his chest, which gave a great view of his neck, but enabled her to avoid getting lost in his beautiful, traitorous eyes.

"She's great. Sit down?" He pointed to the chair next to him and she stared at it and its proximity to him.

It was too close.

She sat in her grandmother's seat across from him. The table served as a welcome barrier. She sat, hands on her lap, resisting the urge to clench them—or whack him. Her blue manicure was chipped, and in this light the color looked decidedly Smurf-like, which was never the intent. She made a mental note to get her nails redone—in a non-cartoon character color this time—and focused on marshaling her thoughts.

"Hannah?"

She raised her head to meet his gaze.

"What are you thinking?"

"I need a new manicure."

He raised an eyebrow. With a sigh, she pushed away from the table.

"I'm angry. I'm angry with Jim for not defending me. This was my shot at a promotion, and he's destroyed it by jumping to the wrong conclusion and doubting my integrity. And I'm angry at you for not telling me you were investigating Fortex in the first place."

"Whoa, you didn't tell me you represented them, either."

Hannah swallowed, acknowledging he had a point. But it didn't make things any better.

Dan reached for her hand and squeezed, but she pulled away. "What can I do?"

"Nothing."

"What will you do?"

"Take myself off the account, I guess. I don't have much of a choice. Even if Jim believes me, the client is always right and he has to placate them. I'll have to hope they put me on an account I like and don't refuse me a promotion because of it."

"You don't want to do something more proactive?"

"Like what?"

"Stand up for yourself, or work with me to find the leak. I'm as upset as you are about this."

"I doubt it!"

"Why?"

She spun away from the table and ran a hand through her hair. He had no idea what he was talking about. "Because your job isn't on the line. Mine is."

"Hannah, the leak came from one of two places— either your office or mine. I can't have leaks in my office. If you help me find the leak, you can show Jim your loyalty."

"I appreciate that you're trying to help me, but you're not in my office. You don't know the dynamics there and you don't know me."

Dan pushed back in his chair, rose, and leaned over the table. His chair fell over from the force of his movements and Hannah's gaze shifted, but Dan stared her down. "What? I don't know you? How can you say that?"

Closing her eyes against the threatening tears, she tried to wish away the day, but her fairy-conjuring powers were lacking. She needed to protect her job in order for her to support her grandmother. She didn't have options, and she didn't have the luxury of letting personal relationships get in the way of professional ones. Letting out a deep breath, she turned to him. "I need a break. From this conversation, from you, from everything."

His mouth opened and closed, and something shuttered behind his eyes. "Then I'll give it to you." He walked past her, his typical straight posture slumped, and the door slammed as he left the apartment.

Her grandmother walked in while she righted the chair. "What can I do for you, *Hannahla?*"

Hannah gripped the back of the chair. "Nothing, *Bubbe*, nothing."

Her grandma cupped her chin. "Okay, but remember what I said about second chances. If you need me, or want to talk, I'm here. Okay?"

She pinched the bridge of her nose to stop the tears that threatened to overflow. "Okay," she whispered.

CHAPTER TWELVE

Hannah dragged herself to meet Aviva for coffee the next morning. As they stood in line for their caffeine fix, she filled her in on the Fortex saga. It was easier to talk about work while standing in line. Once they sat, she told her more details about her split from Dan.

"Oh, honey, I'm sorry." Aviva squeezed her hand. Hannah focused on the froth in her coffee cup rather than Aviva's sympathetic tone, or she'd risk losing it in the middle of the crowded coffee bar.

"I don't know what to do," Hannah said. "I can't talk to *Bubbe*, though she wants me to. I can't talk to Dan. And I can't talk to Jim."

"I'm glad you're talking to me. I think you were right. You do need a break. You need some time to step back and think. Don't make any decisions now."

Hannah nodded and took a sip of her coffee. The nutty aroma filled her nostrils but the warm liquid sloshed in her stomach. She hadn't eaten since Dan walked out.

"I have to say, though, I can't believe Jim did that to you," Aviva said over the rim of her coffee cup.

"I know. I thought he would have believed me. I wish I knew a way to prove him wrong." She pushed the cup to the side and knotted her hands on the table.

Aviva reached across and squeezed her hand again. "Sometimes I hate this job."

"Me too. And Dan's suggestions were out in left field."

"Wait, what did he say?"

When she explained Dan's response, Aviva paused, a wry smile on her face, and shook her head. "That is so typically male. Guys want to fix things. They don't understand anything other than, *you have a problem and I need to fix it.*"

"I know! First he wanted to talk to Jim for me— can you imagine what would happen if my boyfriend called my boss? Then he appeared at my apartment talking to my grandmother. He wanted to have some long conversation about all the different things I could do, and all I wanted was to have the day end, get some space and stop thinking about it. If he, of all people, can't understand, I don't know how I can be with him."

Aviva leaned back in her seat. "I totally understand. He's a pretty closed-up guy and he should be able to deal with your wishes. I think you need to take a breath, give yourself some time and see what happens next week. You don't want to make a rash decision—about your job or Dan."

Hannah sipped her coffee before she answered. It still didn't calm her stomach, but she needed the caffeine. "You're right. In the meantime, I'll get my résumé ready, because while I can't afford not to have a job, I can't work for someone who is ready to sacrifice me the second things get complicated."

"Good for you," said Aviva. "Will you see if there's an opening in another department? I'd love to have my best friend work with me."

She shook her head. "Don't you remember what happened to Regina? She had a problem in one department, switched to another and became the office pariah."

"Oh, right. I don't know how I forgot about her."

"Must be getting old."

Aviva made a funny face and stuck out her tongue. "Going back to Dan, take some time to think about him too. He seems like a great guy. I'd hate for you to regret your decision."

Monday as he dressed, Dan's phone buzzed. He looked at the ID on the screen, clenched his jaw and let it go to voicemail. Turning it off, he stuffed it in his briefcase and left for work. Hannah wanted a break?

Every time he recalled her saying it, a dark cloud enveloped him and he couldn't breathe. But she'd said she needed a break, so he'd give her one.

He'd spent more time working on his puzzle this weekend than he thought possible, and made zero progress on it.

Because he couldn't stop thinking about her.

His anger burned hot. Every time he tried to distract himself, he was reminded of her. The bright colors of the puzzle reminded him of her hair and her eyes. Shopping with Tess reminded him of their trip to the flea market. Eating reminded him how much he wanted to cook for her. But he learned something too. He could be inundated with thoughts of her without losing control.

Even if she drove him crazy.

Lisa was waiting for him when he arrived at the office. "We have a problem."

Great, eight-thirty in the morning. He motioned her inside.

"You know how we said we needed to keep the information about Fortex quiet until the last possible minute?" Lisa asked.

Swallowing the bitter taste in his mouth at the mention of the company, he nodded. "Yeah."

"Well, one of my interns knows a junior reporter at *The Journal* and leaked the information to her."

Dan swore to himself. The leak came from his office. "Why the hell would he"—he looked at Lisa for confirmation and continued—"do something like that?"

"He wanted to impress her and thought this was the way to do it."

"Idiot. Are you sure it was him?"

"Positive. I made phone calls this weekend after you and I talked."

"Can I assume you've already taken care of him?"

"I fired him and warned the rest of the staff what would happen if they ever did something like this."

"The only thing that saves us is we're far enough along in the process to move on what we have. This can't ever happen again, though."

When she left, he opened the report and began his review, accelerating the timeline. He'd have to let Hannah know. Clenching his teeth, he drafted her an email.

The leak came from my office. An intern with a reporter friend. We took care of it. You can tell Jim you had nothing to do with it.

He stared at the words on the screen. Before he could do anything he'd regret—like beg her to take him back—he hit Send. An hour and a half later, his office phone buzzed. "Yes?"

"Daddy?"

"Tess?" His stomach tightened at her unexpected voice and his throat went dry. She never called his office phone. "Why are you calling my office line?"

"Because I've tried your cell and it goes straight to voicemail."

With a start, he looked at his briefcase and pinched the bridge of his nose. He'd turned it off to avoid Hannah.

"I'm sorry, sweetheart. I turned it off by mistake. What's up? Why aren't you in class?"

"It's lunchtime and I got an A on my math test."

Background noise of teen chatter reminded him of the ridiculously early times of high school lunch. "That's great! Want me to bring home something to celebrate?"

"Something chocolate?"

Dan rubbed the nape of his neck. He'd spent so much of their lives limiting his enjoyment of things, and it didn't just affect him. It affected her, too. It was time to change. "Great idea."

"Really? Yay! Love you, Daddy!"

"Love you too, Tess. See you later. And I'm sorry about my cell phone." He hung up and glanced out the window. The sun shined over the buildings and gave Dan a strong urge to go outside for fresh air. Grabbing his phone—this time, he turned it on—and stuffing it into his back pocket, he picked up his cane and left the office. Outside, the brisk air rejuvenated him, helping to cool some of his anger. He slowed his steps and took deep breaths as he tried to relax.

He wandered down the sidewalk, staring into shop windows without seeing anything, avoiding other pedestrians out of sheer luck. A few blocks down the street, the hot dog vendor set up in his usual spot on the corner. Dan's stomach tightened as he thought of Hannah.

It had been four days and his heart felt as if a piece of it was missing. He wasn't hungry, but passing the hot dog vendor, smelling the salty scent, and remembering his lunch with Hannah made him salivate. His anger fizzled. Yeah, he was hurt and wow, he missed her. How much longer did her break need to last?

That night, Hannah dialed Dan's apartment. By Sunday, she'd cooled down enough to think about him and his suggestions, and she itched to talk to him. She hadn't been fair. He'd tried to help and she'd pushed him away. She'd let her anger over her boss infect their relationship. But he didn't answer and he didn't return her messages. Her need to hear his voice drove her crazy. When he didn't answer, she realized she didn't just need to talk to him. She needed to see him.

Grabbing her purse, she raced out the door. When she got to his building, she followed someone else in, raced to the elevator and rode to the third floor. Knocking on his door, she listened for noise inside. The door cracked and Tess peeked through.

"Hannah?" She closed the door, undid the chain, and pulled it open wide. "I didn't know you were coming over." She didn't look pleased to see her. Was it too late?

"Hey, Tess. I'm sorry to barge in like this. I didn't know I was either but I need to talk to your dad." At Tess's look of uncertainty, she continued. "I hurt his feelings and I need to apologize."

Tess's face cleared. "That explains his mood. Yeah, you can come in." She turned to call him, but Hannah stopped her.

"No, I'll just pop in. Where is he?"

"We just finished celebrating my math test, which means he's probably in the guest room, working on his puzzle."

"Congratulations!" Hannah tried to show interest, though every nerve in her body thrummed in agitation.

"Thanks." She twirled her hair.

Hannah gave her a quick hug and raced down the hall. From the doorway, she saw Dan seated at a table, focused on the puzzle. She couldn't make out the details, only that there were bright colors. He held a piece in the air, looking as if he waited for a magical pull from some part of the puzzle to indicate where the piece belonged.

"That's quite a puzzle." She walked in, her feet leaden now that she was here.

He jumped. Surprise crossed his features before he schooled them into...nothing. "What are you doing here?"

"I came to talk to you."

When he didn't react, she swallowed and walked toward him. The solidity of his shoulder beneath her hand grounded her. Trying to control her breathing, she inhaled his scent and a keen longing to be in his arms overtook her.

"Daddy?"

He jumped and Hannah's hand fell from his shoulder.

"Yes, Tess."

"I'm leaving."

"Leaving? Where are you going?"

"The JCC. Tutoring. Don't you remember? We talked about this."

"Oh, right. Okay. Text me when you get there and when you leave."

Hannah waited until the front door clicked shut. "I was wrong." His hand stilled over the puzzle, but he continued to avoid looking at her. "I was angry at Jim and I took it out on you."

His hand tightened around the puzzle piece and she watched his knuckles whiten.

"I'm sorry. I didn't want solutions; I wanted understanding. I should have told you what I needed."

He raised his head, face still averted from her, and she waited. His jaw was tense and his Adam's apple bobbed when he swallowed. She wanted to caress his face, run her hands through his hair, but she didn't dare. When he turned toward her, his gaze was wary.

"I didn't know you wanted me to just listen."

"I know. I shouldn't have expected you to read my mind."

"I should have given you time to explain."

She took his hand, which was clenched around the puzzle piece, and he twisted it until his fingers clasped hers. His fingers were longer than hers, but also thicker, and hers stretched around his. The puzzle piece was trapped between their palms, and dug into her hand.

"I was overwhelmed. I should have shown more appreciation for your attempt to help me."

Dan pushed his chair back and pulled her onto his lap. "I'm sorry."

"Me too." She rested in the comfort of his arms.

After a moment, he spoke. "Have you figured out what you'll do about work?"

She leaned into his shoulder. A faint scent of aftershave lingered about his neck and his heart beat against her back. "Well, I told my boss and showed him your email. It didn't seem to make much difference, so I updated my résumé and sent it to some of the headhunters who have been calling me."

He craned his neck to look at her. "So you'll quit your job?"

"Not necessarily, and not without having a new one first. I want to see what happens where I am. But I also want to be prepared."

"Sounds like you've got a plan."

She nodded. "I couldn't have done it without your help."

Frowning, he adjusted her on his lap so they could see each other better. "I don't see how I helped much."

"Look, at the time we talked, I wanted to vent and to have a supportive listener." At his crestfallen expression, she stroked his cheek. "You kept suggesting ideas for things I should do. Although I didn't want to hear it at the time, once I'd gotten over the emotion, I remembered what you said and was able to use those ideas to formulate a plan."

He rubbed a lock of her hair between his thumb and forefinger. "So...you're no longer looking for a break from me." His tone was matter-of-fact, but he wouldn't meet her gaze. Her chest tightened as she witnessed his pain.

She caressed his shoulder, studying his face and wishing he'd look at her. All she could see was a frown line between his brows and his mouth set in a straight line. "No, I reacted in anger. I wanted to push everyone away, even you, but with time to calm down and think things through, I realized pushing you away was the last thing I wanted."

He rubbed her back. "I need you to be more careful. With me. Because I don't want to have to wonder every time we get into an argument if you'll break up with me because you're angry."

"I will. I promise. It was childish and unfair to you."

He leaned in and kissed her, his lips gentle. His hands threaded through her hair, grasped the nape of her neck, drawing her closer, before letting her go.

She exhaled for the first time in four days.

CHAPTER THIRTEEN

He'd forgotten about Tess. Twice. Dan stood at the window and watched Hannah turn the corner toward her apartment. First he'd been so focused on avoiding Hannah's calls, he'd made it difficult for his own daughter to reach him. What if there had been an emergency and he hadn't found out about it? Tess was his primary responsibility. She should always be able to reach him, no matter what.

Then, he hadn't remembered Tess was leaving. If Tess hadn't come in to remind him, he would never have known she'd left. What the hell kind of father did that? Memories from seven years ago flooded through him. He trembled. He couldn't go through it again. More importantly, Tess couldn't.

He and Hannah had had their first fight, had set new ground rules, and he was thrilled. But also, terrified. How could he balance a relationship and fatherhood?

He turned on the TV and settled in to watch a crime show, needing a break from his thoughts for a moment. At the first commercial, he reached for his phone. He should call her. Frowning, he put it down. She'd left not ten minutes ago. She wasn't home yet, and he didn't want to be clingy.

He tried to focus on the TV show. Ten minutes later, he still couldn't follow the plot. He turned it off and went into his office. His puzzle was there, almost finished, and he sat to work on it.

Except sitting here reminded him of when Hannah had sat on his lap, her bottom pressed against him, the side of her breast against his arm. He'd rested his hand on her back, felt her spine and her bra strap through her shirt. Her vanilla scent had filled his senses and even now he could smell it. He couldn't afford to let his desire for Hannah overtake everything else. And he had no idea how to balance things. He groaned. Concentrating on the puzzle would be futile as well.

Glancing out the window, he noticed the dark sky. She'd walked home right before the sun set, but she'd gone alone. It made sense to call and check on her safety. It was the right thing to do. Armed with this new excuse, he dialed her number.

"Hi." She sounded like she was happy to hear from him.

"I wanted to make sure you got home safely."

"You're sweet. Yes, I'm home safe."

Sweet? He shook his head. "I'm glad. What are you doing now?"

"Working on my résumé."

"If you want a second pair of eyes, I'm happy to look at it."

"How about I email it to you when I've done a draft?"

"Sounds good." He should hang up before he got too accustomed to her voice again, before he made a fool of himself, before...

"I've missed you," she said. "Can I see you this weekend?"

His mouth dropped. She wanted to see him. It wasn't just him. Maybe this pull was normal. He nodded, and remembering she couldn't see through the phone, croaked, "Yeah." It was the best he could do.

"Do you want to include Tess? There's a great pumpkin farm not too far away where my grandmother and I go to sometimes."

This was why he loved her. She provided balance when he couldn't. "She might be going out with her friends, but I'll check with her and let you know."

"Oh, I don't want to ruin her plans."

"You won't. Thanks for thinking of her."

They made plans for the weekend and said good-bye. He bowed his head and held the phone against his forehead. What had he ever done to deserve this, and how could he prevent himself from screwing it up?

Hannah climbed into Dan's car Saturday; Tess sat in the back seat, a mutinous look on her face. "Hi, Tess."

Tess turned and looked out the window, arms folded.

"Tess!" Hannah jumped at Dan's roar. "When Hannah says hello to you, you answer. Do you hear me?"

Eyes filling with tears, Tess mumbled a hello, stuck in her earbuds, and stared once again out the window.

Hannah placed a hand on Dan's hand over the gearshift. He flinched, but after a moment, covered hers with his own. "Sorry about that," he said under his breath.

"Would it be better if we change our plans?"

"No, I'm not caving in to a fourteen-year-old."

"But if she doesn't want to be with me..."

He turned and caressed her arm. "It's not you. She's mad at me because I took away her phone."

Hannah frowned and glanced toward the backseat. "But I thought..."

"That's her old iPod. I'd take it too, but it would end up punishing me more than her, since I'd have to listen to her complain."

"I can hear you, you know," Tess said.

Dan started the car. "If you're not careful, I'll take away Halloween."

Wow, he threatened to cancel a national holiday. Either he possessed way more power than she'd given him credit for, or he was having a bad day. Hannah resolved to make sure everyone enjoyed themself today.

He pulled onto the road, and they headed out of town. Hannah craned her neck toward the backseat. "So, Tess, this farm has great pumpkins and it's pick your own. We can get anything we want. I went here last year to get harvest decorations for our *sukkah*."

Dan glanced at her before he returned his focus to the road in front of him. "You have a *sukkah?*"

"Yeah, a bunch of us build the three-sided hut on the roof of our building, decorate it with pumpkins and mums and eat in it during the *Sukkot* holiday. It's fun."

"Sounds like it."

When Tess continued her silence, Dan shifted his gaze to the rearview mirror and opened his mouth, but Hannah shushed him. "I hope they still have bushels of apples for sale. My grandma makes a great apple pie, and I want to bring some apples home for her."

"I like pie." Dan grinned for the first time since Hannah had entered the car.

She laughed. "Well, if you behave, maybe I'll share with you." She ignored the snort from the backseat. "But I doubt it."

"Why not?"

"Because her apple pie is amazing and I want it all for myself."

"I helped you with your résumé."

She glanced sideways at him. His cheeks were lifted in a grin and his hands, which gripped the steering wheel, relaxed.

"Depends on what it's worth to you."

His eyebrows rose and Hannah bit the insides of her cheeks to keep from laughing.

"Not sure I can say anything in the car with my daughter in the backseat."

A groan from behind made Hannah hunch and cover her face in embarrassment. She remained that way, wondering how to respond, until Dan pulled her hand away from her face and squeezed.

The car bumped along the dirt road as Dan navigated to the parking area. When they stopped, Hannah jumped out of the car, with Dan following at a slower pace. Tess remained inside. Dan and Hannah met at the back of the car; he glared at Tess. Hannah leaned into him and wrapped her arms around his waist. "Relax," she whispered and stroked his back. Pressing her lips softly to his, she teased his mouth until his body loosened and he sighed.

He leaned his forehead against hers. "I know. It's just...it's like she's pissing me off on purpose."

"Of course she is."

He frowned and pulled away, but Hannah wouldn't let him. Instead, she played with the hair at the base of his head. It was soft and freshly trimmed, and she loved the feel of it on her fingertips.

"Come on, she's fifteen. She's doing this to get you back. Don't rise to the bait. Ignore it and eventually she'll come around." She unclasped her hands and ran them down his chest.

His face smoothed out. "It's like you're the parent of a teen."

She shook her head. "Nope, but I'm a little more objective than you."

He kissed her. "Okay, I'll try not to ruin things."

Trailing her hand down his back, she winked at him before opening the door for Tess.

Tess stared at her for a moment and climbed out. Ignoring her father, she walked ahead toward the weathered gray barn and stopped in front of the hand-written Pick-UR-Own sign.

"What kinds of pumpkins should we pick? Large or small?" Hannah asked.

Tess shrugged and out of the corner of Hannah's eye, Dan moved. Waving him away, she turned to Tess and grinned. "How about we start with large ones, since they're great for carving Jack-o-lanterns, and if there's time we can look for smaller ones too," Hannah said.

They took a wagon and walked toward the pumpkin field. The ground was rocky and uneven, and Hannah slowed her natural pace to accommodate Dan. Tess walked next to her and rolled her eyes, but she slowed too and Hannah breathed a sigh of relief.

Once they reached the field, Tess walked ahead, and left Hannah and Dan to follow.

"This looks like a good area, Tess," Dan called. There were lots of pumpkins on the ground.

She ignored him and chose an area farther across the field. Exchanging looks, Dan and Hannah stayed silent, but joined her as she examined a variety of pumpkins. Around them, families raced around, called to each other and picked their perfect pumpkin. A little girl sat on one, while her older brother tried to lift it with her on it. Her mom laughed. The loamy scent of soil wafted around them; the bright sunlight beat upon their heads.

Hannah turned a pumpkin over. "This looks good." She held it up. The pumpkin was heavy and she jostled it, trying to keep a grip on it. Dan reached out a steadying hand and she gazed at him, offering a silent thank you. He maintained eye contact and for a moment, it was as if the two of them were the only ones in the field. A bead of sweat dripped down her back and the spell was broken. Darting a glance toward Tess, she added the pumpkin to the wagon.

"I like this one better," Tess said. She carried another, rounder, pumpkin over and placed it in the wagon.

"I like that one too," Hannah said.

"So, you really live with your grandma?" Tess asked.

"Yup."

"Why?"

"Well, she has a big apartment with room for me, and sharing it helps both of us keep costs down. She saves me time by cooking and I help her out with the laundry. It lets me take care of her, kind of payback for all she's done for me."

"Cool. So, how many more pumpkins do we need?"

Hannah looked at the two pumpkins in the wagon. "Up to you all. I need a large one for the *sukkah*, although I also want to grab some smaller ones and some gourds. But if you two want more, we can keep going."

"Let's find the smaller ones," Dan said. "Tess, do you want to pick out some gourds? You know, the weird looking things."

"Yeah." Her mouth dropped as if she realized she'd violated her own "No Talking To Dad" rule, but she grabbed the wagon and walked ahead of the adults toward the smaller pumpkins.

"Progress," he said.

Hannah put her arm around his waist and walked with him. When they'd picked out a few smaller pumpkins and gourds, as well as a bushel of apples for Hannah's grandma, they headed toward the car.

"Dad, you can't eat Hannah's apples," Tess said as she spied him sneaking one out of the basket. "They're for her grandma's pie."

"It's only one. I'm hungry."

Tess took the basket away and looked at Hannah. "Can I trust you?"

The question, asked as a joke, stunned Hannah and her chest tightened. Because it seemed like more than a question about eating apples, at least to her.

"Yes."

Tess handed her the basket. Hannah turned away and wiped her eyes.

"She likes you," Dan whispered.

"*Bubbe*?" Hannah led Tess and Dan inside her apartment. "We have apples!"

Her grandmother greeted them, hands clasped. "Oh wonderful!"

She tried to take the bag from Hannah, but Dan intervened. "Here, let me." He looped the bag on his arm and gave Hannah her pumpkin.

Bubbe beamed. "Thank you so much. Here, you can put them on the counter. You all must be hungry and thirsty after spending time at the farm. Can I get anyone anything? Tess?"

Tess shot an uncertain look toward her father. Putting down the pumpkin and the bag of gourds, Hannah walked over to her. She put her arm around her shoulders. "My grandmother loves to feed people. Don't be shy." She brought her into the kitchen with her grandmother, who offered her a soda.

With a smile, Tess took it and leaned against the counter. "Hannah says you make amazing apple pie."

Bubbe nodded. "It's one of my specialties. Do you like it?"

"I've never had homemade."

Bubbe arched a brow at Tess and turned to Hannah. "Well, we'll have to fix that right away. Want to help me make it?"

With a shy nod, Tess joined *Bubbe*.

Seeing Tess happily occupied, Hannah sidled up to Dan. "The living room is free, if you'd like to sit."

As he sank into the sofa, Hannah couldn't help notice his flicker of pain. "I'll be right back." She returned a moment later with a heat pack in one hand and an ice pack in another. "Pick one."

He clenched the hand into a fist that had massaged his knee.

"It's fine, Hannah. I'm fine."

"Really? I could swear we've done this before. Okay, take both then."

With a quick glance toward the kitchen to make sure her grandmother wouldn't see her sitting on the table—a pet peeve of hers—she perched on the coffee table across from Dan and held both options, like Lady Justice balancing the scales. She waited.

Finally, as she was about to give up, he reached for the heat pack. Their fingers touched and heat zinged up her arm. His pupils widened, then narrowed. Their arms remained frozen, the heat pack suspended over his knee, fingers touching, until she lowered her hand. When she touched his knee, he flinched, but she didn't know if it was from pain or surprise. With utmost gentleness, she slid her hand out from beneath the pack, but rather than move her hand toward his knee again and maybe cause more pain, she brushed her hand up his thigh. His jeans were soft, the muscles beneath them hard. He inhaled and his free hand covered hers, holding it in place. Heat from his skin warmed her, like her own private furnace. After a moment, he let go.

Dropping the ice pack onto the table, she turned and joined him on the sofa. When she'd gotten herself settled, he reached for her hand. She squeezed and he rested against the sofa.

She sat there, quiet, and listened to the noises from the kitchen. Her grandmother's voice was gentle as she instructed Tess on how to make the perfect piecrust. Hannah smiled.

"My memories of Jewish holidays are all tied to food. I remember arriving at my grandmother's house early on Rosh Hashanah and rushing into the kitchen to 'help' cook. No matter how much food she'd already prepared, she always left something for me to make with her. And my brothers and I would crowd around the table as she passed around *hamentaschen* on Purim. Those were Jeff's favorite cookies. I don't know if they still are." She swallowed at the idea of not knowing her own brother anymore. Maybe tomorrow would change her understanding of him.

Dan's body relaxed next to her. She leaned against his shoulder and she continued. "And whenever I spent a weekend at her house, I'd always arrive early enough on Friday to help her braid challah for Shabbat."

"My grandfather used to make a big deal over our Passover *seder*," Dan said. "As the only grandchild, he asked me to read the Four Questions in Hebrew every year during our celebration and his chest would puff up with pride as I chanted them." He nodded toward the kitchen. "Sounds like they're enjoying themselves in there."

"I think I might be a little jealous."

He chuckled. "Your grandmother is great. Tess doesn't get this kind of extended family attention with me."

"No, but she gets other things."

"Like stubbornness."

The sheepish look on his face was endearing. "There is a familial resemblance. Hold on." Hannah ran into the kitchen and returned a moment later with her phone. "Here."

His face widened into a grin. "How did you get Tess to let you take a photo of her?"

"I just took it. I thought you two might like it. If you keep scrolling, there are a few I took today while she picked fruit too."

He swiped the screen a few times, swallowing and almost caressing the screen, before handing the phone to her. "Can you send them to me?" His voice was hoarse and Hannah saw a faint wetness in his eyes. He blinked and it was gone.

"Sure," she said.

"Guess you're able to work your magic with both of us."

"I don't know if I'd call it magic, but whatever it is, I hope it helps me when I check out my brother's place of employment tomorrow."

Dan turned her face toward him, his fingers gentle along her jaw. "So you're really doing this?"

"I need to know if I can trust him, and this is the first step."

"Do you want me to go with you?"

Every fiber of her being screamed, *Yes!* "No, I need to do this on my own."

CHAPTER FOURTEEN

Sunday morning, Hannah stood on a sidewalk in New York City's Hell's Kitchen, across the street from Mike's Restaurant, a dive of a coffee shop, from the looks of the place. As it got later in the day, sidewalks would be busier, but for now, only a few local residents populated the area.

Although she looked at the restaurant with the dull neon Open sign where her brother worked, she hadn't seen him enter or leave the place during the ten minutes she'd watched. She wasn't sure if she was relieved or disappointed. Hannah crossed the street and walked past the façade. The outside wasn't impressive. A large, frosted window with *Mike's* painted in blue letters in an arc. She couldn't see inside, but wondered if they could see out. The door was glass as well, and it wasn't frosted, but the vestibule appeared dark and she didn't want to stop and stare. So she paced a few times.

This was crazy. Decide. In or out.

The door opened and a man stuck his head out.

"I wondered if you were going to come inside, or wear out the sidewalk."

She stepped back. "Excuse me?"

"You're Jeff's sister, right? You look just like him."

"And you are?"

"Mike." He came outside and held out his hand. Tall and wiry, his head was shaved, he wore an earring and his eyes were bright green. He smiled at her, displaying a gold-capped tooth. "I don't bite."

Despite her nerves, she took his outstretched hand. It dwarfed hers and her gaze trailed up his muscular arm, taking note of the tattoos, which disappeared under the sleeves of his gray T-shirt. His grip was firm.

"Come on in. I'll make you a cup of coffee and we can talk."

"How do you know I want to talk?"

He pinned her with his gaze and turned around.

Biting her lip, she followed him in. It took a moment for her vision to adjust to the darkened room after the bright sunshine outside. She paused between the vestibule and the dining area of the coffee shop. It smelled of bacon, coffee and grease, and her stomach growled. There were metal tables and chairs, black and white photos on the wall, a TV perched high in the corner, and a counter running the length of the room.

Mike stepped behind the counter and poured two cups of coffee. His movements were spare and precise. He whistled while he worked, like some oversized dwarf waiting for Snow White. He pushed a cup across the counter and raised an eyebrow toward her. As she walked over, he slid a metal creamer and a bowl of yellow and white sugar packets toward her. She side-climbed onto the stool and fixed her coffee.

"So," he said.

"Hi."

"Hi."

"I'm Hannah, by the way."

"I know. Jeff talks about you."

"Oh." Her face heated.

He nodded.

"So...is he working today?"

"Are you asking because you want to see him, or because you want to avoid him?"

"Tell me again who you are?" She looked at him through lowered lashes as she stirred her coffee.

"Mike. He didn't mention his sister being hard of hearing. Or forgetful."

"I'm not. I'm trying to figure out why you're asking such personal questions."

He leaned his elbows on the counter. "Because I look out for him."

"Yeah, my brother needs a lot of looking after."

He turned and wiped the spotless counter with a rag. "Less than you think."

"How would you know?"

"Because I'm also his sponsor."

Hannah froze, the wind knocked out of her as if she'd been punched in the stomach. Except Mike hadn't moved from behind the counter and no one else was there. This guy was her brother's sponsor?

He folded his arms across his chest and raised an eyebrow. "Which surprises you more—that I'm his sponsor or that he has one?"

Her face heated again as she recognized the truth in his question, and at how easy it was to read her. "Both, I guess."

He shrugged. "Well, you're honest at least."

"You seem to think you know me."

"Only from what Jeff has told me."

"What did he say?"

"You sure you want to know?"

She wiped her palms on her knees and glanced around the room before she returned her focus to Mike and nodded.

"He said he betrayed you by being an addict. You don't believe he's clean, or that he'll ever be. He'd like to make amends with you, but you won't give him an opportunity."

That her brother cared enough about her to regret his treatment of her was something she'd have to examine another time, in private. "And how, exactly, does that show you know me? Did you form some mental picture of me in your mind based on his description?"

Mike gave a half-smile. "You're just like him, you know."

"Except I'm not an addict." Hannah cringed inside at the words she blurted. She possessed more tact under ordinary circumstances, but anything having to do with Jeff brought out the worst in her.

He stared at her until she wanted to break eye contact, but she remained firm and he looked away first. "I did form a mental picture of you."

"Which is?"

"You're not forgiving, which means he hurt you. You're afraid of getting hurt again; therefore, you don't want to get too close to him. And based on what I see now, you don't want to fall for any of his shit again, either. Am I right?"

"Yeah."

"Great, why are you here?"

"Because he told me he had a job and I wanted to know if he was lying or not." *And maybe because I want to forgive him.*

"So you're curious."

"My grandmother thinks he's changed and I don't want to see her get hurt." *Or me.*

"Ah, you're here for her."

She didn't bother to answer. She had nothing to prove to this guy. Bracing herself against the counter, she started to slide off the stool.

"I have a habit of being an ass," he said.

Hannah laughed. It was either laugh or tell him he was right. "I might have deserved some of it."

"So, what do you want to know about your brother? Of course, you need to recognize there are only certain things I can say as his sponsor."

She returned to the stool. "How long have you been his sponsor?"

"A year."

Her eyes widened. "Really?"

"Are you going to doubt everything I tell you?"

"I'll stop doubting when you start breaking that habit you apologized for."

Mike let out a roar of laughter and his gold tooth glinted in a shaft of sunlight. "Touché. Yes, for a year."

"How serious is he about recovery?"

"He's been clean for a year."

"And?"

"He's putting in the time. He calls me when he needs support. He goes to meetings twice a day. He works here and he gets paid and he doesn't use the money to buy drugs, although he's tempted."

"It's the temptation that worries me."

"We're all tempted, sweetheart. But he's fighting. Hard."

"Where is he now?"

Mike looked at his watch. "At a meeting. His shift starts in an hour if you want to hang around."

She climbed off the stool. "No, I don't."

"Now imagine how he feels."

Hannah stared without seeing at the TV that night. Her focus remained on her earlier conversation with Mike. For all the attitude he'd given, he'd clarified a few things. Her brother was trying. He was clean. And he was as scared as she was.

Maybe her grandmother was right. It was one thing to enable him and ignore his flaws. It was another thing to ignore all the work he did and continued to do, and to punish him for a past he was trying to fix. Moving on would require her to set aside all her hurt. Could she do it?

Hannah's phone rang. When Dan's caller ID popped up, she muted the TV. "Hey there."

"Hannah, it's Tess."

She started. "Oh, hi, sweetheart. I thought it was your Dad. How are you?"

"I'm fine, but I wanted to ask you a question."

Hannah leaned forward and clenched her hands into fists. Tess never called. "Sure, what's up?"

"My school is hosting an art exhibition. I wanted to know if you'd like to go. I have a few pieces in it and they serve snacks and drinks. They sort of arranged it like an art gallery opening and the money is used to fund art in our school."

Hannah gripped her phone tight and blinked multiple times. Out of all the people Tess could invite, she chose her? Her chest expanded. "I'd love to go! What kinds of pieces are you displaying?"

"I'm taking a charcoal sketch class, and mine will be from that portfolio."

"I can't wait. When is it?"

"December third. Are you sure you're free?"

"Hold on, let me check my calendar. Yup, totally free. Thank you so much for the invitation." Hannah hung up the phone. Tess invited her to her art exhibition. She cared for Tess more each time she saw her, and it gratified her to know her feelings were reciprocated.

"Hannah, where are you going?" her grandmother asked as she emerged from her bedroom, knitting in hand.

"Tess invited me to her art show," she said. "Can you believe she wants me to go?"

"Of course I can. You've made a good impression on her. Can I come too?"

"I don't know. Let me ask." She hit redial and when Tess picked up, she asked, "My grandmother wants to know if she can come too."

"Sure!"

Hannah smiled at the excitement in Tess's voice as she hung up the phone. "Yes, *Bubbe*, Tess said you can come too."

As she was about to tell her grandmother the date and time, the phone rang again. This time, though caller ID said Dan, she answered with care. "Hello?"

"Hi, what's wrong?"

At the sound of Dan's voice, she relaxed and stretched out on the sofa. "Nothing, I wasn't sure it was you." She filled him in about Tess's phone call. "Is it okay with you? I don't want to infringe on any-thing..."

"Hannah, it's great. I want the two of you to have a relationship, and I'm thrilled she invited you."

Hannah let out a deep breath. "Okay."

He chuckled.

"What's funny?"

"Not funny, so much as...I don't know. I love the way you are with Tess. How you mix our family in with yours without question."

"You make her sound like an ingredient," Hannah said.

The deep laugh on the other end of the line sent chills down the nape of her neck and warmed the pit of her stomach.

"Well, I am partial to food," Dan said, "so maybe it's not such a bad thing. But in all seriousness, thank you."

"You're welcome. I enjoy getting to know her."

"So...I...I missed your voice. And I wanted to know how it went at your brother's job."

"It was...weird." She lowered her voice, walking into her bedroom and shutting the door. "I haven't told *Bubbe* about this yet. Mike is Jeff's boss and his sponsor. He says Jeff is clean and has been for a year."

"Do you believe him?"

She rose and paced around the room. "There's a big part of me that doesn't believe he can do it. But I can't continue to ignore evidence. I'm not sure what that makes me, though. Mike wasn't too complimentary."

"Hannah, you're a good person. You've been hurt. You have every right to distrust Jeff. The fact you're trying to look at the evidence and conceive a reason why you should believe him is admirable. Mike doesn't know you."

"Well, here's the thing. He was brash and forward and he knew me, or acted like he did, and somehow I responded to him. It was like I wasn't surprised at the way he talked to me. Or maybe I was surprised. I didn't know what else to do, so I answered him rather than calling him out on his behavior. Well, for the most part."

"At least you got some answers."

"Yeah. I have a lot to think about, and I have to figure out how to go forward with Jeff and with my grandmother. I think I want a relationship with him, I'm just not sure how much of one I can handle."

"Give it time. You don't have to decide right away."

Hannah closed her eyes, letting Dan's voice wash over her and calm her. He was right.

"Speaking of decisions," he said, "did you send out your résumé yet?"

"Yeah, I have an interview on Tuesday with another PR firm."

"That's terrific. I can't wait to hear about it."

Shivers ran down her spine as his happiness for her deepened the timbre of his voice.

"You know, Tess is out tutoring again tomorrow night," he said. "If you want to come over, I could help you prepare for your interview. Or we could relax..."

She'd have him all to herself. Desire coursed through her. "I'd love to come over."

As she hung up the phone, her stomach tightened. Last time they'd been alone, Dan stopped them because she'd been upset about Jeff. This time, there would be no more excuses.

CHAPTER FIFTEEN

The ring of the doorbell echoed through the lonely apartment. Dan paused before he answered the door. Hannah was on the other side. Tess liked her. Was he ready? Maybe he was making a big deal out of nothing. Maybe he should let himself go this once. If Hannah was ready to give her brother a chance, maybe she could overlook Dan's mistakes too. Hadn't he paid enough for them? And if she could, there was no reason to hold himself back from her.

Squaring his shoulders, he pulled the door open. Raindrops spattered her jacket and darkened the ends of her hair to chocolate. She smelled of rain, vanilla, and something unique to her, and heat pooled low in his belly. She was here. They were alone at last. All the times he'd thought about her, dreamed about her, desired her, coalesced into one hot ball of need. He grabbed her hand and pulled her inside. His groin tightened and he pulled her close, capturing her lips with his as he tangled his fingers through her silky hair. She was his and she was glorious.

When she opened her mouth, he thrust his tongue inside, tasting her sweetness. He groaned. He hadn't realized how much he'd missed her, how much he needed her, until this minute. If he were smart, he'd go slow, talk about his feelings, double check hers, make a plan. Running his hands down her back, his palms rounded over her backside. He pressed her against him and all thoughts of being smart, all thoughts, period, disappeared. Her sigh, or was it his, tickled his mouth as she moved her hips back and forth against him. He'd waited so long for her, wanting to make sure everything was perfect. Her movements were sure. Her desire was as great as his. The friction was exquisite torture. He couldn't wait anymore and he backed her against the wall.

"Slow down," she whispered against his lips. "We've got plenty of time."

He trailed kisses down her neck. She whimpered as she tilted her head, exposing more of her skin for him to taste. For him to own.

"I need you," he groaned, and ran his hands up and down her body, memorizing her curves as need built inside of him. He wanted to be inside of her, to be one with her. Preplanning be damned. Candles, roses, wine, they all could wait. His pulse pounded. He hardened as he pressed against her. He couldn't breathe, couldn't think, couldn't focus on anything but her. He couldn't wait.

She wiggled against him and he fought to maintain the little control he had left. Oh god, he would lose it right now if she kept that up. Pulling away from her, dizzy with desire, he took her hand and led her farther inside his apartment. Hands shaking, he pushed her jacket off her shoulders, leaving it where it dropped on the floor. He stared into her eyes. Her lashes were long and her pupils were dilated, surrounded by bright green rims. He slid his fingertips beneath her sweater. Her skin was warm and smooth, begging him to explore further, but he wasn't a barbarian. Pausing, he waited for her response. She bit her lip, raised and lowered her hands. When she nodded, he raised her sweater over her head, flinging it aside to join her jacket. He stared at her, breathless.

Creamy skin with a light smattering of freckles. Breasts that fit perfectly into his hands. She was perfect. He cupped her breasts through her navy lace bra and her nipples puckered at the contact. It was him. He was doing this. He was making her react to him. His chest swelled. As he admired them with his touch, she tugged at his T-shirt, pulling it out from his jeans. Thank God, she wanted him as much as he wanted her. Her hands on his bare skin made him hiss. Her touch was like a brand. He raised his arms over his head for her to continue undressing him. Never before had he wanted to be naked with someone as much as he did with her.

Bare chest to bare chest, their hot skin touched, igniting a fire of need in him that matched what he saw reflected in her eyes. Pupils dilated, lips parted, she kissed his brow, down the bridge of his nose and across to his cheekbones. His skin burned beneath her lips and coherent thought fled.

He shut his eyes, let the feel of her lips take over. Their noses touched, their cheeks brushed against each other as she mapped his face with her kisses. When she finally reached his mouth, he opened it hungrily, devouring her, thrusting his tongue against hers, battling for ultimate control.

He clenched his stomach as the backs of her fingers slipped between his pants and his stomach. A tugging at his waistband made him open his eyes. He stretched his mouth in a wicked grin as he reached for her jeans, unbuckling her belt and the metal clasp. He couldn't wait for them to be naked together. When she pulled away from him, the cool air shocked him. He stifled a protest at the space, space he didn't want between them. His disappointment disappeared when she shimmied out of her jeans. He watched her, his gaze drawn to parts of her she kept hidden. She stood there, motionless as his gaze moved from her toes to her head and down again. Her skin blushed along with his gaze and she stepped forward.

"You're wearing too many clothes," she murmured and reached once again for his waistband.

Reality returned as he realized his leg needed more support than the middle of the room could provide him. He cupped her jaw and gave her a searing kiss before he moved to the sofa. She followed. Standing in front of him, she unbuckled his belt. She pulled it out of his belt loops with agonizing slowness. He closed his eyes when her hands pulled at his zipper. The waiting was torture. The speed with which she'd met his demands disappeared. As if in slow motion, she pulled his jeans over his hips, inch by torturous inch. Finally, she lowered them over his hips. The physical evidence of his arousal was obvious. He ached for her to touch him. Instead, she spent what felt like hours staring at him. His pulse pounded in his ears. Goosebumps rose on his exposed flesh. She reached forward and touched him. Sheer bliss washed over him. It was all he could do not to come right there. She followed him as he sank into the sofa. This time, he wasn't letting her go. He reached for her to draw her into his lap, but she shook her head. Instead, she knelt in front of him. His eyes widened. She pulled off his pant legs, and traced his scar along his leg with her tongue. He shivered with desire so great, his hips bucked. Her tongue traveled up his leg. He'd never been so turned on. His breath came out as harsh gasp as he panted with need. When he could bear it no longer, he pulled her against him, letting her body slide against his, friction setting off sparks of desire with increasing potency. They leaned sideways, and stretched out with her on top of him.

He clasped her bottom with shaking hands. Their mouths joined, his tongue plunging inside her. Their bodies rocked together. He bucked beneath her, unable to wait a moment longer.

"Hold on," he ground out. He fumbled for his jeans and pulled out a condom.

"You're such a boy scout," she whispered. "Always prepared." Eyes filled with longing, she shimmied out of her panties. He fumbled with the condom wrapper. Who the hell made them so small and well-sealed?

She took it from him with a gleam in her eye, her hands sliding over his.

"Mine," she said.

He almost lost it right there. She ripped open the package and slid it on him, the ache of her touch exquisite torture. He wanted her. He needed her right now.

He pulled her toward him, but she arched away. She was a tease, touching him only with her lips on his mouth. His body shook with desire. Her tongue plunged deeper, imitating what he longed to do to her.

"Hannah, I can't bear this," he groaned against her. More than just the physical coupling, he needed her to become one with him. He needed the connection.

He jerked as her fingers circled him. His head pounded with every massage and squeeze she gave. No longer able to let her take complete control, he inserted his fingers into her wetness. Now it was she who shuddered. She wriggled and gasped beneath his hand. When he couldn't hold out a minute longer, she rose on her knees and came down upon him.

She was tight and warm and perfect. This is what he had been waiting for. He fit inside her as if their bodies were meant for each other. They rocked together, finding their rhythm. He climbed higher and higher, eking out every last bit of pure pleasure. He could see the peak, feel it. His muscles contracted, his focus narrowed. But he needed her to come first. She deserved that much consideration at least. He listened to her moans of desire, and they increased his own pleasure. He caressed her breasts, rubbing his thumbs across their peaks. She flung her head back and screamed. It was all he needed. Pressure built deep within him. Blood pounded in his ears. Oh God, the wait was over. He closed his eyes. Lights flashed behind his lids. His body exploded, and he shouted his release.

Collapsing on top of him, Hannah buried her head into his neck and he wrapped his arms around her, holding her close. His breathing was ragged and matched hers. Against his chest, her heart pounded. Her back was slick with sweat as he trailed his fingers up and down her spine. He inhaled her scent as peace descended around him. More than just joining their bodies, they'd joined their souls. He hadn't felt this close to another woman in years. He loved her.

He drifted on the edge of sleep, enjoying the weight of her body on top of him, uniting them. After a while, she kissed his jaw. He turned his head toward her, blue eyes meeting green. She caressed his forehead. He kissed the palm of her hand and stared at her pink flushed cheeks.

"You're beautiful," he whispered, and pulled her into the crook of his arm. He thought about saying "I love you," but the words stuck in his throat. He needed to tell her the truth first.

"So are you," she said.

He drew her close and they rested against each other. They dozed and when he finally woke up, she lay next to him, staring at him.

"That was amazing. And unexpected." She looked like she wanted to say more, but he wasn't sure he wanted her to.

"Well," he said, "spontaneity is a good thing, right?"

She stroked his cheek and he studied her face, trying to see what she was thinking. Flashes of emotion danced across her eyes—happiness, confusion, and something he couldn't define. They'd just had sex. Their bodies had become one. He should know what she was thinking, what the unidentified emotion was. But he was afraid to ask. He didn't want to spoil the moment. His stomach growled and he chuckled with relief. He reached for his clothes. "Can I make you something to eat—omelet?"

"Perfect."

And it would have to be. For now.

Hannah was supposed to think about tough interview questions, like, "What are your worst qualities?" or "Why are you leaving your current job?" Instead, as she stuck gold loops in her ears and redid her hair for the fourth time, she thought about sex. Sex with Dan, to be specific. And what it meant, or didn't.

The first time they'd fooled around, he hadn't wanted to have sex because it needed to mean something.

Well, they had sex last night, and he didn't say anything about what it meant. Or what she meant to him. She climbed in the cab and gave the driver the address. Was she too emotional, thinking he needed to declare his feelings for her, or define their relationship, after having sex?

She didn't tell him she thought she was falling in love with him, so why did she expect him to say something to her?

Because she'd been about to say something, and he'd changed the subject with food. And she let him. She was no better than he was, but her pride still stung.

Hannah traveled alone in the elevator, watching the floor numbers tick upwards and feeling her palms dampen as she approached twenty-one. When the bell dinged and the door opened, she squared her shoulders and stepped into the reception area of the boutique PR firm.

She hadn't interviewed since she'd left college five years ago and her heart beat fast in her chest. With a quick glance around the cream and taupe reception area, she walked to the desk and smiled. "Hi, I'm Hannah Cohen. I'm here for an interview with Barbara James."

The receptionist directed Hannah to a plush dark taupe sofa to wait. To keep occupied, she studied the magazine covers framed on the walls—case studies and publicity for clients and maybe the firm, if she had to guess.

"Hannah, I'm Barbara James."

A small, plump, friendly looking woman held out her hand. Hannah rose, grasped it, and couldn't help but smile in return. "Nice to meet you."

"Come on back to my office. I'm impressed with your résumé. You've experienced some wonderful opportunities for someone so young."

Barbara's office credenza was filled with photos—people Hannah assumed were family, friends, and clients. On the walls were more magazine covers and articles.

"I remember that campaign." Hannah pointed to a start-up technology company. "I loved the way you turned the tide from a cold technology company to a company whose products reflected the need to care for the community."

Barbara smiled. "It was one of my favorites. I try to convey warmth and connection in both my personal and professional life. My employees are like family, as are my clients. If I can't relate to a person, I don't want to hire them or work with them. We specialize in what I like to call *Hallmark* moments, although I shouldn't call them that since they're not our client." She grinned and pointed Hannah to a seat across from her blond wood desk.

Hannah crossed her legs. "So you create stories for your clients that convey emotions."

"Exactly. We want the public to patronize a company because it makes them feel good, because they admire their values—whatever those may be—because they're more than an economic beast."

Hannah bit her lip. This was exactly what she wanted, but she'd tried to do it with Fortex and look where that had landed her. If Barbara did any investigating into her previous job, she'd never hire her.

Barbara reviewed her résumé and asked questions about her experience. When she reached the end, she laid it on her desk, folded her hands and pinned her gaze on Hannah. "So, why are you leaving your current position?"

Hannah's neck grew warm and a drop of sweat dripped down her back. How honest could she be? An image of Jim flashed through her mind. If she couldn't be honest with her boss, and if her boss couldn't believe her, she didn't want to work with him or her. With a deep breath, she told Barbara about Fortex, leaving out the names of everyone involved.

Barbara leaned back in her chair. "Based on what you just told me, I think you're a perfect fit."

Hannah's mouth dropped.

"While I understand the difficult situation your boss was in, the difference is, here I will always back my employees. While the client is *always right*, it doesn't mean my employees are always wrong. I am selective in what companies I take on and I do an exhaustive check into their backgrounds before I agree to represent them. In your boss' position, I would have dropped the client, not you."

"But how can you run a business that way?"

"You'd be surprised." She slid a folder across her desk to Hannah. "Take a look at who we are, what we do, and what you would do if you worked here. Let's both take a few days to think and talk again on Friday. In the meantime, I'll check your references."

Speechless, Hannah nodded and left the office.

Later that night, she reviewed the company folder. Her favorable opinion of the boutique firm increased. She'd gain valuable experience by broadening her duties and responsibilities. The campaigns the firm created and the companies they represented were impressive. And she'd be getting a pay raise to boot.

She'd be on pins and needles until she heard back from Barbara. For the first time in a long time, she was excited about her job.

Dan scrolled through financial statements, but his brain wasn't focused on numbers. It had been two days since he'd seen Hannah—two days too long. He missed the touch of her hand—the way her skin felt smooth beneath his, the unexpected delicate feel of her bones when their fingers were intertwined. She was strong, stronger than she looked. The contrast intrigued him.

He missed the closeness he'd experienced when he was inside of her, arms and legs entwined. Their breaths mingled, their hearts beat together and their bodies moved as one. They connected in a way he hadn't shared with anyone in a long time. She was the first person he'd wanted to have sex with since his wife.

He missed her vanilla-scented perfume when he buried his face in her neck, the berry flavor of her mouth when he kissed her. He missed the peace that settled over him when she leaned into him. Hell, he missed how she pushed him to test his physical limits and made his leg ache when he was with her, how she was solicitous yet not pitying.

Dammit, he missed everything about her, which was ridiculous, because they'd been together on Monday. And they would see each other this coming weekend. He was a grown man. Why couldn't he be away from her?

Fear settled in the pit of his stomach. His hands grew cold. He wasn't dependent on her, was he? It was one thing to care about someone. It was a different thing to be unable to be away from them. He'd been drawn to her from the start—it was a relief when he realized she felt the same way. But was this something more? Like someone testing a wound to see how painful it was, he poked and prodded at his feelings for

Hannah and his desire to be with her. Maybe not seeing her for the next few days was a good thing.

He pushed away from his desk in disgust and ran a hand over the top of his head. His phone rang. Spinning around in his chair, he banged his leg against the desk. With a muttered oath, he answered the phone.

"Dan Rothberg."

"Whoa, it's Lisa. Not sure who you're mad at, but it can't be me."

He let out a whoosh of air. "Sorry, Lisa. What can I do for you?"

"Did you look at the affidavits from the charities?"

"Yeah, I did. Great work. We've got everything lined up. Thanks." He massaged his knee.

"Okay, let me know if you need anything else. Or if you need girlfriend advice."

He sputtered. Was it that obvious? Her laughter told him it was. Except the advice he needed—determining if his attachment to Hannah was healthy—couldn't come from her. "I will. Thanks."

"No problem. But next time I might persuade you to tell me details."

He shook his head as he hung up. He was losing it. The phone rang again, but this time it was his cell. Hannah. His heartbeat increased. "Hey, I was thinking about you," he said. In a matter of seconds, all his anxiety melted away.

"It must be why my nose is itching. Or are my ears supposed to ring?"

He laughed. "I have no idea, but it sounds like allergies and that can't be good."

"Not as good as your kisses."

His face heated. He glanced at the door to make sure it was shut. Pulling his collar away from his neck, he cleared his throat.

"Oh, did I embarrass you?" She sounded surprised. "I'm sorry."

"It's okay. Just didn't expect it."

"Mmm, I'm full of surprises."

This was the Hannah he'd missed. *His* Hannah?

"So, I have news and I'd rather tell you in person," she said. "I wish it wasn't so long until the weekend."

He glanced at his calendar. "Want to slip away and meet now? It's almost lunchtime."

"Can we do that?"

He laughed again. "We're adults. In theory, we can do whatever we want." There was silence on the other end of the line, interrupted by a keyboard clicking.

"Okay, let's meet in Chelsea, the corner of 5th Avenue and 30th Street, in say, twenty minutes?"

"Great." He hung up, told his assistant he was going out, and made his way to the subway. He had no idea what her surprise could be. Nineteen minutes later, he waited on the agreed-upon corner, hand tapping the top of his cane. A flash of red caught his eye and he turned in time to see Hannah in a red coat, her smile illuminating the entire street corner.

"I'm glad you came." Placing her hand on top of his cane for balance, she stood on tiptoe. Berry lips met his, vanilla engulfed him, smooth fingers caressed the nape of his neck. He was drowning. The knot tightened.

With a groan, he pulled her close, feeling her soft breasts against his chest, her narrow hips against his. He nipped her lips, stroked her hair, entwining strands around his fingers. Soft and silky, her hair twisted around his wrist. With reluctance, he pulled away. "God, I can't get enough of you," he said, his voice hoarse with longing. That was his problem.

She stroked his cheek and her blue eyes sparkled. "You're pretty irresistible yourself."

He raised his cane. "Yeah, a total babe magnet." Because she couldn't be as desperate for him as he was for her.

She took it out of his hands and used it as a shepherd's crook to reel him in. "You're good just as you are."

He exhaled, took back his cane, and stepped out of the line of pedestrian traffic that flowed around them. "So, what news do you have?"

She told him about her job interview, described Barbara and the company philosophy. "Can you believe what she said?"

"I think she makes some interesting points," he answered when she finished her recitation. "It's heartwarming to hear about a company with honor. Have you looked over her materials yet?"

"Last night. I'm going for a second interview. I hope they offer me the position. I *really* want this job."

"They'd be lucky to have you. Even if you don't take this job, it's nice to know other alternatives are out there."

She shrugged. They continued walking, hand in hand, until she stopped in front of a gallery. "Look at these pictures. Do you have time to go in?"

"Sure."

Entering the austere white-on-white space, the owner invited them to look around. With a nod, they walked the perimeter of the room and studied the photographs hanging on the walls. Most were black and white portraits. Dan admired the poses and composition when he wasn't analyzing his attraction to Hannah.

Was a never-ending desire to be with her normal? Did other people in love feel this, or only former addicts?

"Look at this one," Hannah said. She pointed to one of a mother and baby. He dragged his focus away from his thoughts and followed Hannah's finger. The photo showed half of their profiles, noses touching.

"It's excellent, but did you notice the one over there?" He led her to one of a couple sitting on a bench, facing away from the camera. Through the slats of the bench, you could see their arms entwined around each other. How attached to each other were they? How would it compare to his feelings for Hannah? "Something about this reminds me of us."

"Is it the grey hair?" Hannah asked.

He shook his head at her, unable to speak.

She gave him a hug. "I like it also. I was teasing."

"I know." Or he hoped.

They waved to the owner.

Outside the gallery, Hannah paused. "You seem off today," she said. "Did something happen?"

They strolled along the street, window-shopping. "No. I just...." He turned to her and kissed her lips. "I just missed you." *And I'm terrified about what it means.*

She gave him a look like she knew he was leaving information out. He was, because he remembered the last time he'd felt this pull, this lack of control. And it had almost cost him his daughter.

CHAPTER SIXTEEN

That weekend, Hannah's stomach fluttered with anticipation as she approached the movie   theater. Dan waited for her outside, scanning the crowd. In these few moments before he noticed her, she watched him. About a head taller than those around him, he was easy to spot. Broad shoulders, trim waist, ever-present cane. Light glinted off his hair, giving him a silver halo.

Dan as an angel. She stifled a snort. Approaching from behind, she reached her hands around his waist, moved her hands to his muscular chest, and leaned her cheek against his back. He started, but must have realized it was her, because he covered her hands with his own. He leaned against her.

His chest expanded as he inhaled. His heart beat against her hands, making her smile. Peeking around his body, she tilted her face toward him. "Hi."

"I missed you," he said.

"I missed you too."

He took her hand in his, brought her fingers to his lips and kissed the backs of them. A shiver ran down her spine as his heated breath fanned her skin.

Coming around to his front, she hugged him. He pulled her tight against him, burying his face in her neck. While she loved being close to him, it felt as if he was afraid to let her go. This wasn't like him.

"Are you okay?"

Pulling away, he looked at her, longing reflected in his gaze. "I am now."

"We don't have to watch a movie, you know."

"No, you want to see it and I do too." Taking her hand, he led her into the theater. He didn't break contact with her the entire time. Not while buying tickets or popcorn, not while finding seats, not while settling in to wait for the previews to start. She liked the closeness, but it was odd.

"Are you sure there's nothing wrong?" she asked as the previews started.

"I've missed you."

She took his face in her hands. His eyes flashed in the dim theater. "I'm right here, okay?"

He kissed her, his lips making the lightest contact with hers. It was the whisper of a kiss, and it left her wanting more. "I know," he said.

Resting in the crook of his arm, she settled in to watch the movie.

When it was over, she grabbed his hand to keep him in his seat. "Talk to me."

"What about?"

"You. You're not acting like yourself."

He stiffened, but she wouldn't back down. Not this time. Instead, she waited. He pulled at his collar. "What do you mean?"

"You're more attached to me than usual." At his shocked expression, she hurried to continue. "Not that I mind. I love being close to you, and if that's all it is, you wanting to be close to me, fine. But it seems like it's more than that."

He swallowed, opened his mouth, and closed it. After a moment, he spoke. "I'm sorry. I like being with you, that's all. I don't mean to smother you."

She raised an eyebrow. His face darkened, but he didn't add anything further. Squeezing his hand, she rose. "You'd tell me if it was something, right?"

He pulled her against his chest, his heart beating against her ear. It was strong and steady, like him.

"Yes."

She believed him.

Hannah hugged herself as she let herself into her apartment. It was the only way she could contain the feelings bubbling inside her, threatening escape.

"*Hannahla?* Is that you?"

"Yes, *Bubbe*, it's me." She walked into the living room and frowned. "What are you still doing up?"

"I couldn't sleep, so I decided to wait for you."

"Oh, I'm sorry I kept you up."

Her grandma laughed. "Not to worry. I read our next book club book. It's good. Did you have fun tonight?"

She sank onto the sofa next to her grandmother. "Oh *Bubbe*, I did. He makes me so happy, I can barely contain myself. Although he was a little weird tonight, I know I make him feel good." At her grandmother's raised eyebrows, Hannah tipped her head away. "I don't mean that, *Bubbe*, although that's good too." Now it was *Bubbe's* turn to blush and look away. "I mean...when I got there, he didn't see me. I snuck behind him and put my arms around him. He could have reacted any number of ways, but instead, he leaned into me and stayed there, like he didn't want to break contact. Or like I was helping him in some way. It's hard to explain..."

"Like you've become a part of him?"

Hannah's eyes widened. "Exactly! And he's become a part of me." She leaned toward her grandmother. "I think I love him." She wrapped her arms around her stomach, trying to contain the feeling inside her.

Her grandma's face broadened into a grin. She clasped her hands together, looking as excited as Hannah felt. "Oh *Hannahla*, I'm happy for you. I'll admit, I was reluctant at first because he's older than you, and he has a daughter."

"I know, *Bubbe*, I was too. But Tess has accepted me, and Dan isn't old."

"If you love him, he must be wonderful."

"He is. He still doesn't talk to me as much as I'd like him to, but he's made progress."

"Sometimes men take time. Tess is a doll. Only a good man could raise someone like her. When will you invite them to Shabbat dinner?"

"Soon, *Bubbe*, soon."

A family dinner with her grandmother, Dan, and Tess. In the past, she would have been nervous. But this felt right. And she'd tell him she loved him.

Dan looked out the window. The full moon's light shined into the darkened spare room, pooled onto the puzzle table, and spilled onto the wood floor. He hadn't been able to sleep since he came home from the movies with Hannah.

Like he did when his leg bothered him, he tried to distract himself with putting together the puzzle. But the bright-colored sea creatures reminded him of her laughter. The moonlight reminded him of her creamy skin. The stillness around him reminded him of her breath on his neck when she leaned around to kiss him.

He couldn't get her out of his mind.

He rubbed his knee. What would it be like for Hannah to massage him? He closed his eyes, imagining her soft hands on his skin, their cool touch against his heat. He hardened. Opening his eyes in frustration, he stood and walked around.

A vision of Hannah's blue eyes, wide with sympathy, sparkling with humor, darkening in passion, flitted through his mind. He shook his head, trying to clear it.

He loved her.

He jerked to a standstill. He loved her? When did that happen? Was it when she'd cleaned the tomato sauce off of his cheek? Charmed Tess? Made him feel like a man even as she figured out a way for him to rest his leg? Confided to him about her brother?

Her brother.

There was no possible way this could work. Now that he knew he loved her, he had to do what was best for her.

He recognized the signs. An inability to get her out of his mind. An inability to sleep. His need to see her, talk to her, touch her.

He was addicted to her, as if she were a substance. Like before.

Her brother was a drug addict.

He was too.

She didn't deserve that.

He'd broken his oxy habit, because it almost killed him and harmed Tess. Now he had to break things off with Hannah. No matter what it cost him.

CHAPTER SEVENTEEN

Hannah looked at her phone for the third time that day. Dan still hadn't returned her call. She'd called him in the morning. When she reached his voice mail, she suggested he and Tess come over next weekend for Shabbat dinner with her grandmother. He hadn't called back. Now, it was ten at night. They talked every day. It was weird. Maybe there was something wrong with his leg? Or Tess?

She picked up her phone and weighed it in her hand. She didn't want to seem needy, but she also wanted to talk to him, to make sure he was all right. Deciding to compromise, she sent him a text.

hi

She was about to give up when dots flashed across the screen. He was typing.

Hello

She breathed a sigh of relief.

missed you today

Again, there was a pause.

I missed you too.

did you get my message

Yeah, sorry, busy day.

what's wrong

She stared at the phone. You didn't have to be a genius to figure out he wasn't in the mood to talk. With a sigh, she turned her phone to vibrate.

When she woke the next morning, there was a message from Dan declining the dinner invitation—he and Tess were busy. For the next couple of days, he answered only if she initiated conversations, without giving away information. If she called, his phone often went straight to voicemail. This was getting ridiculous. Her fingers jabbed the text buttons on her phone.

i think we should talk

She didn't expect an answer, not after how he'd been avoiding her. After a few seconds, the dancing dots appeared on her phone. She held her breath, waiting.

About what?

i'd rather talk in person

There was such a long pause she was convinced he'd tossed the phone aside, like he seemed to be doing with her.

Okay.

The breath she'd held whooshed out of her.

vinnie's at 7:30 tonight

A few seconds later, he responded.

See you then.

Vinnie's Coffee Shop was popular with the commuting crowd, so by 7:30 on a weeknight it began to empty out as people headed home for the evening. Hannah walked into the restaurant. Not seeing Dan, she found a seat near the window to wait. A minute or two later, he entered. She waved.

He didn't smile.

She swallowed.

As he eased into the chair across from her, she wondered how his leg was, but at a time like this, it would be a bad idea to ask him. She swallowed again and stared at the menu in front of her.

"Do you want to order something?" Her stomach was queasy. She wasn't sure what she could eat.

"No."

Great, this was going well. She took in the tense set of his shoulders, the frown line between his brows, his hand clenched on the table.

"What did I do?" Her voice was low. She tried hard not to make it whiny. Days of silence from him had given her too much time to think. She needed answers.

He looked out the window. His Adam's apple bobbed as he swallowed.

"Does this mean I did nothing, or you won't tell me?"

Dan expelled a breath. He met her gaze. "It's not you."

She gave a shaky laugh. "Don't start with the *it's not you, it's me* crap. That's a brush-off and I deserve better."

His face colored. "You're right. I can't be the man you want, the man you deserve."

"Did I miss a conversation, Dan? Because I don't remember listing the things I wanted in a man. You don't get to decide what I deserve." Hannah's heart pounded in her chest. Her nostrils flared as she tried to squeeze air in past the anger blocking her lungs.

Dan swore under his breath. "Dammit."

Hannah took a sip of water. It sloshed in her stomach.

"I thought I could do this," Dan said. "I thought I could be a good dad and have a relationship. But I can't, Hannah. I just can't."

"You're a great dad. I've never asked you to choose between me and Tess." Hannah paused. "Does Tess not like me? Is that the problem?" Tears prickled behind her eyes.

"No, she loves you. But I can't manage the relationship right now. I'm sorry."

She gripped her water glass. The icy temperature permeated her skin, traveling through her veins to her heart. "You don't want to try to work this out?"

"I can't. I know you don't want to hear me say this, but you deserve someone who can devote his entire self to you. I'm not that guy."

If she opened her mouth, she'd scream. Her scream would shatter the water glass, the windows, and the lights above. But it would be nothing compared to what Dan did to her heart.

Hannah rose and gripped the edge of the table. "Maybe you're not that guy. Right now, I don't know who you are, because you're not the Dan I've gotten to know these past six weeks. You're not the Dan I fell in love with."

"I don't understand it, Aviva," Hannah said at lunch two days later. She rubbed her brow, trying to relieve the headache she'd had since leaving Dan. "I know I should just forget about him, but he broke up with me without giving me a reason."

"Could something have spooked him?"

"I don't know. I told you he acted weird the last couple of times we were together."

"Maybe there's something going on he can't talk about right now."

"Can't or won't? I don't understand why he won't share his feelings with me, and I can't be with someone who doesn't."

"You deserve better."

Hannah shook her head. "Now you sound like Dan."

"I don't mean it like that." She reached for Hannah's hand. "You shouldn't be with someone who won't talk to you."

"No, I shouldn't. I just wish I knew what went wrong. He hasn't spoken to me since Monday. Yesterday doesn't count. Part of me wants to completely forget about him. The other part..." She watched the light glint off the stainless-steel spoon handle. "The other part wants to force him to explain himself. And I have no idea what to do."

"Did you call him?"

She sighed. "I did."

"He didn't answer?"

"Nope."

"Did you leave a message?"

Hannah averted her gaze. "No."

"Why not?"

"Because I didn't want to sound like I was begging. He knows I'm angry and hurt. Leaving a message will make me sound like some petulant child. He already has a teenager; he doesn't need to date one—not that Tess is petulant, because she's great." She sighed and sipped her coffee. It was tasteless. Or maybe it was her.

Aviva tipped her head. Hannah was reminded of a sprite. She kept her mouth shut—her friend hated being called that. She bit the inside of her cheek to keep from smiling. It was the first time she'd been in the mood to smile in days.

"I see your point, but you should have left a message. The only way you two will work is if you communicate."

"That's just it. I don't know if there's anything *to* work. He won't communicate."

"Neither will you. You should call him again."

"Ugh, I hate this. I really do."

Aviva gave Hannah a hug. The two of them returned to their offices, where Hannah contacted Barbara to confirm her follow-up interview. Although excited about the prospect of a new job, thoughts of Dan dampened her feelings. She hoped Aviva was right, but she had a sinking feeling in her stomach there was something else going on.

It had been 72 hours since Dan had talked to Hannah. 4,320 minutes. 259,200 seconds. Granted, their latest bout of "talking" had been him breaking up with her. But his limbic system didn't care. Even now, despite the shitty way he'd treated her, when he thought about her, his heartbeat increased and his palms sweated.

After tossing and turning all night, he'd gotten up early on a Saturday morning to make coffee.

The ring of his phone made him jump. He looked around to make sure Tess didn't see him. *Wimp.*

He looked at the cellphone screen. Hannah. Guess he wasn't the only one not sleeping. A shot of guilt ran through him for causing her lack of sleep. Then reality returned—maybe he wasn't causing her any problems. Maybe she just wanted to yell at him. He should let it go to voicemail. He stuffed the phone back in his pocket. *Coward.*

No, he wasn't a coward. He was trying to end the addiction before it became a problem he couldn't overcome.

The phone continued to play Radiohead's 2+2=5 ringtone. His hand started to shake. Would it be bad to talk to her? It was early on a Saturday morning. Maybe she needed something. Swearing under his breath, he yanked the phone out of his pocket. The movement made him twist wrong and he shouted as blinding pain shot up and down his leg. His phone clattered to the floor. He grabbed blindly for the countertop as he fell.

CHAPTER EIGHTEEN

Insistent knocking on her bedroom door pulled Hannah out of bed Saturday morning, much earlier than she'd intended on waking. Actually, she'd been up for a while. She'd called Dan, but as usual, he hadn't answered. Still, she'd been hoping to relax a little longer...

"*Hannahla*, are you up? Hannah?"

"I'm awake, *Bubbe*." She rubbed her face. "What's wrong?"

Her grandma walked in holding the apartment phone. "There's a call for you."

On the home phone? No one called on the home phone. Her grandmother and telemarketers used it. If this was a telemarketer at eight-flippin' thirty on a Saturday, they would pay.

"Hello?"

"Hannah, it's Tess."

Hannah sat up straight. "Hi, Tess."

"Um, I'm sorry to bother you..."

"It's okay, sweetheart. What's wrong?"

There was a gasp, sobs, and words she couldn't make out. Her heart beat fast in her chest. She clasped the phone tightly. Her grandmother frowned. Hannah shook her head, covered the phone, and whispered, "I have no idea what's going on." Uncovering the mouthpiece, she waited until there was a pause in the noise on the other end. "Tess, honey, I can't understand what you said. Take a deep breath and start over."

"It's my dad."

A frisson of fear trickled down her spine. She jumped out of bed, trying to untangle the sheets around her legs. "What happened?"

"His leg hurts. I mean, it always hurts, but it's much worse and he fell and I can't get him up and I don't know what to do. Can you help me please?"

"Of course, sweetheart. Did you call 911?" She grabbed clothes and started to put them on.

"I wanted to call, but he yelled at me not to. He's fallen before when his leg gives out. He'd kill me if he knew I called you, but I'm scared. I haven't seen him like this in a really long time."

"Okay. Give me about fifteen minutes. And Tess? I'm glad you called."

Hanging up, she finished dressing. With a few quick words to her grandmother, she raced the ten blocks to Dan's apartment. Her hand was poised to knock on the door when Tess jerked it open.

The teen fell into Hannah's arms and trembled against her shoulder.

"Shh, it's okay, honey." Hannah rubbed her back. She'd never seen Tess like this, but she couldn't show her how freaked out she was. After a moment, Tess pulled away. Her face was splotchy, her eyes red, and she pulled her hair forward to cover her embarrassment.

"Tess, you did the right thing by calling me."

Tess blew her hair out of her face. "You were the first person I could think of. I'm sorry I worried you. He's fallen before and it's not usually a big deal, but he's been acting weird lately and I just wanted you to be here."

"Don't worry about me. Why don't you take me to your dad."

As she led her inside, she looked over her shoulder at Hannah. "He'll be really mad at me for doing this."

Hannah patted her shoulder. "Don't worry. I'll handle it."

"He's in there." Tess pointed to the kitchen from the safety of the hallway.

Hannah peeked around the doorway. The counter was messy and things had fallen to the floor. An overhead light brightened the room. It wasn't until she stepped in that she saw him, sitting in a chair brought in from the dining room. His face was contorted in a grimace. His good leg was bent and he was trying to lever himself to a standing position. He moaned.

A shiver of fear passed through her. She knelt by his side, hand on his arm. "Dan?"

He opened his eyes, locked his gaze with Hannah, before he shut them again. His face turned a dark red. "What are you doing here?"

"Tess called me. Are you okay? What happened?"

"I don't want you here. I'm fine." He tried to stand up, winced, and sat back on the chair, hands fisted on the edges of the seat, jaw clenched. He ignored Hannah's outstretched arms.

Tess spoke from the doorway. "Daddy, you needed help and she was the only—"

"Tess, I'm fine," he ground out as Tess entered the kitchen.

Hannah led Tess out of earshot. "Bring him a pillow for his head and maybe another for his leg. Give him pain killers—"

"He won't take those."

Seriously? "Okay, how about ibuprofen?"

Tess shook her head. "He won't take anything at all."

"But he needs it!"

Now Tess raised her hands.

"Okay, give him an ice pack and a heating pad. Alternate between the two in twenty-minute intervals."

"I can do that." Tess bit her lip, before backing out of the room.

When she was gone, Hannah turned her attention to Dan, trying to assess his injuries. There didn't seem to be any obvious ones, which only made her feel a little better. She stroked his wrist.

"I said go." He took short breaths through his teeth, which were bared in a grimace. He pulled his hand away. "She's a teenager. The last time I checked, adults didn't have to listen to them."

"Smart ones do, though."

He blew a breath through clenched teeth. "Why are you being so stubborn?"

"Because Tess is scared and I'm trying to do what's best for her." *Which means helping a man who doesn't want it.*

Dan pushed himself forward, one arm braced against the counter. His face was pale. Beads of sweat popped on his forehead. "And you think I'm not?"

Hannah's eyes widened at the tone of his voice. "Dan, this isn't a me-versus-you thing. She's worried about you."

"For the last time, I'm telling you I don't want your help."

She rolled back on her heels and dropped his wrist. She searched his face, looking for some hidden desire for her to stay, a trace of his affection for her. There was nothing except anger. She tried to squelch her own anger and hurt simmering below the surface. No matter how horribly he was behaving, he was in pain. Now was not the time to discuss her feelings.

"Are you sure you don't need to go to the hospital?"

"This has happened before, I'm fine."

That damned word again. "Fine." She strode out of the kitchen. "Tess," she called, as she returned to the living room, "your dad..." What the heck was she supposed to say? Did she even know they'd broken up?

"What? Is he okay?" She held an ice pack and heating pad in her hand.

Hannah shrugged. "I don't think it's anything other than his normal leg pain, albeit more severe. I think he'd be more comfortable without me here."

"He kicked you out?"

"No, but I don't want to make things worse." Hannah gave her a hug. "I'm sorry you have to deal with this yourself. I wish there was something I could do. He'll be fine." She hoped she spoke the truth. She was trying to comfort a teenager. Short of arranging for a boy band to serenade her, she didn't know what to do. But her words seemed to do the trick. Tess nodded and seemed to relax.

"I'm going to go. If you get scared, you can call me. I'll check in again with you later." She turned to look at the math and science books strewn across the sofa and glass coffee table. "What do you need to do today? Anything I can help with?"

"No, I just have homework. I might go over to the JCC later to tutor, depending on how Dad is feeling."

"Do you have enough food in the house? Did you eat breakfast? What about lunch?" Tess looked at her askance and Hannah laughed. "I sound like my grandmother, don't I? Well, you know Jewish grandmothers—not having enough food is a sin."

Tess shook her head.

"You don't know that? Okay, well, trust me. My grandmother would forgive me for murdering someone. However, if I didn't have enough food, I'd be banished from the family."

At Tess's wide-eyed look, Hannah patted her back. "Well, practically. Anyway, the point I'm trying to make is if you need anything from the grocery store, I can get it."

"Nope, we're good for today."

"Tomorrow too?"

"Yup."

She gave Tess a last hug, tossed a glance toward the kitchen and left. Dan was being an ass. She didn't know why or for how long, but as soon as he could string two sentences together without gasping in pain, she was getting answers.

Dan lay in bed that evening, listening to Tess putter in the kitchen. Okay, he hoped she was puttering, rather than whipping up a poison milkshake to murder him. The sounds coming from the direction of the kitchen sounded harmless enough. For now.

She was angry.

He saw it in the set of her shoulders, in her flashing brown eyes every time she looked at him, right before they switched over to a combination of fear and anxiety. The fact she could manage any anxiety at all, no matter how delayed, killed him.

After Hannah left, Tess had helped him hobble into the bedroom. He wasn't sure who suffered more—Tess straining under his weight, or his pride for having to depend on his daughter. But they'd managed.

"I thought you'd be hungry. I made some scrambled eggs and toast," she said without making eye contact. She'd found a tray and arranged his meal on it to look like something straight out of the 1950s. The eggs, which were fluffy and perfect, sat in the middle of the plate, which sat in the middle of the tray. To its right was a glass of orange juice; to its left was a small plate with toasted bread, buttered lightly. All it needed was a flower.

Dammit. His daughter was not supposed to be the caregiver.

"Thank you. I am." He raised himself to a seated position and spread the blanket on his lap in order to put the tray on top of it.

"Oh, I forgot silverware and a napkin. I'll be right back."

After not eating breakfast or lunch, he was starving. The aroma from the food made his mouth water. She might be a kid, but she made mean scrambled eggs.

Returning to his room, she placed the silverware and napkin on his tray without making eye contact. He reached for her and she looked at their clasped hands. He waited. After a few moments, she met his gaze.

"Are you all right?" she asked. "Do you need something else?"

He needed Hannah. Despite what a bastard he'd been to her. That was the problem. "No, I'm fine. I feel better. Thank you."

"You're welcome." She tried to pull away, but he held on. She frowned.

His heart squeezed in his chest. "I want to thank you for all you did for me today, sweetheart. I know you were scared. And I'm sorry. I'm sorry for scaring you, and for the way I treated Hannah."

Uncertainty flickered in her expression, her chest heaved, her nostrils flared. He could see the gold flecks in the brown irises, the individual eyelashes curl from her lids, the arch of her eyebrows. She was losing her "little girl" look and he caught a glimpse of the woman she would be. His hand lifted of its own accord, to bring her toward him in a hug, but he paused mid-lift and lowered it on the bed. He couldn't bear the rejection he knew he would get.

He could tell by the set of her shoulders she didn't want a hug from him.

What he wouldn't give to go back ten years when life made sense. Before Beth died and he'd fallen apart, when Tess had been a little girl and everything could be fixed with a kiss. This time, he couldn't fix things. He couldn't explain to Tess why he needed to send Hannah away—it would scare her. So he stayed quiet, to absorb Tess's anger and hoped they could move past it together.

From outside, thunder boomed. They both jumped. Lightning flashed, and rain—the same rain that had hovered since yesterday, and had caused him such knee pain—pelted the window. Another clap sounded, another flash of lighting seared through the window.

"Storm broke." Even to his own ears, his voice sounded raspy. He cleared his throat.

Tess shuddered. "I hate the noise. I hate what you did to Hannah."

He should explain...if he even had an explanation. But how could he discuss his fears about becoming addicted to Hannah to his little girl, who was growing up and would be trying to figure out her own way of loving someone soon?

Before he could figure out what to do, Tess rose and turned toward the door. With a wary glance out the window, she spoke. "I'll let you eat in peace."

"You don't have to."

"Yes I do. I'm Facetiming Lexi for homework. I have to go to the JCC to tutor."

Dan's stomach dropped. She was leaving. "You can't go out now. You'll get soaked."

"I'll wear my rain jacket. It has a hood."

She left without another word. Later, he listened to the soft giggles from his living room as Tess talked with Lexi, and wondered for the hundredth time how things had changed so fast.

CHAPTER NINETEEN

There was no way Hannah's heart and mind could reconcile breaking up with Dan after she admitted to falling in love with him. The pain was a physical ache in her heart, her head, and her joints, even two weeks later. She'd thought Dan was old? She swore she'd aged fifty years since she'd left the coffee shop. Eating and sleeping were distant memories. Mascara was the most useless thing on the planet—even the waterproof kind—unless she wanted to look like a raccoon. Her grandmother took to whispering into the phone to God-knew-who, and staring at her with a worried expression.

Now she needed to put all of it aside for the first day of her new job.

Hannah took a deep breath before walking into her new office building. Giving her name to the receptionist, she waited until Barbara came into reception, a warm smile on her face.

"Hannah, welcome! I'm glad you've joined us. Come, let me introduce you around."

She followed Barbara inside, shook hands with her new colleagues and tried to smile. Fifteen minutes later, she reached her desk, a pile of paperwork to be filled out in front of her. Letting out a breath, she sank into her chair. Pretending to be happy was exhausting.

She tried to focus on the task in front of her, but her mind spun in a million directions—most of them Dan-related. The forms took longer than they should have.

A few hours later, Barbara stopped by. "Want to grab some lunch?"

It wouldn't do to refuse her new boss. They walked a few blocks to a cozy book and teashop and sat at a quiet table in the back. Bookshelves stacked with books of all sizes and genres lined the walls of the shop. Lower bookcases separated the room into sections. Small, round tables and spindly chairs filled in the middle spaces. A spiral iron staircase disappeared below. Sounds of dishes clinking told Hannah it led to the kitchen. The scent of vellum and leather mingled with tealeaves, and she took her first deep breath in days.

"This place is amazing." She sat across the white lace tablecloth from Barbara.

"It's this little hidden treasure where I love to come to get away from everything. I thought after the activity of meeting everyone this morning, you might appreciate the quiet."

Her new boss was perceptive. "Thank you."

"Since it's too soon to ask how things are going," she said with a smile, "I'll just ask if you're okay. Because you don't seem quite yourself. I'm not complaining. It could be your adjustment to a new place. But I thought I'd ask in case anything is wrong."

Hannah gripped the leather-bound menu tighter. Was she that transparent? If she told her she'd just broken up with her boyfriend, what kind of an impression would she make?

Before she could formulate an answer, Barbara reached across the table and covered Hannah's hand. "Relax. I recognize the value you bring to the company. Like I told you when you interviewed, I care about my employees. So if you ever need to talk, I'm a good listener."

"Thank you." She needed to change the subject before she burst into tears on her first day of work in front of her brand-new boss. She swallowed over the enormous lump in her throat. "So, what kinds of projects do you envision me working on?"

Barbara said, "Well, my thought is I'd like to give you several projects to work on. They'll be in different areas and once we see how you do and where your strengths lie, we'll narrow your focus."

"You have the flexibility to do that?"

Barbara nodded. "I do this with all my new hires. The chemistry of a team is important and I want to make sure you mesh well with the people you work with. Based on our conversations and where I think you would do the best, I'll give you three different projects—I've got a non-profit that needs straight publicity, a tech firm launching a new piece of software to help amputees, and a pharma company raising awareness of women's health issues. Sound good?"

"I think the non-profit and the pharma interest me the most, but I'm happy to work on any of them."

"You can look over the project information after lunch and get to work tomorrow. It's a quiet week because of Thanksgiving so things won't ramp up until after the holiday. I'll observe you and talk to your teammates and you throughout the next month and based on feedback, we'll determine your best fit."

When the waitress brought their salads and sandwiches, Hannah and Barbara stopped talking about work. Hannah found out Barbara and her wife, Janet, were parents to a three-year-old daughter and a five-year-old son, and Hannah told her about her grandmother.

"I love the generational thing you have going there," Barbara said. "That's wonderful!"

"Yeah, my grandma and I have always been close. I love living with her. Plus it lets me pay her back in a way for all the things she did for me."

Later, Hannah, fortified by her garden salad and tuna sandwich, reined her attention in and brushed up on the three projects she'd start work on tomorrow. As she made her way home, a desire to tell Dan about her wonderful new job washed over her and she leaned against the wall as flashes of his eyes deep with understanding and bright with interest invaded her thoughts. Swallowing the lump in her throat, she let herself into her apartment.

"*Hannahlah*, is that you?"

She counted to five and put her keys on the side table. "Yes, *Bubbe*, it's me." She sniffed and walked into the kitchen, where Sylvia was making soup. "Mmm, smells delicious."

"There's bread warming in the oven. How was your first day?"

Hannah set the table and told her about her new job. "I like it." Hannah described the office, Barbara, and her co-workers.

Her grandmother gave her a hug. "I'm so glad. Barbara sounds different, and wonderful."

"She is," Hannah said. "I feel like I'm starting over in exactly the right place.

The next day at work, three people asked Hannah if she was dating anyone, two others mentioned the status of the single guys in the office, and two more offered to introduce her to them. The conversation was like sandpaper against her heart.

"Wow, these people are worse than my grandmother," Hannah said to Stan, her new officemate.

He laughed. "Being the only gay man in the office has its benefits."

"My grandma and her best friend could set you up," she said with a wink.

He held out his hands. "My boyfriend wouldn't like it." He pointed to a photo on the desk and Hannah looked at the two handsome men with a dog.

"I'll leave you alone, if only for the dog's sake."

"Roscoe appreciates that."

After putting in a few hours of work, she walked into the break room for a cup of coffee. Turning around, she almost crashed into a guy who'd walked in behind her. Her coffee sloshed over her hand. With a cry of pain, she ran it under the faucet.

"I'm sorry," he said. "Here, let me help." He rummaged through a drawer and pulled out a first aid kit. Opening it, he tossed Band-Aids, lotions, antiseptic and an assortment of stuff onto the counter. "There must be something here for burns."

She dried off her hand with a towel. "No, it's fine. I think the air is the best thing for it. But thanks."

"You can't thank me. I'm the one who made your coffee spill."

"There was enough milk in it to not burn too badly. Really, I'm fine." She turned her hand this way and that to inspect. A slight redness, but even now the pain had receded.

"At least let me pay for your dry-cleaning bill."

She looked at the stain on her grey peplum skirt and back into his eyes, which squinted in concern. She suspected he wouldn't let this go. "I appreciate it."

When she returned to her desk, Stan whistled. "Oh no."

"I didn't realize there was someone behind me. I'm glad I didn't get him as well."

"Him?"

"I didn't catch his name. Average height, brown eyes, curly brown hair..."

"Probably Marc. He's a bit of a klutz, but nice. Single too if you're interested," he said with a wink.

"He's covering my dry cleaning. Let's leave it as is."

Stan shrugged. "Relationships have started on less."

Later that afternoon, Hannah jumped as someone knocked on her office door. "Geez, I always startle you. I realized I didn't introduce myself. I'm Marc Lang." He held out a hand, which Hannah shook.

"Hannah Cohen."

"I'm serious about the dry cleaning. Make sure you give me the bill. I don't suppose you'd let me make it up to you and buy you a drink?"

"You're already cleaning my clothes, Marc. It's not necessary." She looked at Stan, kind of hoping for an out.

"Don't look at me. I wasn't invited for drinks." He winked at Marc, who laughed.

"You can come too, Stan," Marc said.

Hannah hoped he'd say yes. If Stan came, would be more of a social activity, which she was more ready for than a date.

"Nah, I've got plans."

Her hopes fizzled.

"Hannah?" Marc's gaze reminded Hannah of a puppy. A cute one, but a puppy, nonetheless.

She couldn't help but compare him to Dan, which made her sad. Clearly she wasn't ready to start dating. But all she did at home was mope. Instead, she thrust back her shoulders. If she were ever to get over Dan, she needed to start somewhere. "Sure, that'd be great. Thanks for the invitation."

"I can make sure you get home okay after, if you want."

She blushed as Stan stifled some sort of noise. "Um, we'll see what time it is, but thanks."

He nodded. "Okay."

Marc left and Stan covered his face, shoulders shaking.

"You're awful, you know that?" Hannah said. "Marc seems like a nice guy. Going out will distract me and maybe fill me in on the workings of this place."

"So you need a distraction?"

"I do."

"Well, I'm running outside to grab something from one of the food trucks. Hungry?"

Her eyes filled as she remembered how she and Dan had met. Blinking to prevent tears from falling, she shook her head. "Thanks, though."

After a full day of meetings with her project leaders, research and a little writing, Hannah was more than ready to leave the office when Marc picked her up. "Ready?"

As they walked to the bar, Hannah glanced sideways at him. He was average height with broad shoulders. In khakis and a button-down, his muscular arms filled out his shirt sleeves. He walked with ease, dominating the sidewalk. Was this the guy Stan called a klutz? At a different time in her life, she might have found him attractive.

"Here it is." Marc held the door for her.

Walking past him into the bar, Hannah paused while her vision adjusted to the darker space. The room was long and narrow, with a bar on the left and tables against the wall on the right. She'd never been to a place like this with Dan—their dates were more subdued. Music played. People talked at the bar. It would be difficult to have a serious conversation here. Maybe this wasn't such a good idea...

Before she could change her mind, Marc put a hand on her arm. He introduced her to everyone and seated her next to him—it was pretty clear he'd staked his claim.

"What'll you have?" he asked as he pushed through the crowd at the bar.

"Beer." Dan knew what she drank.

"Any particular kind?"

"Surprise me," she said.

A minute later he returned with two bottles of Yuengling. He tapped his bottle to hers and took a long pull. She watched him swallow, his Adam's apple bobbing. Again, she thought of Dan. Blinking, she sipped her drink and looked around. She recognized faces, but the names were a blur.

She turned to the woman on her left. "Hi, you're Jill, right? What department do you work in?"

"I work in healthcare. Do you live around here?"

"Hoboken. You?"

"Jersey City. We can go to the PATH station together if you want."

"That would be great." And it would relieve her of having to depend on Marc.

The waitress interrupted with plates of wings and skins, which she distributed along the table. Everyone paused their conversations to help themselves to plates, food, and pitchers of beer.

"Do you have everything you need?" Marc asked.

"I'm good." He was sweet. Hannah tried to keep an open mind. "Do you all do this often?"

Marc put his arm around the back of her chair. Hannah flinched, but he didn't seem to notice.

"About every couple of weeks," he said. "We're a pretty social group."

"That's nice. Thanks for inviting me."

A guy on the other side of Jill leaned forward. "Hey, Hannah, I'm Travis. How do you like the place so far?"

"Everyone is friendly. I'm getting my feet wet on the accounts. We'll see what happens."

"Well, I'm in your tech group. If you have questions, don't hesitate to ask."

Conversations about movies, music, and sports swirled around her. Hannah participated as she could, listening more often than not.

Focusing on the talk around her kept her from thoughts of Dan. Or it should have. Her mind drifted to him on occasion—when she saw Alan's blue eyes, she was reminded of Dan's, except Dan's were darker; when Marc laughed at something, she compared his mid-level tone to Dan's deeper one; when Kari twirled her hair, she thought of Tess. Each time her mind drifted to Dan, she tried to steer it to this restaurant, these people. It was exhausting.

She turned to Marc. "Is this your go-to after-work place?"

He nodded. "I prefer it on weekends. They have live bands on Saturday nights and sports on the weekends."

"Sounds fun."

"We should go sometime."

Hannah smiled. He meant well; maybe she could drag Aviva and Jacob with her. She took another sip of her beer. "How long have you worked at the office?"

"About five years. I worked at a larger firm for about three years before that, right out of college. How about you?"

"I was at my previous firm for just under five years."

"What made you leave?"

Hannah played with the beer bottle. Office gossip wasn't her thing. Still... "I wanted a change and the timing seemed right."

From the knowing look in his eye and the way his lips twitched, she thought he knew she was putting him off. "I like to keep things exciting, too. It's why I live in Manhattan. Lots to do, lots of people, always something happening."

She swallowed. Life would be much easier if she could fall for him. She couldn't get Dan out of her mind.

For the next half hour, she made an extra effort to participate in the conversation around her. She laughed at jokes, gave opinions when asked and accepted an offer to shop with some of the other women at the table. Marc ran through descriptions of colleagues. His perceptions were pretty good. Some of them made her laugh. She started to relax.

"Your officemate, Stan. He's a trip. One of the smartest guys I've ever met. Has an innate knowledge of what will work with the public and what won't. But his sense of humor? Oh boy. Do not, I repeat, do not, drink around him when he speaks."

"You mean I have to add him to the list?"

Marc looked at her blankly for a moment before he shook his head. "Yeah, between the two of us, your dry-cleaning bills will be pretty high."

"Or yours will be." She winked.

"Hey, I haven't done anything yet. Can I ask you a personal question, or are you going to change the subject back to work again?"

Hannah let out a deep breath. "How about this. I'm reluctant to get too deep into personal questions at this time. But you can ask, and if I'm not comfortable, I won't answer. Deal?"

"Deal. Every time someone new starts, there are questions about whether they're single or not. So, are you? Single, I mean."

Her chest tightened. She shouldn't be. She didn't want to be. But she was. "Yes. Newly so."

"Ah, that explains it."

"Explains what?"

"Something in your expression whenever I get personal."

"Probably."

Marc turned away. When he turned back, he looked at her. "Whoever he was, he was a fool."

Except, he wasn't.

"How's your new job?" Aviva asked Hannah when they met for brunch that weekend. The blue-and-white restaurant, decorated with cows, was known for its amazing pancakes, and both women ordered them as soon as they were seated. Now, with coffee poured, they waited for their food to arrive.

"I like it." Hannah described the office, Barbara, and her co-workers.

"I love Stan! You'll have to introduce me to him. Any other interesting men in the office? Straight ones?"

Hannah fidgeted at Aviva's pointed look. "Not really."

"Which isn't a definitive no, so tell me!"

Hannah rolled her eyes and told her about Marc and their drinks. "It was weird and awkward. Especially because I tried to keep things work-related and he didn't."

"Well, give him a chance. He might be someone you want to get to know better when you're ready to date again."

"I don't think I should date a co-worker. Look what happened before."

"Oh come on. That was Jim being an asshole. No one can believe he did that to you. Barbara sounds different."

"Still, it wouldn't be wise for me not to learn from previous mistakes."

"So you think Dan was a mistake?"

Hannah circled the rim of her coffee cup with her finger. "I miss him." She looked across the table at Aviva, who grabbed her hand and squeezed. "You should have seen me at the dinner table on

Thanksgiving, trying to figure out a way to express gratitude, when I don't feel it."

"I know, sweetie. But he's got obvious issues and you don't need someone like him in your life."

"But it doesn't mean I don't miss him. I miss Tess. I was supposed to go to her art show, but I can't now. And I wish I could."

"I know but it doesn't mean you can't enjoy yourself with Marc, or someone else, even, if he makes you happy. I'm not saying you should. With all the unwanted matchmaking my roommates did for me, the last thing I'd do is force my best friend into a relationship."

Hannah smiled.

"But I will say keep your mind open. You never know what might happen when you least expect it."

Their pancakes arrived and the two women changed the subject as they ate. When they'd finished, they hugged outside on the sidewalk.

"I miss having you around every day," Hannah said.

"Me too. Let's get together again soon. Okay?"

As Hannah headed home, she tried not to let melancholy wash over her. Between losing Dan and no longer working with Aviva, she was lonely.

CHAPTER TWENTY

Dan's luck evaporated.

He swept the puzzle pieces to the floor. Multi-colored, multi-faceted pieces scattered across the Berber carpet like confetti. He swore under his breath. This was not working. No matter how many pieces he added to the picture, no matter how he focused on each piece, thoughts of Hannah invaded his mind. His throat went dry.

It had been three weeks since he and Hannah had broken up. Three weeks watching the clock all day wondering what she was doing. Three weeks of him staring at his phone, willing himself not to call her but hoping she'd call him. Three weeks of smelling those damn hot dog vendors and getting nauseated.

If he'd thought he was addicted to her before, he was positive now. Except his addiction appeared to be getting worse, not better. Ending his relationship with her hadn't worked. Now it was time for more drastic measures.

Grabbing the garbage can, he swept the remaining puzzle pieces from the table into the receptacle. He dropped to the floor and picked up all the ones that had fallen, adding them to those he'd already collected. When he was finished, he hoisted himself upright. His gaze darted from the tabletop to the trashcan. His fingers itched to remove the pieces from the garbage. What would he do without his distraction? With a muttered curse, he grabbed the can and brought it out into the hallway, dumping its contents down the building's trash compactor. He folded the box and sent it into the recycling bin. Returning to his apartment, he strode to the window. He looked out at the street scene below as he tried to clear his mind.

All he saw were flashing images of Hannah reflected in the window, like some torturous slideshow. He raised his hand to pound the glass, thought better of it and lowered it again to his side. The only thing he'd accomplish would be a sore hand. Staring at his fist, he wondered if the pain would make things better. This was ridiculous. His heart pounded. Sweat dampened his brow. Maybe he was feverish?

The scrape of a key in a lock pulled him out of his self-examination. Tess entered the apartment. "Hi, Dad. Uh, are you okay?"

"Fine, why?"

"You don't look like yourself."

"I'm fine. How was shopping?"

"Good, I got lots of stuff."

"Show me?"

"Later. I told Lexi I'd FaceTime her."

"You shopped all day with her. What else is left to say?"

"Dad!"

Dan shook his head. He watched Tess stride down the hall in a huff. If Hannah were here, she'd make some joke to lighten his mood. She'd go after Tess. Everyone would laugh and get along, like the characters in a Disney movie. She'd probably have Tess model the clothes. But if Hannah were here, he wouldn't be in this mess in the first place. Hannah wasn't here. She wouldn't be here ever again. His chest constricted and his head ached.

He walked into the kitchen to get a drink. When he opened the freezer for ice, he found one of the pies Hannah's grandmother had made. His eyes burned and before he could stop himself, he'd thrown the pie into the garbage, right before Tess walked into the kitchen.

"What's for dinner tonight?"

"I haven't thought about it. How about pasta and meatballs?"

"Great. And can we defrost the apple pie?"

Did the entire universe conspire against him? "No, we don't have it anymore."

"You ate it?"

"I got rid of it."

"Why?"

He didn't have a good answer for her and her expression flattened after a minute. "Because it reminds you of Hannah, right?"

He had nothing to say, so he shrugged.

"I hate this."

"Tess!"

But she'd left the room and he was alone. Again.

CHAPTER TWENTY-ONE

The apartment phone rang just as Hannah got home from work the next day. She swallowed when she recognized the name. "Hello, Jeff."

She hadn't expected him to call, especially when he was a no-show for Thanksgiving. Her respect for her brother had increased a smidgeon. But she still dreaded this conversation.

"I know you don't want to talk to me, but I'd like to talk to you." She heard him swallow. "I wondered if maybe we could meet somewhere?"

She expelled a deep breath. Everyone told her to talk to him. Well, everyone but Dan, but he didn't count anymore. Her eyes filled with tears, but she didn't know if it was from thoughts of Dan or from the sound of Jeff's voice. Either way, she couldn't let them fall. She counted to ten before she spoke. "Whenever is good for you."

"That'd be great. Wow, thanks. Does tonight work? Or tomorrow? We could meet at that diner in the city on Third."

"Tonight is fine. Seven?"

"Seven is great. I'll see you then. And Hannah? Thanks."

She clicked off her phone, not trusting herself to speak. It was a start.

That night, Jeff waved from a table near the door as soon as Hannah walked into the red and gold diner at seven on the dot.

She must have swallowed a trampoline, because her stomach was doing flip-flops. She pressed her hand against her belly in an effort to calm it as she walked over to him.

He rose and waited to sit until she sat. This was new.

Hannah stared into his clear, focused, and maybe a little nervous, blue eyes. His clothes were clean and neat. He no longer looked skinny as a rooster, like when he was using. His cheeks were filled out; his neck had lost its stringiness. When he folded his arms on the table, Hannah resisted the urge to push up his sleeve to look for track marks. Instead, she noticed how clean his hands and nails were, how healthy his skin looked.

She let out a breath. "Hi," she said.

"Hi." His voice was deep and smooth. "I'm glad you came."

She bit her lip.

"Should we order first?" When she picked up her menu, he added, "My treat."

Her eyes widened.

"I have a job and you're my little sister. My treat."

Something in the way he looked at her reminded her of Dan, when he desperately tried to hold onto his dignity as he knee flared up. "Thank you."

The air between them crackled and they studied the menu in silence. After the waitress took their orders and they were alone once again, Hannah sat back.

"I wanted to apologize," he said. "I've done so many bad things and hurt you. It's gone on for years. I know needing to make amends isn't enough for you. I know a simple 'I'm sorry' won't cut it, but I hope this can be the start to my fixing things with you."

Her stomach rolled. "I'd like to say okay, but I'm scared, Jeff."

He reached across the table and took her hand. It was warm, rough from work, but it reminded her of when they were kids and he'd boost her into their tree house or give her a hand climbing the jungle gym when she needed one.

"Me too."

She squeezed his hand. He smiled. "I heard you met Mike."

"Yeah, he's, um…interesting."

The laugh that burst from Jeff caused the patrons nearby to stare. Jeff waved and shook his head. "Yeah, it's one way to describe him. He said the same thing about you."

"I guess he could have said worse."

"Actually, he said I was pretty lucky to have a sister like you. He's right."

She didn't know what to say. She started to look away, but a tug on her arm returned her focus to Jeff.

"I want you to know I set up a repayment plan with Grandma. It will take a few months, but I should have all the money I took repaid. It's what we talked about those times I visited."

Her pulse rushed in her ears. "Mike said he's your sponsor."

"Yeah, he saved my ass."

"He said you've been clean for a year."

"Three hundred and twenty-five days, to be exact. Long enough for me to be long overdue in fixing things with you."

"Why?"

"Why what?"

"Why did you get clean?"

He waited while the waitress handed them their "breakfast for dinner"—him eggs and hash browns, Hannah French toast. When she left, he took a bite, swallowed and spoke. "I OD'd. In all honesty, I'm not sure if it was accidental or on purpose. The way my mind was at the time, I'm not sure it matters. It happened outside Mike's restaurant. He took me to the hospital, got me cleaned up and told me his story—told me he could help me, but I needed to want help. I wasn't sure if I wanted help, or if I wanted company. I'd done a pretty good job isolating myself from everyone. Something told me this was my last chance. He's a hell of a sponsor, let me tell you."

"That's all it took? Some stranger telling you to get clean? I tried for years, so did *Bubbe*. We love you. You're supposed to love us. How come our attempts didn't work?" She couldn't keep the hurt out of her voice.

"I don't know. The only thing I can think of is I was afraid of disappointing you and Grandma, of having to deal with your opinions of me. If I failed Mike, he'd get over it."

She gripped her fork and watched her knuckles whiten. Around her, the sounds of the diner filtered through: cutlery clinking, people talking, chairs scraping the floor. Aromas wafting from the kitchen should have made her hungry. But Jeff's words prevented her from eating.

"So your not getting clean was our fault?"

"No!" Jeff jumped up and came around to her side of the table. "It was all my fault. I was too ashamed to try and fail, so I didn't try at all. I had other issues too, issues I'm getting help with, which made me think doing drugs was the best thing for me." He put a hand on her shoulder. For once, she didn't flinch. "I'm sorry. If I live to be a hundred, I'll never be able to apologize enough for what I put you through. But I'll do anything to prove to you I've changed."

"So what happens next?"

Jeff returned to his side of the table. "Whatever you want."

"Whatever I want?"

He nodded. "Look, if I had my way, we'd pick up where we left off and everything would be fine and dandy."

Hannah couldn't believe what he said. She opened her mouth to speak, but he held out a hand. She waited.

"However, I also know a few things. One, I don't know where we left off, and going back in time has its own set of problems. Two, I don't deserve to be treated as if nothing happened. I've caused too much damage. While my apology is a start, it can't wipe the slate clean. Three, my readiness and yours are two different things. It's up to you. I'd like for us to have a relationship, but I understand you might not want one with me."

She stared at him, trying to read him, but the only thing she noticed was resignation, mixed with a little bit of hope. Hannah folded her arms around her waist. "I don't know what I want. I don't want everything to be so hard."

He nodded. "Okay, what can I do to make things easier for you?"

"Not be a jerk?"

He pulled away a little, but when she smiled, he shook his head. "Yeah, I can work on it."

For the first time, Hannah got a glimpse of their old relationship. "So, you're really clean?"

"I am."

"What happens the next time you want to use?"

He pinned her with a look. "Han, I want to use every minute of every day." He reached for her hand. "But I want to be clean more."

She watched him, waiting for him to look away or make some excuse or joke. But he sat there, holding her hand, and waiting for her. Squeezing his hand, she swallowed. "Can I maybe call you sometime?"

"I'd love you to call me. Anytime."

He gave her his phone number. "Can I have yours too, or would you rather I didn't? I mean, I already know the home phone, but..."

"No, it's okay, you can have mine."

With numbers exchanged, it seemed like a weight lifted from his shoulders. He sat straighter with the familiar twinkle in his eye. If she let herself, she could pretend the drugs had never happened. For the rest of the meal, they made small talk, which was only a little awkward.

"Grandma says you have a boyfriend."

Hannah clenched her fork tight. "Had. We broke up."

"I'm sorry."

"Me too. He was a great guy."

"What happened?"

She shrugged. "I don't know. He seemed into me and all of a sudden, he wasn't. How about you? Do you have a girlfriend?"

He shook his head. "No. I can't focus on anyone else yet. I'm almost there, but not quite. How's your job? Grandma says you started at a new place."

"You have the direct line to my life through her, I see."

He reddened. "We talk."

"Good." She told him about her new firm before she looked at her phone. "Wow, it's getting late. I should head home."

Jeff flagged the waitress with his debit card. When Hannah tried to pay, he shooed her away. "I told you. My treat."

Could he afford it? He nodded. "Yes, I can afford it, don't worry."

"Thank you. Nice mind reading."

"It's amazing the things I notice when I'm not high." At the door to the diner, Jeff stopped her. "Can I give you a hug?"

She nodded. He wrapped his arms around her and she fought the tears that threatened. When they pulled away, his face was red.

"Thank you for meeting me, Hannah. You'll never know how much it means."

Unable to speak, she raised a hand to flag a cab.

"Will you be okay getting back?" he asked.

One pulled up and she started to climb in. "Sure. Will you?"

He nodded and raised his hand in salute. As the cab drove away, she watched him from the back window until he faded into the distance.

Maybe her brother was back.

He was an addict, just like Hannah's brother. He couldn't give in to what he wanted—desired—craved—the most. Once, it was pain pills. Dan shut his eyes. Images from that horrible day flashed through his mind. Downing the last of his pain pills with shaking hands. Going out in the driving rain to get his fake prescription refilled. His apartment, door ajar, when he returned—he'd left it open when he left. The fear when he couldn't find Tess. His own recriminations as he looked around the apartment for the items stolen while he was gone.

It could have been Tess who had been taken. But somehow, she'd been spared, no thanks to him. He'd gone cold turkey as a result, never taking another painkiller of any sort again.

Like the drugs he'd eventually gotten out of his system, his desire for Hannah would fade too.

Even if it'd intensified in the weeks since she'd been gone.

The irony struck him. This time, he couldn't have Hannah because it would hurt *her*, not *him*. Dan looked in the mirror that evening, rubbed his hand across his jaw, swore under his breath. No matter how much he missed her, he couldn't get her back. He'd been the one to suggest she distance herself from her brother. How could he justify Hannah spending time with him? Every time she looked at him, she'd see his past and be reminded of her brother. He loved her too much to hurt her that way. No, it was better for her that they remain apart, even if right now, the separation felt like it would kill him.

He turned in a circle and looked for a distraction. Under normal circumstances, he'd retreat to his puzzles. But he'd gotten rid of the one he'd been working on and hadn't replaced it yet. He walked into the hallway. Tess's door was closed; he debated knocking to see if she wanted to watch a movie. Ever since his breakup with Hannah, she'd been moody. While he understood her disappointment, he wasn't up to dealing with her now. Walking into the living room, he looked around aimlessly. His gaze fell on the bookshelves. A book. He needed a book to read. Stores didn't close until nine; it was only eight. With a shout to Tess telling her was running out, he grabbed his keys and wallet and left his apartment.

The elevator landing jarred his leg. He clenched his teeth. Dammit, this was not what he needed now. Awkwardly stepping off the elevator and out of his apartment building, he headed down the street and around the corner to the independent bookseller. As he walked, he noticed the couples on the sidewalk. He tried not to stare as they passed him. He missed that. With a sigh, he opened the door of the bookshop. The cheery bell announced his presence.

"May I help you?"

"No thanks, I'm just browsing."

He headed toward the mystery aisle. The latest John Grisham beckoned, but he'd already read it. He continued along the aisle, stopping to look at books that caught his interest. With two in his hand, he moved into the Sci-fi aisle, but found nothing he wanted to read. As he turned toward the counter, the self-help aisle diverted his attention. With a quick look to see if anyone noticed, he walked over. Two books side by side made him shake his head at the coincidence. One was on managing addiction. The other was on dealing with teenagers. Apparently God was paying attention. Before he could talk himself out of it, he grabbed both, paid for all four, and left the store.

Outside, he paused. He didn't want to return home right away. Instead, he headed toward the Hudson River, found an empty bench, and sat. He pulled his jacket closer against the biting wind. Seagulls screamed and local traffic added background noise. Pulling out the book on managing addiction, he began to read using his phone's flashlight. At the end of the chapter, he frowned and flipped to the back cover blurb. After reading it, he looked for the author bio. He tossed the book in his bag and looked out over the water.

Only one chapter in and the author already recommended self-help groups. They weren't what Dan needed. Sure, he was an addict, but his addiction was seven years ago. He'd been clean ever since. He knew how to manage his life. Didn't he?

Hannah didn't have a clue how to make the ache go away. Everywhere she looked, happy couples surrounded her. She didn't begrudge them their joy, but she wished she could partake in some of it.

If the sappy look on Marc's face as he stood in her office door was any indication, he wanted to help.

"Hey, Hannah. There's a great movie playing at this little independent theater in Greenwich Village. Want to go see it Saturday night?"

"Oh, I'm sorry, Marc, but my book club meets then." *Haven't read the book, but not skipping the meeting now.*

"Too bad, maybe another time?"

"Sure." She turned toward Stan. "Can you help me with something?"

Taking his cue, Marc went back to his office. Stan, however, was less willing to let the matter drop.

"He is so into you."

Hannah shook her head. "Don't make it worse please."

"Book club? Really?"

"Really. Although I confess I didn't read the book."

"Why not go out with him?"

"Because I'm not interested, and my grandmother is counting on me."

"Honey, if your grandmother is the best you can do, you need to get a social life."

"I'll ignore your diss of my grandmother because she's awesome, but you may have a point about my social life."

Hannah went back to work, until Dave called her into his office.

"We're impressed by your work on this project, Hannah. We're going out to Chicago to make a presentation to the client and we'd like you to come with us."

Hannah blinked. "I'd love to. Thank you!"

"We're going February third. I'll have my admin make your travel arrangements."

As Hannah returned to her office, she couldn't stop a smile from spreading across her face. Her personal life might be a disaster, but her professional one was looking up.

That night when she got home, she told her grandmother about her upcoming business trip.

"*Hannahla*, how wonderful! I'm so proud of you. I knew this new job would be right for you."

"I have much more responsibility and my bosses and co-workers care about me. It's such a nice change."

"You know what's also a nice change?"

"No, what?"

"Your new attitude toward Jeff."

Hannah looked at her dinner plate before meeting her grandmother's gaze. "He told you?"

Sylvia's expression softened. "Hannah, he was so pleased, he cried on the phone to me. I don't think you realize what your forgiveness means to him."

"I haven't fully forgiven him yet."

"I know. He knows it too. But you will. In the meantime, you've helped him."

CHAPTER TWENTY-TWO

Dan stood in the living room, looked at his watch, and glanced at Tess's door, which was still closed. He tapped his foot and pulled out his phone. Glancing again at her closed door, he scrolled through emails. Finally, he gave up.

"Tess, we need to go or we'll be late!"

As expected, there was no answer. Two minutes later, her door opened. "I just have to fix my hair."

He bit his tongue rather than ask why she hadn't already fixed it. Fathers of fifteen-year-old girls knew better than to ask those questions. With a sigh, he sat on the sofa. Five minutes later, she emerged.

"You look beautiful. Ready to go?"

Actually, she looked no different than earlier that day, but having already proven he was no dummy when it came to parenting teenaged girls, he didn't mention it.

Tess headed to the door, Dan behind her. She was silent the entire trip to school. Only when she found her friends who were also displaying their work at the art show in the school commons did she smile and talk. Never once to Dan.

He greeted the other parents he recognized, introduced himself once again to her art teacher, helped himself to some snacks, and wandered the show. Tess's work was fantastic. Her charcoal drawings of people were phenomenal. But it was her last piece that knocked the breath out of him.

It was a portrait of him and Hannah at the pumpkin farm. The field was in the background. She'd captured them mid-stride, Hannah holding one of the pumpkins. Dan held her hand. The entire picture was charcoal, except for the pumpkin, which she'd colored with pastel.

His vision blurred. It was the most stunning picture he'd seen.

"Beautiful, isn't it?" Her art teacher walked over and talked about the portrait as if its existence was the most natural thing in the world.

He could only nod and he gripped his cane so hard he'd swear the wooden handle became one with his palm.

The art teacher moved on. Dan willed himself to walk away. Anywhere, as long as it was far from this portrait. At the refreshment table, he pretended to be interested in the sweets—as the ones he'd already eaten roiled his stomach—until his heart rate returned to normal and his palms stopped sweating. It took another minute or two to release his hold on his cane, and he opened and closed his hand in an attempt to regain circulation.

Spying Tess across the commons, he headed toward her. "Are you ready to go?"

"Not yet."

They were the first words she'd spoken to him all day. Rather than argue, he took another turn around the exhibit, avoiding the picture of him and Hannah, before motioning to Tess they needed to go. With a roll of her eyes and a flip of her hair, she stormed past him out the door.

Great.

By the time they reached their apartment, Dan had had enough. As Tess brushed past him to go to her room, he let loose. "Hold it!"

She stopped, her back to him.

"Turn around, please."

She turned in a slow circle, her face a stony mask.

"Come here, please."

Her gaze fixed somewhere beyond him, she walked toward him.

"Can you please tell me what your problem is?"

"It's your fault."

"What's my fault?"

"They weren't there."

"Who wasn't there?"

Tess bit her lip and Dan blew out a breath in frustration. "I can't fix anything if you don't clarify the problem."

"I invited Hannah and her grandma to the art show and they didn't come. All because you had the stupid idea to break up with her. I hate you!"

Racing past him, she ran out of the apartment.

Tess burst into tears at Hannah's door. "I hate him!"

Hannah pulled Tess against her as she led the girl into her apartment. All of Hannah's own pain leaked out of this girl. Hannah's heart ached anew. She led the sobbing teen to the sofa. Together, they sat until she calmed down. Drawing gasping, stuttering breaths, Tess accepted the glass of water Hannah's grandmother offered. *Bubbe* sat across the room, silent, but watchful.

"Don't hate him because of me, Tess," Hannah said.

"I don't. I mean, I do because of that also, but it's not the main reason."

Feeling stupid, Hannah shrugged. "Okay, do you want to tell me why you hate him?"

"Because he hates me."

"Oh, honey, no he doesn't."

"Yes. He does." She pulled away from Hannah with a glare.

"Okay, why do you think he hates you?"

"When he thinks he likes something too much, he gets rid of it. It's why he broke up with you. He doesn't want to tempt himself to overdo it, to become addicted to it."

Addicted.

Bubbe made a sound. Hannah started to shake and clamped her jaw to suppress her teeth from chattering out of her head.

"It's why I hate him. Because he must hate me or he wouldn't want me around either."

Hannah grasped Tess's face between her hands, forcing the teen to look at her. "You may be right about everything else, but I know he loves you more than life. Never, ever doubt him. You're the one person in his life he'll never throw away. In fact," she drew a deep breath, "I think it's why he got rid of everything else. Because he wants to make sure he can take care of you." No matter what she might think of him, Dan was a great father.

Dissolving into tears, Tess leaned into Hannah and Hannah held her while she tried to brush off what Tess had said. It was just a turn of phrase, she told herself, as Tess launched into a second round of sobs. Dan couldn't really be an addict. Teenagers were dramatic. When the second round of sobs quieted, Hannah smoothed Tess's hair away from her face. "What happened to make you fight?"

"Why weren't you at my art show?"

Hannah's stomach dropped. The art show. It was on her calendar, but she'd assumed Dan wouldn't want her there. She also assumed Dan would explain things to Tess.

"Oh sweetheart, I'm sorry. I assumed we were no longer invited. I didn't realize you'd still want us there."

Tess picked a piece of lint off her sleeve and Hannah pulled her into another hug. "I'm sorry."

"I am too," *Bubbe* said. "Does your dad know you're here?"

Tess shook her head.

"You should text him to make sure he doesn't worry about you," Hannah said.

"He won't care."

Hannah shook her head. "Tess, I'm telling you, you're wrong."

"You don't want me here?"

"Of course I do. I've missed you. You're welcome to stay as long as you want. But your dad needs to know you're safe."

Hannah suppressed a laugh at Tess's dramatic sigh as the teen texted her dad. Her phone buzzed immediately.

"Was that him?"

Tess nodded and stuffed her phone in her pocket.

"Do you have photos from your art show?" Hannah asked.

Tess's face brightened. "Most of them." The three women sat on the sofa and looked through the pictures. Tess's talent impressed Hannah, and she complimented her. A knock on the door interrupted their study of the artwork. Hannah rose to open it and stood face to face with Dan.

Her mouth went dry. Her heart thudded in her chest. His wood, musk and spice scent wafted around her and created a longing deep in her soul.

"Where's Tess?" Dan looked past her into the apartment.

Hannah swallowed. All desire fled. He'd thrown her away. No matter what reason Tess gave, the sooner Hannah got over him the better. She stood back and pointed down the hall, and followed him as he rushed toward Tess, unsteady, but faster than she'd ever seen him move.

"She's in the living room."

When he stopped at the entry to the living room, he wobbled. She reached out a hand to steady him.

He shook her off and barked at Tess. "Come on, Tess, we're going home."

"No."

"Tess." He ground out the word between clenched teeth. Hannah sucked in her stomach at the anger he tried without success to bank.

Tess glowered at him and folded her arms against her chest, sinking into the sofa as if she planned to become one with the chenille cushion. "I don't want to go anywhere with you. I want to stay here."

"You're fifteen. What you want doesn't matter." His hand shook. He clenched it at his side.

Hannah's eyes widened. Under normal circumstances, she'd disappear with her grandmother into the kitchen, to give them the privacy they needed. Dan would understand it. He might not acknowledge it, but he'd realize her motives. However Tess wouldn't. She already thought Hannah abandoned her by not going to the art show—an unintended casualty of the breakup with her father. What would Tess think if Hannah walked away now?

Tess's eyes filled with tears. "I hate you."

"I know." Dan remained motionless except for the tic in his jaw.

With a mutinous look on her face, Tess flung herself off the sofa and marched past her father out the door. Hannah watched them go. As Dan reached the door, *Bubbe* pressed something into his hands. He stiffened and left.

"What did you give him?" Hannah asked her grandmother.

"Help."

He gripped the pamphlet Sylvia had given him as he sat in the cab next to Tess. *Next to* might be a slight exaggeration. Tess huddled against the opposite door, leaving as much space as possible on the ripped vinyl seat. He had a feeling if there were a way for her to melt into the door, she would. Actually, if there were a way for her to throw him out of the cab, she'd probably do it.

Once inside their apartment, he forced his fist open and looked again at the pamphlet. Narcotics Anonymous. Crumpling it between his fingers, he threw it in the trash. He didn't need their help. He'd conquered his addiction. He was fine.

As long as he paid no attention to the paralyzing fear he'd felt when Tess disappeared. Assuming she'd gone to Lexi's, he'd waited ten minutes, giving her a chance to calm down before he'd walked down the hall and knocked on Lexi's door. When he found out she wasn't there, the building tipped. He'd had to use all of his strength to remain standing. Flashbacks from when he'd found the apartment ransacked years ago clicked through his mind on an endless loop, broken only by the concern of Lexi's mom. With a brief nod, he'd limped to his apartment to figure out what to do next. In the thirty minutes it took for Tess to text him, he'd crafted a plan to find her that would have been the envy of SEAL Team Six. Only when her text dinged had he calmed down. Now, he told himself for the fifth time—or was it the sixth—he was fine.

Someone disagreed with him, though, because throughout the rest of the week, the damn pamphlet, wrinkled but readable, reappeared in the strangest of places—the kitchen counter, the bathroom mirror, under his pillow. Each time he found it, he threw it away. Each day, it reappeared somewhere else. The most creative place was his pants pocket.

He let it continue because he knew this was Tess's way of communicating with him, and if she was communicating, he wouldn't stop it. Especially since she'd given him the silent treatment for the past four days. But when he opened his briefcase in the middle of a meeting at work and found it, he put an end to it. After a quick trip to the shredder in the mailroom, he knew he'd won.

He had a sneaky suspicion it was a pyrrhic victory.

That night for dinner, he brought in Tess's favorite—Thai food. She picked at it and wouldn't look at him.

He sighed. "When are you going to talk to me again?"

"When are you going to get help?"

"I don't need help, Tess. I'm fine."

"I don't need to talk to you. I like the silence." She stuck a forkful of rice into her mouth and rose to clear her plate.

"You won't win this, Tess."

Standing facing the wall, she replied, "I lost this a long time ago. I lost it the day you chose drugs over me. Even though you cleaned yourself up, you got rid of anything you cared about. But you kept me."

The Pad Thai threatened to come right back up as she turned, shoulders slumped. "No matter what Hannah says, I'll never win."

If she stomped out of the kitchen, maybe he'd feel better. But she slipped out, barely making a sound, as if there was no point anymore. It scared the hell out of him. Her door clicked shut; he hobbled after her and opened the door. She lay face down on the bed, shoulders shaking. He sat next to her and patted her back. "I love you, Tess. How can you doubt me?"

"Because you get rid of everything you care about. You threw away your puzzle. You no longer eat chocolate. You stopped talking to your friends."

"I could never get rid of you. Ever."

"It's obvious you don't care about me as much as you do anything else."

"Tess, you don't understand."

"You're right, I don't. And since you won't get actual help, I never will understand."

"I'm not addicted anymore."

"Then why don't you trust yourself?"

It was a great question. One for which he didn't have an answer.

CHAPTER TWENTY-THREE

Hannah's phone rang the next morning on the way to work; her eyes widened at the caller. "H...hello?" Her stomach dropped. Maybe seeing her yesterday made Dan miss her. Maybe he'd explain what Tess meant about his being an addict.

"What did you tell Tess?" Dan's voice was frantic.

Her heart rate quickened as the voice she'd missed gave no indication of his care for her. "Excuse me?" No hello, no how are you. An immediate accusation. The man she'd loved was gone.

"Tess told me you said something to her. What was it?"

Hannah leaned against the building as commuters rushed past her. "I said a lot of somethings to her. You'll have to be more specific."

He remained silent for a minute. Hannah wondered if she should hang up. They weren't together anymore. He didn't miss her. If Tess was right, he was an addict. She didn't have to deal with him or his issues. The only reason she talked to him now was because of Tess.

"Tess accused me of getting rid of everything I love, except her. She said you told her something, but you're wrong. What did you tell her?"

She blinked the tears out of her eyes. "I told her no matter what she might think, you loved her more than anything, and everything you do, no matter how much it might not make sense, is for her."

Again, there was silence.

"Dan? Are you there? Because I need to get to work..."

"Thank you." His voice was hoarse. Despite everything, his obvious pain hurt her. She shook her head. Making him feel better was no longer her concern. He'd never wanted it when they were together, he wouldn't want it now. He'd been more than clear on that one. Getting involved would only make her suffer.

"I have to go, Dan." She hung up and took a deep breath. She had a presentation today and she needed to focus.

After the presentation, Stan stopped her on her way out of the conference room. "Hannah, got a minute?"

"Sure." She pulled out a tall-backed black leather chair and sat at the table across from her friend.

"That was a great presentation today. You nailed it."

Hannah's chest filled with pride. "Thanks. I appreciate you saying so."

He squared her papers, picked them up, and walked to the conference room door. "You okay, though?"

"Yeah, why?"

"You don't seem yourself."

"Just stuff going on at home. I'm fine."

Stan turned and put a hand on her shoulder. "I'm available if you want to talk."

Hannah blinked. "Thanks, I appreciate it."

As Stan walked away, he called over his shoulder, "Whoever he is, he's not worth it."

Sighing, Hannah headed to her office. The problem was, he was.

Dan closed the door to his office and sat at his computer. His hand hovered over the touchpad. He rubbed his forearm as he contemplated what he was about to do. His stomach roiled.

He closed his eyes and images of Tess laughing played in his mind. He hadn't heard her laugh since had broken up with Hannah.

Tapping the touchpad, he opened his internet browser:

```
Nar
```

He stopped. He was fine. *Sure you are, as long as you keep away from everything and everyone you enjoy.*

He let out a breath and typed:

```
cot
```

It shouldn't be this difficult. He didn't need it. *Except Tess says you do and she might be right.*

He slammed the keys with his fingers:

```
ics anonymous
```

Information popped up on his screen. He jumped as if it was going to explode out of the screen and rain burning sparks around him. He pushed his chair back and looked at his door. Still closed. Scooting forward, he searched for meetings in his area. There were three locations close to him—one near his home and two near work. He didn't want anyone to see him, but based on the times of the meetings, one of the churches near his office was the most convenient. He checked his calendar and made a small notation. He'd see what happened between now and then.

CHAPTER TWENTY-FOUR

Two weeks later, Dan finally found the time to go to the church. Okay, found the time might not be the right terminology. More like got up the nerve. Still, he walked past the church three times before he stopped across the street and thrust his hands in his pockets.

The church itself was pretty with grey stone and beige arches. Big brown plank doors with iron trim work and handles faced him. A plastic sign on the right listed mass times and clergy names. A chalkboard in front announced the location of the NA meeting.

He'd cleared his schedule. He'd found this church. He couldn't enter, though. At least, not today.

Tess talked to him now, albeit without excitement. She hadn't yet gone back to saying, "I love you," but she said "goodnight" and "hello" and "goodbye." When he asked questions, she answered with minimal eye rolls, quite a feat for a teenager. It was progress. *But she sounds more like a roommate than a daughter.*

If Hannah were here, she'd know how to fix it. She possessed an innate ability with Tess. He shook his head. He shouldn't think about her.

He paced the sidewalk across from the church. This was stupid.

"Are you going in?"

Dan swung around and swore under his breath as his leg protested. A woman had stuck her head out of the diner. He frowned at her.

She opened the door wider. "I've seen a lot of people hesitate about going to meetings, and I've served a lot of coffee to them as they considered. If you'd like a cup, you're welcome to it."

He shook his head. "No. I—"

"—could probably use a seat to give your leg a break." She tilted her chin toward his leg, held the diner door open wider and he relented. Pointing to the first table in the corner, she smiled. "Regular or decaf?"

"Decaf."

She brought it over, patted his shoulder and left. He nursed his cup, inhaling the nutty scent and stared out the window. Who would have thought entering the church would be so difficult? He'd made it this far. He'd postponed long enough. Tess needed him to do this. Hannah did too. Hell, he needed it. The waitress returned and he asked for the check. Instead, she sat across from him. "Coffee's on the house for newbies," she said. "When you get your one-year-clean chip, come back, and make a donation for someone else's cup. We've done this for years." She rose and turned to him. "You're not alone."

The thought of not being alone, like invisible strings, pulled him out of his seat and propelled him across the street. He entered the church, and followed the taped paper signs for the meeting. As he descended the stairs into the basement, gripping the handrail and moving one step at a time, he shook his head. Funny how an obligation over one cup of coffee could convince him to do what no one else could do. He didn't want to think too long about what it said about him. He was tired of overthinking. He was tired of wondering.

He was tired of everything.

The doorway to the classroom where the meeting was held was open. He entered the room and sat in the back. No one's attention was focused on him as the meeting had already started, and he remained inconspicuous until they made for the coffee machine.

A blonde woman approached him, hand extended. "Hi, I'm Darlene."

He shook it, feeling uncomfortable, as more people looked him over. "Dan."

"Nice to meet you, Dan. Are you joining our group?"

"Well..."

"We don't bite, although the coffee might, depending on who made it."

He nodded. "I'm good. I just drank some."

"Across the street? Jewel is a gem, pun intended." She looked him up and down. Dan wasn't sure what to make of her. Was she flirting? Trying to decide why he was here?

"You owe her now, so you have to come to at least one meeting."

"I'm here, aren't I?"

"Doesn't count unless you arrive on time and participate. We have another one tomorrow at lunchtime. Why don't you come then?"

Sometimes anticipation was worse than the actual event. He'd hemmed and hawed enough. "Okay."

That weekend, Dan examined the brochures he'd found on display at the meeting and the booklets his NA group suggested. There was a lot of information to take in. He wasn't sure what to believe. According to his initial conversation with the people at the NA meeting, and the brochures he'd started to read, he'd gone to the extreme. Cutting off the drugs cold turkey had been admirable. Eliminating everything he loved in his life was overkill. The books and brochures, written by addiction experts, backed them up. Scientific data, case studies and recommendations for moving forward filled his brain. He'd cut things out he'd only needed to limit, ignored things he liked rather than embraced them.

"What are you reading?"

Dan jumped at Tess's question. He held out the materials. She grabbed a brochure and plopped next to him on the sofa.

"NA, huh?"

He swallowed. "Yeah." She'd wanted this. He shouldn't be self-conscious, but he was.

Her eyes lit up. "That's really good." She gave him a hug and he inhaled her shampoo and One Direction perfume. His eyes watered—he'd blame it on the perfume. More importantly, she'd hugged him again. "I'm really glad you're doing this."

He nodded, throat thick with too many things he should say, but couldn't.

"I'm going to the JCC with Lexi to tutor."

There went the moment. "Don't you mean, 'May I go tutor with Lexi, Dad?'"

She sighed, the long, deep, drawn-out sigh perfected by teenagers everywhere. "Yes, Dad."

He waited.

"May I go to tutor with Lexi, Dad? Please?"

With a smile, he nodded. She jumped off the couch and slammed the door. As he reabsorbed the silence after she left, he thought about what he'd read and the discussions he'd had. It had only been one lunch meeting, not including the one he'd arrived half way through. Now it was up to him to be brave enough to go ahead with it. Before he could change his mind, he grabbed a coat and left the building. Entering the drug store on the corner, he went to the pain relief section, grabbed a bottle of ibuprofen.

It was over-the-counter. It was non-habit forming.

He purchased a small bottle, the hairs on the nape of his neck prickling. Except this time, he had no reason for shame or embarrassment. Ibuprofen wasn't illegal. He brought the bag home and placed the pills in the medicine cabinet.

As he prepared dinner, his mind drifted to the pills. Would he take them? Should he? Wasn't this what he'd tried to avoid? He pulled the phone number of the group leader off one of the brochures. Swallowing, he dialed. "Darlene? It's Dan. From...NA."

"Hi, Dan. What can I do for you?"

"I bought the ibuprofen."

"Okay."

"I can't stop thinking about it. Doesn't this prove I'm addicted to it? I know it's not physically addicting, but I don't want to feel like I have to lean on it, like a crutch, in order to get through my day. And these constant thoughts about it can't be healthy."

"Dan, you know ibuprofen isn't addictive. You're thinking about it because it's new. Take two pills and see how you feel. I think it's the anticipation that's worrying you. You'll feel better having taken the plunge. Trust me."

He swallowed two pills before he could change his mind. "I don't feel anything."

"You're not supposed to. They're not like the painkillers you were on before. As long as you follow the directions on the box, you'll be fine. If you need to talk to me again, call anytime. The next meeting, we'll see about getting you a sponsor."

For the next two weeks, Dan went to lunchtime meetings every day. He didn't take any more ibuprofen—he was used to the ache in his leg. He began to believe maybe what they all said was right: just because you wanted something with all your soul, didn't mean you were addicted to it. But he couldn't be sure, so he couldn't risk calling Hannah. Too bad ibuprofen couldn't cure the ache in his heart.

He did a lot of listening. He listened to the other recovering addicts in the meetings when they told their stories. He listened to Tess talk about school and friends. He listened to his coworkers talk about their families and life outside of work. For the first time in a long time, he considered the possibility of developing friendships with some of them. And he listened when his sponsor, Brian, suggested he develop some outside hobbies.

"I used to work on puzzles," he said.

"Puzzles are great. You should continue them if you enjoy them. But also try to develop something you can do with other people."

"I stopped the puzzles, though."

"Why?"

"I was afraid I was too dependent on them."

Brian put down his soda and tented his fingers. "Some attachments are healthy, like exercise. People who exercise feel a physical need to do it, due to a chemical the brain produces that makes them feel good. That's not a bad thing. In fact, it's excellent. If you feel a need to work something out when you're in pain, a puzzle can be an excellent form of therapy. You want to replace your need for painkillers with something else. As long as you're healthy about it, it's fine. Don't be afraid of developing an addiction to everything you like."

"How do I know? How do I know if it's a healthy attachment or a dangerous addiction?"

"You need to learn to trust yourself. You need to be honest with yourself and decide if you need to talk to a professional. And you have to be able to depend on those around you. In general, I've found if I need to hide something, it's dangerous."

Dan stirred the straw in his Coke and listened to the ice make a whirring sound as it spun around the glass. When he stopped moving the straw, the ice cubes clinked against each other, changing the liquid from a smooth whirlpool to choppy waves. Kind of like his thoughts these days—choppy, jumping from one thing to another, without any consistency.

"You know," Brian said. "You're supposed to do things to make you happy. As long as those things don't cause harm to you or to those you love, it's usually okay. Replacing bad habits with good ones is the goal. If you take away everything that makes you happy, life is pretty grim."

Grim. It was a good description of his life. Perhaps it was time for a change.

CHAPTER TWENTY-FIVE

Hannah walked to her apartment, deep in thought. Aviva was engaged. She'd asked her to be a bridesmaid and Hannah accepted with pleasure. But as she walked into her building, a weight sat on her chest and made it hard to breathe. She wasn't out of shape. She hadn't walked long. It was cold, but she was bundled well.

It was sadness.

No matter how happy she was for Aviva, she was sad about her own life. And she shouldn't be. She was young. She was intelligent. And when she looked in the mirror, she didn't cringe. She worked for a great company where people respected her work and her. She'd met people there with the potential to be good friends. Aviva was her best friend, and she liked Jacob, her fiancé. She lived with her grandmother and they adored each other. By all accounts, she had a great life.

But she was lonely. There was a Dan-shaped hole in her heart, with an accompanying Tess-shaped one too. And no matter how she tried to plug it, nothing fit right. Aviva's engagement emphasized her own loneliness.

Voices from her apartment greeted her when she opened the door and she craned her neck to see who was there.

"*Hannahla*, is that you?"

Chicken, spices, and onions wafted from the kitchen.

"Yes, *Bubbe*." She walked into the kitchen, where her grandmother and Jeff stood together. Her grandmother stirred a pot on the stove. The smell of the chicken soup made her mouth water.

Jeff stiffened, a guarded expression on his face. "Hi, Hannah. I was just—"

"No, it's okay." She gave her grandmother a hug and smiled at Jeff. "What's up?"

"Just saying hi, and—" He stopped, his gaze switching from Hannah to his grandmother.

"Go on, ask her."

Hannah's gaze shifted between the two of them. "Ask me what?"

"My one-year anniversary is this week. We're allowed to bring guests to our meeting, and well, I wondered if you'd come. You don't have to. I'll understand if you're busy or if you'd rather not go."

The hope on her grandmother's face mirrored Jeff's, and Hannah's heart melted. No matter what she'd lost, she'd gained her brother. He'd disappointed her so many times, but she could see he was trying. "Of course I want to go!"

This time, her grandmother's teary expression mirrored hers. Hannah blinked before she stepped toward Jeff. His arms wrapped around her and the tears fell. She sobbed into his shoulder and he patted her back, rocking a little from side to side. When she quieted, she stepped away and looked at him. His eyes could not be described as dry either.

"I hope all those tears weren't my fault," he said.

She shook her head. "No, they're just...life. I'm honored you'd want me there and I'm proud of you. Really."

Taking a shaky breath, he handed her a card. "Here's where the meeting is. Thank you. Thanks both of you."

"We wouldn't miss it for the world," *Bubbe* said.

For the first time in a long time, Hannah agreed with her grandmother.

That night, Hannah and her grandmother went to their monthly book club meeting at Karen Black's apartment. Her grandmother and Karen were best friends and had invited Hannah and some younger women to join them. After discussing the book for a half an hour, Karen began *kvelling* about Jacob's engagement to Aviva.

"My son is marrying the nicest girl," she said. With a glance at Hannah, she amended her statement. "Well, one of!"

"It's okay, Karen, I love Aviva, too."

For the next ten minutes, Hannah listened to descriptions of the ring, how he proposed and what their plans were. Karen, who used to speak sharply about her son not having time for a relationship, now changed her tune and was convinced he'd be an intrinsic part of all the planning. When Hannah reached her limit, she excused herself and walked into the kitchen, on the pretense of getting something to drink.

Leaning against the counter, she let out a sigh.

"Don't worry, *Hannahla*, it will happen to you," Sylvia said as she followed her in.

"I know, *Bubbe*. And I'm thrilled for both of them. They're perfect for each other and are so happy. I'm just sad right now."

Sylvia hugged her. "You still haven't heard from Dan?"

"I won't. We're done."

"I don't understand. He seemed like such a nice man. And the way he looked at you? It was just like the way Harry used to look at me."

"At this point, I don't think I care anymore about the 'why.' I'd like to get past him so I can move on with my life."

"It takes time, sweetheart."

"Oh, sorry, am I interrupting?" Becca, one of Hannah's friends, walked in.

"No, I'll leave you two alone," Sylvia said, kissing Hannah's cheek and returning to the rest of the book club.

"Had enough of in there?" Becca asked and cocked her head toward the other room. "I know I have."

Hannah rolled her eyes. "I feel like a horrible person."

"Oh please, you're the nicest person I know. But there's only so much engagement gushing I can take from the *yentas* before I go nuts."

"You too?"

"Totally. None of them will come out and ask if I'm going to marry my girlfriend—they're open-minded, but afraid—but they keep giving me looks. Especially when you're not there to get any of them yourself."

"Ha! I'm trying to avoid the questions right now."

"You and Dan broke up, right? I thought I overheard someone whisper about it."

"Great. Yes, we did."

"Sorry, that sucks.

"It really does." Hannah opened the refrigerator while she blinked back tears and poured herself a glass of wine. "Guess I'd better go out there. You coming?"

"Yeah. Think we can get them to talk about the book some more?"

Laughing, Hannah linked her arm through Becca's. "I doubt it, but we can try."

Tuesday night, Hannah and her grandmother took a taxi to the church where Jeff's meeting was. A big chalkboard sign stood on the sidewalk with a hand-drawn *Welcome* in large blue letters, *NA meeting inside* in smaller pink ones.

As she was about to open the side door, *Bubbe* pulled on her elbow. "I'm pleased you're doing this, Hannah. It means a lot to Jeff."

Inside, a printed sign on the wall directed them to a classroom downstairs where chairs were arranged lecture-style.

Jeff stood near the window. When he saw them, he rushed over, hands jammed in his front jeans pockets. "Thank you both for coming tonight. It means a lot."

"We wouldn't miss it," Hannah said.

"Most of our meetings are closed to visitors, but we have occasional open meetings where we celebrate anniversaries. No one will give big confessions, but we'll have a speaker talk about the NA organization. There's some food in the back for a little celebration. It's not much, but..."

Hannah looked around. A blue-plastic cloth covered a table with plates of cookies and brownies, and urns of coffee and tea. "It's perfect."

They took their seats as the meeting was called to order. After the leader spoke a few words, the speaker told everyone about the organization—its history, purpose, and goals. Then the meeting leader walked to the front again.

"I'd like to take this opportunity to recognize one of our members. Jeff is celebrating his one-year anniversary clean." Everyone clapped. Tears prickled behind Hannah's lids. "Jeff, would you like to come and say a few words?"

Squeezing Hannah's hand, he walked to the front and faced everyone. "I've been a drug addict for longer than I can remember. I lost everything. Myself, my job, my family." He looked at Hannah. "I never thought I'd get clean. This group has helped me realize I can get clean and stay clean. It's been three hundred and sixty-five days. It's a struggle every day. But thanks to my sponsor, Mike, I'm here celebrating today."

Mike approached Jeff and gave him a hug and a handshake before he returned to his seat.

"I'd also like to thank my grandmother for never losing faith in me. And finally, my sister. Hannah, you loved me enough not to enable me. You forced me to see I needed to clean up my act. Thank you for letting me back in your life. I love you."

A cough sounded behind her, but before she could turn, Jeff grabbed her in a hug. The tears she felt earlier trickled down her cheeks as she whispered in Jeff's ear, "I love you too."

"Come on, let's get something to eat," *Bubbe* said.

She followed her grandmother and Jeff toward the table in the back. A crowd blocked the aisle and when she tried to get past, she knocked into someone. "I'm sorr—"

The words died in her throat.

It was Dan.

CHAPTER TWENTY-SIX

He should have left the moment he heard Hannah's name.

He'd imagined her everywhere. When he'd walked in and thought he saw her sitting in the audience, he'd attributed it to an overactive imagination, grabbed a cup of coffee, and sat in the back row.

Now, face-to-face with her, he wondered how he could ever have imagined he saw her anywhere. Her hair was more luxurious, her eyes brighter, her skin more luminescent than anyone he'd mistaken for her. And she was as surprised as he was.

Her eyes didn't glow with happiness at seeing him. They didn't sparkle with excitement. They were wide with shock.

He suspected they mirrored his own.

When Jeff celebrated his year of being clean, Dan didn't think anything of it. He still didn't know people's last names. But when he'd thanked his sister, Hannah, Dan had inhaled with such sharpness he'd choked. Still, he'd convinced himself it was a coincidence. When he'd turned away from the coffeepot and almost banged into her, he lost his equilibrium. Thank goodness for his cane, because without it, he'd be flat on the floor.

Only now, seeing her in this room, did he fully make the connection.

She was here. In this room. With him.

He wanted to grab her in his arms and never let her go. He wanted to apologize for being an ass. All he could do was stare, because she was here. So was he.

His joy at seeing her slowly evaporated.

She was here for her brother. He was here for himself. If she hadn't already figured it out, she would in a moment. Any dream of a future with her he might have clung to would disappear. She already had a drug addict for a brother. Why would she want a second one in her life?

He swallowed the bile that threatened to rise in his throat. She didn't move. She shut her eyes. She knew.

Unable to stand it a moment longer, he swung around and left the room.

For a moment, the room spun and Hannah shut her eyes. When she opened them, Dan was gone. She turned, caught a fleeting glimpse of grey hair out in the hallway, heard the faint tap of his cane on the linoleum floor. Why was he here?

"Hannah, are you okay? Sit down, *Hannahla*, you look pale." *Bubbe* helped her to a seat, and she followed without seeing anything. Dan was here.

"What's wrong?" Her grandmother took her icy hand and rubbed it.

She opened her mouth to speak, but nothing came out. Swallowing, she tried again. "I think I saw Dan."

"Are you sure?"

"Yes." He'd stared at her like he'd seen a ghost. Once again, he hadn't said anything to her.

Her grandmother left, returning a moment later with a cup of water and Jeff. "Drink this." Without waiting for Hannah to say anything, her grandmother described Dan and asked if Jeff knew him.

"Not personally, but I've seen him at meetings. He's pretty new."

Dan came to NA meetings?

"Why does he come?" Hannah asked.

Jeff looked at her. "I can't tell you what goes on here, Hannah. I'm sorry. The only reason you're allowed here tonight is it's a public meeting. Most are private."

"The only people who come here are drug addicts, right?" She bit her lip. She couldn't think clearly enough to be tactful.

He sat next to her and took her hand. "Yes. Do you know him?"

Her eyes filled with tears and she looked at her grandmother.

"He was her boyfriend."

"I'm sorry, Han. You didn't know he was an addict?"

She shook her head. In the back of her mind, little things fell into place. He never drank. He never took anything for pain. And there was Tess and her outburst. All of a sudden everything she'd ignored made sense.

Her hands shook with rage. He'd known her feelings about her brother and never told her. She'd asked why he didn't drink or take pain meds and he'd changed the subject. He'd lied to her.

"Hannah, I'm sorry," Jeff said.

His gaze reflected sympathy and understanding. Blinking, she took a deep breath. This was Jeff's night. She wouldn't ruin it. With a wobbly smile, she stood and squeezed his hand. "Don't worry about it. We should go celebrate, shouldn't we, *Bubbe*?"

"You're right. Jeff, where do you want to go?"

"How about the diner across the street? They have great desserts, and I think Hannah could use a sweet treat right about now."

The three of them left the church and entered the diner. Warmth blasted them when they opened the door. As they passed the cash register, Jeff handed the woman across the counter a five-dollar bill. She nodded, and put it in a jar.

"What's that for?" Hannah asked.

He shrugged. "Just a tradition we have here."

At the table, they picked up the heavy vinyl menus. Hannah's mind churned.

"Hannah, are you ready to order?" She started as she heard her name. The waitress stood next to her, pen poised over her pad.

"Oh, ah, I'll have a cheeseburger, medium." Her grandmother and Jeff frowned. "What?"

"Nothing," Jeff said. "It's just that we ordered desserts. But if you're hungry…"

"Oh, no, I'll have chocolate mousse pie instead."

The waitress left. Hannah stared into space.

"So, Han, how's your new job?"

"It's good…" She'd been there about six weeks. Dan knew nothing about it. Dan knew nothing about anything in her life. Dan had lied to her. Her eyes filled. She felt pressure on her arm. Her grandmother's bony fingers gripped her elbow.

"Hannah, honey, go to him."

"No. We're eating. Besides, I want nothing to do with a liar."

"When did he lie to you, *Hannahla*?"

"So many times, *Bubbe*." Mostly by omission, but he'd had plenty of opportunities to tell her.

"Maybe he had a good reason."

"Doesn't matter what his reason was." All those times she'd talked to him about Jeff and he'd never said anything.

"I've heard him in the couple of meetings we both attended, Hannah. You need to talk to him."

"I'm not the one who has to talk. He's in meetings! He never said anything to me, and believe me, I gave him plenty of opportunities."

Jeff blew out a breath and took Hannah's flailing hands. "Look, I don't know him well, but he seems like a pretty earnest guy who's trying to do the right thing. Don't waste time on who should be the one to initiate the conversation. Just have the conversation."

She straightened her shoulders. Her brother was right. She and Dan had avoided this conversation for too long. It was time to face him. She rose. "Maybe. Do you mind if I go now? I don't want to ruin your celebration, but I have something I need to do."

She hailed a cab and took it to Dan's apartment, rehearsing the entire ride what to say. Should she speak first or ask questions or let him start? Anger, hurt, confusion warred within her, drowned out the hint of hope she'd felt when she stood in front of him. Before she'd formulated what she'd say, the cab pulled up in front of his apartment. The doorman recognized her and let her in without calling upstairs. Outside his door, she paused. Taking a deep breath, she knocked. Tess opened the door.

"Hannah!" The girl gave her a bone-cracking hug.

Despite her anger, Hannah smiled. "Hey, Tess. I missed you."

"I missed you too. Wait, what are you doing here?"

"I came to talk to your dad."

Tess's face brightened. "Are you two getting back together?"

Hannah shook her head. "No, sweetie. But I need to talk to him. Is he here?"

"He went to a meeting and he's not back yet."

Hannah paused. The meeting ended an hour ago. Disappointment flooded her. She'd finally gotten up the courage to confront him, and now she'd have to wait for another time.

"Do you want me to have him call you?" Her face was eager.

"No, I'll try him another time." She wouldn't involve Tess in this. "It was good to see you, though, Tess."

"You too, Hannah. I miss you."

She gave Tess a hug. "I miss you too." With a sigh, she left.

Outside of her apartment, she searched her purse for her keys. As the cab pulled away, she looked up and dropped her purse.

Dan stood on the sidewalk under a streetlamp outside her building.

The evening chill did nothing to prevent sweat from dotting his brow. Cold brick dug into his back through his wool coat and his leg stiffened as he stood outside and waited for her.

Leaving the meeting without talking to Hannah was the latest in an endless string of acts of cowardice, which began with his addiction and ended with leaving the meeting. But his cowardice would end, because tonight he would tell Hannah everything.

He'd never been so scared in his life. Well, maybe that one time with Tess.

He'd started to shake when Sylvia and Jeff got out of a cab, but calmed down when he realized Hannah wasn't there. His heart dropped to his toes. He'd frozen against the wall, unsure of what to do next.

"She went to your apartment," Jeff said, after he told his grandmother to go inside.

"What?"

"You're Dan? She went to your apartment."

"But I'm not there." His reactions were slow and he wanted to smack himself upside the head for his stupid response.

"Clearly." Jeff smiled. "She'll be back."

"I'll wait."

"Probably the smartest decision you've made, other than coming to a meeting."

"She'll never forgive me."

"I used to think that too."

Dan closed his eyes and pinched the bridge of his nose. A pat on the arm made him open them again. He was alone on the sidewalk.

Now, Hannah stood in front of him, the streetlight turning her hair a beautiful deep red color his fingers ached to touch.

Her purse dropped onto the pavement. He stepped forward to help.

"Don't."

He froze. She was pale and her breath made white puffs in front of her. His ice queen was beautiful.

His hands shook and he fisted one at his side, the other around his cane, as he nodded toward her bag. "You going to pick it up?"

"Go to hell."

They both jerked. It was only the surprise on Hannah's face that kept Dan from turning around and walking away.

"I'm already there."

Hannah bent to pick up her purse. Her hair fell forward, curtaining her face from his view. Her narrow shoulders shook.

He groaned. "Please, Hannah, can we talk?"

She rose. "Why?"

"Because I owe you...so much...but at the very least an explanation."

"You owe me more than that."

Her response took his breath away. He gasped. "I know."

Folding her arms across her chest, she tapped her foot, her face set in a glare. "You never wanted to talk before."

With a look up and down the sidewalk, he motioned to a nearby bench. "Will you sit with me?"

She followed him to the bench and sat on one end, as far from him as possible without landing on the ground. He didn't try to move closer. Resting his cane against the side of the icy bench, he leaned forward, elbows on his knees, hands hanging limp. It was better she sat far away. He couldn't bear to see the condemnation in her expression.

"It was raining that day when the three of us went out. We were running errands. Tess was singing in the backseat." He paused, a brief smile tugging at his lips as he remembered her little-girl voice. "Beth was rummaging in her purse, looking for something to record Tess. The light turned green. I pulled into the intersection." He swallowed, his palms slick with sweat as he rubbed them on his thighs. "The car never slowed." Was there a squeal? Or was it his imagination now? "It hit the front passenger side head-on." He remembered the sound of metal screeching as it bent, the odor of burnt rubber, the excruciating pain. "She died instantly." He took a deep gulp of air, trying to ease the ache in his chest as cold sweat trickled down his back.

"I was hospitalized for weeks. My leg was shattered. The pain was unbearable." His drug-induced haze was filled with psychedelic nightmares, made worse when he came out of it and learned the truth. "They gave me oxy when they discharged me, enough for ten days. Afterwards, I was supposed to move to over-the-counter drugs. For whatever reason, I couldn't." He hadn't been able to do anything— breathing had overwhelmed him. "I'm sure it had a lot to do with losing my wife and becoming a single father overnight. That's not me trying to excuse anything; I'm stating what I've learned. Anyway, I became addicted to it."

He looked at the cracked, dirty sidewalk, across the street at the lit-up lobby of the apartment building, anywhere but at Hannah. His mouth dried and he licked his lips.

"I'd found a way to get it illegally. One day, I was down to my last pill. I'd never make it through the rest of the day without it. Tess was watching TV. She was seven years old and I left without telling her where I was going. I was gone maybe forty minutes, but during that time, some guys who were connected to my pusher broke into my apartment. They knew I had money and they stole a bunch of stuff. But Tess...Tess was there." His voice cracked. Even now, years later, he couldn't tell this story without reliving the horror.

"She'd hidden under the bed. When I found her, I lost it. I cried in front of her. I'd never cried before, not even when Beth died. I promised her I'd never take another drug again. And I didn't." He tried to breathe but his lungs wouldn't expand. "Not even ibuprofen. I didn't want anyone to know. I didn't think I deserved anything other than punishment. So I went cold turkey. I sent Tess to stay with Lexi for a few days and I went through withdrawal on my own." Hannah made some sort of sound, but he couldn't look at her. He pushed on, his head pounding.

"I fought my addiction by being in rigid control of everything I did—no alcohol, nothing I liked too much, like chocolate. I wouldn't allow any kind of drug in the house unless it was medicine Tess needed, and even then, I hated having it in the house. If my leg hurt, I either ignored it, or I worked on puzzles to distract me. I thought I'd beaten it." He paced in front of the bench. His leg ached in the cold. It was nothing compared to the ache in his chest.

"Before I met you, it was like I was dead inside. Oh, I was pretty good at faking it for Tess's sake, but deep down, I was numb. With you, I started to feel again. I wanted you to be a part of my life, to know everything. But you told me about your brother and I knew I could never tell you my secret. You already had one addict in your family. The last thing you needed was another one."

She squeaked, but he ignored her. If he stopped now, he'd never get it all out. "I counted the minutes until I could see you again. I wasn't happy unless I was with you. I couldn't breathe. I thought I'd become addicted to you, so I needed to let you go."

He angled toward her, still not looking at her. He couldn't have seen her anyway through unshed tears. "I pulled away from you. I thought it was best for you and for me, but without you I was miserable. I wanted to talk to you, but how could I do that? I saw that what I was doing was hurting Tess. I'd vowed I'd never hurt her again, and I'd done it without realizing it. So I went to NA. Or at least, I tried."

He sat again and rubbed his knee. He didn't know if it hurt. Everything was painful. "The first time I went, I couldn't make myself go inside. But eventually,

I was able to. I learned how my addiction worked and what was okay or not okay to do. But it was meaningless. Because I'd lost you. I have lost you. You already have one addict in your family. I know how much he hurt you. And I hurt you too. I'm sorry."

He had nothing else to say. His hands shook and he clasped them together. He couldn't meet her gaze. The silence between them stretched like the taut string of a guitar. The only thing he could hear was the rushing of his blood in his veins. His breathing came in short gasps, like he'd run a marathon.

She grasped his clenched hands. Her skin was smooth and cool, and he couldn't figure out why she touched him. Within the surety of her grip, his trembling ceased. He risked a glance. Despite his expectations, there was no horror, no condemnation, no anger. Only compassion.

He bowed his head until it touched her arms and those short gasps transformed into long, shuddering gulps of air. Pressure on the back of his head made him pause. He realized with wonder it was her lips. If he moved, he'd break contact with her and she might never touch him again. He was a selfish bastard. The thought of space between them was enough to keep him motionless. All too soon, the chill air ruffled the back of his neck, she released his hands and she pulled away. He gripped her hands again, needing to maintain at least some contact, and raised his head. His head pounded and his chest ached.

Confessing was supposed to make him feel better.

"You're right," she said. "You don't deserve me."

He blinked. Deep, deep down, surrounded by doubts and self-loathing, when she didn't run away, there was a tiny spark of hope that maybe she'd forgive him. Tell him all wasn't lost. Remind him she loved him. Now the spark of hope died.

He pulled his hands away and rose, gripping his cane as much to transfer the pain as for support. "I hope you can find happiness again with someone who deserves you."

She sputtered. "So, that's it? You're leaving me again?"

He took in her beautiful angry face. "Again?"

She rolled her eyes. "I swear he wasn't a moron when I first met him," she muttered. "You left me. You just came back. And you're leaving again."

"Why would you want me to stay? I've lost you."

"You lost me? I'm not some toy you forget about only to find again one day. I'm a living, breathing person. Someone I thought you cared about. Someone you said you cared about. I've never been lost. It's you who keep throwing me away."

Now he was the one who was lost. "Can we sit down for a minute? Because I'm confused."

She joined him on the bench. He'd give anything to touch her one last time, but it would be cruel to both of them.

"Okay, if you wouldn't mind, start over," he said. "You told me I'm right. I don't deserve you. So why are you mad I'm leaving?"

"Because you're wrong!"

Numbers. Numbers made sense. Hannah, however, wasn't a number. She was a sexy-as-hell woman he would die to be with. He frowned, eliciting a groan from her.

"You're right about hurting me, not losing me, you idiot."

Hurting this beautiful woman should not have made him happy, but it took all his effort not to jump up and laugh. From the expression on her face, even a small smile would endanger him, though, so he bit the inside of his cheek, took a deep breath and focused. The urge to laugh or smile disappeared. "I'm sorry."

"That doesn't make what you did any better. You listened to me when I was upset about Jeff and my job and my grandmother, yet when I could have listened to you, maybe helped you, you didn't trust me enough to tell me the truth."

His jaw dropped. "It had nothing to do with trust, Hannah."

"Oh really? How do you figure?"

"I knew how upset you were about your brother. For you to find out I was no different than him? I couldn't do it to you, no matter how many times I told myself I should. It's a numbers thing. It didn't add up."

"What do you mean?"

He sighed. "Your brother is an addict. He upset you. I'm an addict. It's numbers."

She grasped his bicep. "No, it isn't. Numbers are black and white. All addicts are not the same. You weren't some heroin junkie standing on a street corner who stole from people to get your fix. You didn't trust I'd recognize the difference. Instead, you lied to me by withholding information and deciding about us by yourself."

Dropping his head, he ran his hands across the back of his neck. "Hell, Hannah, I didn't even recognize the difference until a little while ago. It was never a matter of trusting you. It was coming to terms with who I am. I didn't trust me."

"You need to see the shades of gray. I get you didn't want me to think you were like Jeff, but I need you to believe I can see who you are. Who I see is a brave man who made a huge mistake, but did everything possible afterwards to protect his daughter."

He couldn't speak. His throat was thick, his eyelids were heavy, his lungs didn't work.

"I need to know you understand the difference between needing a drug and needing a person. Because they're not the same thing, and if you try to get rid of me every time you think you're too close, all you'll do is hurt me."

Taking a deep breath, he avoided her gaze. "I'm working on learning the difference." He paused. The air around him was cold, but his nerves made him feel feverish. "I'm used to battling this on my own, to figuring out the signs I need to look out for. Sometimes, those signs get confusing."

"You don't have to do this alone."

How could she be this understanding? "I have a knee-jerk reaction to protect myself and Tess. It feels right for me to suffer. Maybe I don't deserve anything else."

She took his face in hers. "You deserve to be loved."

"How can you say that after everything I've done to you?" After everything he'd done to Tess.

She gave a strangled laugh. "Because of those shades of gray. I'm still angry and hurt, but I can see how hard you're trying. If you'll try as hard with me, maybe we can work through this."

He wanted to pull her close, to kiss her and never let go. But he recognized the fragility of their connection right now. He remained where he was, but moved so his hands held hers. "How do I fix this?"

"You give me time and you stop assuming you have the answers to everything. You stop trying to save me from you—I can save myself."

"So I should leave you alone?"

She grabbed the nape of his neck and pulled him forward until their foreheads touched. "Not unless I tell you to. You support me and you let me support you. I don't need a savior, I need a partner."

He inhaled her scent, letting the silky strands of her hair caress the sides of his face. She stroked his cheek. He wanted to do more, but he wouldn't push his luck. However, he couldn't resist one question. "Can we be kissing partners?"

She huffed against him, her breath tickling the skin above his lip. Drawing away, she looked at him solemnly. "Yes."

As he leaned in and met her lips with his, the coiled tension in his shoulders loosened. She didn't yet forgive him. It would be even longer before he forgave himself, but it was a start.

CHAPTER TWENTY-SEVEN

Outside the JCC Manhattan on a cold Sunday afternoon in February after the *Tu B'shevat* festivities Hannah buried her face in Dan's shoulder and shivered. The birthday of the trees. They'd planted seeds and participated in a *seder* using different types of fruit and wines. It was fun, but beyond fun, Dan found a special meaning behind the holiday, which commemorates the season in which the earliest blooming trees in Israel emerge and begin a new fruit-bearing cycle.

His and Hannah's relationship was beginning anew. After several weeks of conversations and meetings, working things out and more conversations—and even some arguments—he and Hannah had finally entered a good place again.

He and Tess were better as well. She was talking to him again, and now, instead of always completing a puzzle to relax, he spent time with her. He was no longer afraid of everything he liked. He was less afraid of love. And he knew what he needed to do to manage his addiction.

He tipped Hannah's head and hugged her close. "I love you," he said.

He'd intended to make a grand gesture with his declaration—wine, flowers, chocolate—with commensurate planning, of course. But somehow, when she turned into him for protection or warmth or whatever her reason was, the feeling swelled in his chest and he couldn't hold it in any longer.

She stared into his eyes. "I've waited so long to hear you say those words to me."

Her fingers gripped his shoulders, her body pressed against him and all he wanted was to never let her go. And he was okay with that. "I'm sorry I took so long," he said. "I needed...I needed to learn loving you didn't mean losing you...or me."

She stroked his cheek. "I know. I love you too."

He'd known she did, but hearing her utter the words made all his broken pieces shift back into place. A weight lifted from his shoulders and tears misted his vision. "Can you forgive me for everything I put you through?"

"I already have."

From inside his coat pocket, he pulled out a small pot in which he'd planted a seed. He gave it to Hannah. "This is for you. The seed is trust. We've planted it and from it, our relationship will grow strong."

This time, her eyes were the ones that were wet. She cradled the pot and his body warmed, as if she cradled him. And in a way, she did. He drew her close again and leaned his cheek against the top of her head.

A few minutes later, when Tess joined them, he pulled away from Hannah and smiled at his daughter. Lacing his fingers together with Hannah's, they walked down the street.

"Oh, those hot dogs smell good!" Tess cried. "Can we have some?"

"We just ate inside." Dan said.

Hannah pulled on his hand and he stopped. She smirked as she looked at him and he grinned at her.

"You know, hot dogs sound great right about now. Especially if you get mustard on your cheek."

Arm in arm, they walked toward the vendor.

He was forgiven. And she was his.

The End

Acknowledgements

Laurie Cooper, thank you for your marketing and relaunch advice. I could not self-publish without your wisdom.

I can't believe I actually have to say this, but this book was written by me, not some AI bot or whatever. A reader's time is too precious to waste.

.

About Jennifer Wilck

Jennifer Wilck is an award-winning contemporary romance author for readers who are passionate about love, laughter, and happily ever after. Known for writing both Jewish and non-Jewish romances, her books feature damaged heroes, sassy and independent heroines, witty banter and hot chemistry. Jennifer's ability to transport the reader into the scene, create characters the reader will fall in love with, and evoke a roller coaster of emotions, will hook you from the first page.

You can find her books at all major online retailers in a variety of formats.

Jennifer started telling herself stories as a little girl when she couldn't fall asleep at night. Pretty soon, her head was filled with these stories and the characters that populated them. Even as an adult, she thinks about the characters and stories at night before she falls asleep or walking the dog. Eventually, she started writing them down. Her favorite stories to write are those with smart, sassy, independent heroines; handsome, strong and slightly vulnerable heroes; and her stories always end with happily ever after.

In the real world, she's the mother of two amazing daughters and wife of one of the smartest men she knows. She believes humor is the only way to get through the day and does not believe in sharing her chocolate.

To learn more, go to http://www.jennifer-wilck.com